THE HORSEMAN'S TALE

THE HORSEMAN'S TALE

a novel

TOM EQUELS

The characters and events in this book are fictitious. Any similarity to real persons, living or dead, is coincidental and not intended by the author.

First published in 2024 by
Four In Hand Press
an Imprint of Trafalgar Square Books
North Pomfret, Vermont 05053

Disclaimer of Liability

The author and publisher shall have neither liability nor responsibility to any person or entity with respect to any loss or damage caused or alleged to be caused directly or indirectly by the information contained in this book. While the book is as accurate as the author can make it, there may be errors, omissions, and inaccuracies.

Trafalgar Square Books certifies that the content in this book was generated by a human expert on the subject, and the content was edited, fact-checked, and proofread by human publishing specialists with a lifetime of equestrian knowledge. TSB does not publish books generated by artificial intelligence (AI).

ISBN: 978-1-64601-265-7
Library of Congress Control Number: 2024912709

Book interior and cover design by RM Didier
Typefaces: Athelas, Lust, Brim Narrow

Printed in the United States of America

10 9 8 7 6 5 4 3 2 1

To my wife, Laura,
my children, Lesley, Mary, Darius, Christina,
and Liana, and an ever-growing crew of grandchildren,
with a special acknowledgment of my deceased parents,
Tom Equels and Patricia Mortimer Simonet, and my
stepdad of over fifty years, Richard Simonet.
Family Forever.

contents

I moved in darkness,
with clumsy fits and starts,
without good light to guide me,
only lust and an inflamed heart.

SAINT JOHN OF THE CROSS

From "The Dark Night," Translated from the Spanish by the Author

chapter 1
WET—Confidential

WHERE TO START? *Written Exposure Therapy*. WET. I took a Veterans' Administration training class on it as part of my post-retirement efforts to curb what was diagnosed as Post Traumatic Stress Syndrome. You know, *PTSD*. I have workbooks, "how-to" programmed texts, that break the therapeutic method down to a fifth-grade level. WET was the only therapeutic option for me. I considered the others. The drugs were mind-dulling and unacceptable. Like an indecisive college freshman, I audited, without participating in, a few group therapy sessions. They felt like a violation of both privacy and good taste. But WET, I liked. I made it my own. I distilled all of it down to my essence. For me, it became a simple process. *Write Every Thought.* No matter how random, how inane, just write it down. Then, days, maybe even weeks, later, find a quiet place and read it. Somehow it all came together.

So, I type, pounding out fragments of my life with each click of my keyboard.

Home. My home. I'm a part of this place, just like the ancient oaks, the verdant pastures, and the spring-fed pond. Ever since Sally died, our farmhouse feels too big and more painfully empty than I ever imagined my childhood home could feel. There was a time when it comfortably housed my parents, Sally, and all three of our children. I spent most of my life on this farm. My roots here run deep.

Before I was born, when my pa returned to the States at the end of WWII, he came back not just a hero but also in possession of a small fortune. No one knew where the money came from, but his first stop on his return was not to my mother (then in Tennessee), but Ocala, Florida, where he bought a racehorse farm—three hundred acres—with a racetrack, starting gate, four barns, and a humble two-room cottage. With that, and a half-dozen top-quality racing broodmares donated by my maternal grandparents, my parents built our racing business.

While I wasn't born in a barn, it was damn near close. April 7th, 1948, was the day. Racehorses have their foals in the spring, and I arrived right in the middle of all the action. My mother oversaw our broodmares. Foaling, and aftercare, was her domain. Ma's water broke and she went into labor while birthing a foal. She rejected my father's insistent demand that she go to the hospital. She refused to leave the foaling barn until her job was done. It was only after the colt was safely delivered that Pa drove her to Ocala Regional Hospital. I was named Jacob Asa Montgomery, after my great-grandfather.

This farm is where my life started, and it's probably where it'll eventually end. It's where my wife's slowly approached the end...an end we took elsewhere, to a place that meant to her what this farm means to me.

When Sally passed, our family was left broken. God, how our children and grandchildren were devoted to her. I was broken. In truth she was my better half, and that better part of me died. When I first laid eyes on her senior year of college, Sally was a cute, tall, strawberry-blonde sorority girl whose effect on me was involuntary and physical, instantaneous and palpable. When I took her hand to introduce myself that first night, my knees went weak, and my skin felt hot. She chose me, somehow, for some reason, thank God.

I still can't believe it. In the evening, all alone, I turn to talk to her, then catch myself. Over time, Parkinson's eventually took her mind and her nervous system, then liver cancer administered the mortal blow. She never had a chance.

Now I'm all alone in this house. My close friends and lovers are dead. All my kids have left: James for Orlando (he's a senior VP—a banker), Cassie for South Carolina (she's a nurse), and Katie for a house just a few miles away. She runs our farm, but "a girl needs her private space," she says.

To keep myself from going crazy, once Katie and all the farm staff have left for the day, I steep myself in routine. In the evening, I start my dinner, usually a frozen precooked meal. I set the timer, and while my food warms in the oven, I walk over to my bar for a tumbler of Johnny Walker Black Scotch whiskey—two cubes of ice. Glass in hand, I move to my recliner promptly at seven to distract myself with the latest in global mayhem, followed by a movie or football at eight.

Tonight, though, my routine is shattered.

As usual, whiskey in hand, fully reclined in my La-Z-Boy, I turn on CNN. It's remarkable how little has changed since I was a boy. Or how much has changed and how quickly it has all regressed back to shit. I'm never sure which it is. The big screen lights up, a CNN Special entitled "The State of Hate," the white supremacists' bloody march in Charlottesville, American Nazis *Sieg Heiling* at a meeting in Chicago, seething skinheads and of white-robed Klansmen marching, all chanting "America first!" Seeing the Klansmen on TV, marching in their costumed regalia, strikes a strong chord. It is a grim reminder of the Florida of my youth. As someone who fought for, and sincerely believes in, our country, our democracy, and our constitution, I'm embarrassed by the resurgence of white supremacy in America today. But as much as I'd like to turn it off, the embarrassment is fueling anger, a welcome distraction, for not much gets me excited anymore. The energy, the emotion, even though negative, feels good.

It feels good to feel something.

But it is the hyped-up law firm commercial, mid-program, that cuts me to the quick. It starts with red-and-gold fireworks that morph into a 3D digital graphic of the Marine Corps globe and anchor emblem. Then an actor, dressed as a USMC Master Gunnery Sergeant, appears, with a warning—"non-attorney spokesperson"—at the bottom of the screen.

"Camp Lejeune's water supply was toxic, contaminated by civilian contractors on base," says the actor. "Were you a Marine or civilian living or working for more than thirty days at Camp Lejeune from 1952 through 1984? If so, and you or a loved one has had a child with birth defects, or contracted Parkinson's disease, clinical depression, leukemia, kidney cancer, liver cancer, or any other cancer or nervous disorder, call now! 1 800...."

I stand and throw the glass of scotch across the room at the television, striking a sloppy but harmless glancing blow to the glowing wall-mounted big screen TV.

"MOTHERFUCKERS! DIRTY MOTHERFUCKERS!"

Thank God the kids aren't home...their worst fears would be confirmed. "The old man has finally snapped," I imagine them saying to each other.

I switch off the TV and cleaned up my mess. My appetite has disappeared, so I turn off the oven and put the meal in the fridge. From the bar, I bring the half full bottle of Johnny Walker Black and a clean glass to the walnut end table next to my recliner. Staggered by a tsunami of emotion, I slump into my seat. I pour three fingers of scotch, neat, and down half of it in one gulp.

Camp Lejeune was where I brought Sally and our young son James to live while I served as a training officer after my first tour in Vietnam. The law firm commercial brought an unspeakable truth home—living at Camp Lejeune caused the death of our second son, a newborn, and many years later, the death of my wife.

Bitterly, I mutter, "They died because of me."

I have Post-Traumatic Stress Disorder, which for me means even random things can trigger explosive anger. Years ago, shortly after I retired from the Marines, Sally begged me to seek therapy at the nearby VA clinic in Ocala. I agreed. As a retired Marine and a combat-wounded veteran, I get 100 percent medical coverage, everything from colds to broken bones. I talked with my primary care physician, and she referred me to a psychologist down the hall. He suggested I join a group therapy session held every week on Thursday to talk about my service in Vietnam. I explained that was not possible, that much of my Marine Corps service is still classified. He nodded his head and asked, "Well, how about just talking to me?" I shook my head no. He then suggested journal therapy, saying, "Write down the things that bother you; go deep into your feelings, not just the combat memories, even your day-to-day things."

I looked at my doctor with a clear sense of purpose, to make him understand. "I cannot write down and give you something, something that is designated SECRET, any more than I can talk about it."

The psychologist laughed. "Well, Colonel Montgomery, I've got you now. The VA thinks of everything. Look right here." He opened a workbook and said, "This here is designed for vets like you, the ones who have things they simply cannot talk about. *Written Exposure Therapy*.

We call it W-E-T, WET for short. Just follow Confidential Information Protocol #2.201(A). That section provides that whatever you write stays confidential, it's for your eyes only, whether it is a military secret or just some highly sensitive personal point. Because it stays private, for your eyes only, you can journal it. Write without fear. No holds barred. The therapy comes from you writing it, not from your therapist reading it. So, after writing, save it, or delete it, and whether you share it with me is strictly up to you."

I remember nodding, but he then went on and on, "WET this" and "WET that." My mind could not accept the repeating of the acronym without an image coming to me. When he said WET, I pictured *wet*. The unrelenting rains of monsoon season in the jungles of Vietnam, being soaking wet for days on end. For me, words often came with pictures... and they were not always pretty.

According to the VA's WET workbooks, truth is an element essential for therapeutic journaling, but such truth is hard to muster. I know. Much of my life has been built on rationalizations, half-truths, and outright lies. I think the most insidious lies—for all of us—are the ones we tell ourselves. Maybe everyone is like that, after so many years, piling little lie upon little lie—things we have done, things we have failed to do, things we hide because of fear or shame. Perhaps life would be unbearable without such rationalizations.

I journal because I want healing. WET taught me that if I wanted healing, I could not be afraid. I could not hide from my truth. I could not sugar-coat the facts. To address my life's hard edges, I couldn't shy away from things, and I couldn't lie. *Easier said than done*, but then again, WET had worked for me. Now when I have my PTSD moments, like tonight's explosion in response to the television commercial, I use WET. I take a deep breath and think, *Wait a minute*, and *Let me write this out*. I try and buffer the blow-up. Then, as soon as possible, I grab my laptop and journal it. In doing so, I ride out the wave of pent-up anger.

I have made up a few of my own rules, though. For example, one of the VA guidelines was, "Do not journal when intoxicated." Probably good advice, but I always write in the evenings, settled into my recliner with whiskey at hand.

Camp Lejeune, Sally's death, our baby's death. I had been taught to start my journal entries by thinking of what made me angry. Sometimes I don't have a clue. I just type aimlessly, accomplishing nothing. With Camp Lejeune, however, the trigger could not be clearer. After another healthy gulp of Johnny Walker, I vow not to stop until I run out of words or whiskey. I let it come to me just as Dr. McGaffen taught: *(1) recognize the trigger; (2) carefully and truthfully expose the event in my mind;* and then *(3) write whatever, and wherever, your mind takes you, even if it seems unconnected, even if it makes no sense. Forget grammar and typos. Just open your laptop and type. In the process, expose on the computer screen the hidden pain that might ultimately lead to healing.*

A road trip with Sally about ten years ago. Ten years. It seemed like a lifetime. We had just received her diagnosis of Parkinson's. We did not know that water contamination at Camp Lejeune could lead to fatal illness...that the cause of those illnesses would be covered up for decades.

We made the trip before Sally became seriously ill. Her doctor told us that Parkinson's changes people and never for the better. As we often had over almost fifty years of marriage, in times of trouble, we drove to the farm she'd inherited from her parents in the Carolina mountains. It was our special place.

My big metallic brown Ford F250 farm truck sped north on Interstate 75, with neither of us speaking, the truth of her disease progression overwhelming us, leaving only silence in the cab. Then I began. Sally was quiet as I rambled…about how important love was in life, how much she meant to me and our family, and how much I loved her. As we began our ascent out of North Central Georgia's red clay flatlands into the foothills at the threshold of South Carolina's mountains, I looked over at her. She had tears in her eyes, streaming down her face. She took my right hand and held it to her wet cheek and smiled.

My mind latched on to a profound feeling flowing from the moment. *Hers were tears of joy.* I saw it. I felt it. In the wetness on the back of my hand, every molecule seemed alive. It was like holy water to me, sanctifying me in her happiness.

Sally looked at me intently and said, "I love that you're talking to me from the heart. That's what I miss the most from when we were kids."

"Really?" I asked, surprised, unintentionally conveying that it had never occurred to me.

"Yes…really," she said with a slight tone of irritation at my ignorance. Then her voice softened, and she asked, "What do *you* miss the most?"

"Honestly?" I asked, inhibited by her earlier tone.

"Of course," she said with a poke of her finger in the air for emphasis.

"Really?" I asked again.

"Of course," she replied once more, now with a quizzical frown. "Come on now, Jake."

"Okay." I paused for composure. "I miss making love in the backseat of the old Impala, Santana on the eight-track."

She laughed.

"My God, Jake, you are still so, so, shallow. Unbecoming in such an old man," she said with a wink. She paused, then, "Remember the time I was on top of you in the back seat? You kicked out the backseat passenger side window with your riding boot!"

"Well, proves my point. That's how good it was," I said with a grin.

"*Was?*" Sally complained. "I'll show you *was*."

She fumbled around with the travel CD case I kept under the seat, placing a disc in the truck stereo. Sally and I went back ages in technology. When dating we listened to FM and eight-track tapes. After we married it was cassette tapes, then CDs. Of course, now I have playlists on my phone.

As Carlos Santana sang "Black Magic Woman," she leaned over, her hand massaging my lap, and whispered in my ear, "How fast are we going?"

"Eighty," I said.

"You aren't going to crash the truck, are you, Big Boy?"

I savored the question but slowed to seventy as she went down on me.

Just a few minutes later, I spied a State of Georgia highway rest stop, and pulled into a remote shaded corner of the parking lot. Sally sat up and smiled knowingly. I placed the reflective thermal sunscreen I always carried across the inside of the windshield and left the truck running. A diesel engine can idle for days without overheating. We had the air conditioning on and the stereo loud.

Without saying a word, Sally doffed her panties and pulled up her tunic-style dress to her waist. I reclined the driver's seat as far back as possible and pulled my pants to my knees. Nimbly, Sally crawled on top of me. One of the advantages of more than forty years of sexual union was that there was no fumbling around. She started moving her pelvis, rocking to the Santana beat.

Suddenly, she stopped moving and asked, "What if the police come?"

"Well," I replied, "if someone taps on the window, I'll tell the trooper we are taking a nap. That is what sixty-year-olds do."

She grunted at the reference to our age and then started grinding to the rhythm of the music again. I knew from the series of high-pitched chirping moans that were unique to her that she was on the verge of coming. I slid my hands up under the loose-fitting dress, along her waist and to her breasts. I pushed the cups of her bra up and over. I knew her, what she wanted and when she wanted it. My index fingers moved with feathery pressure around her nipples. I could feel them, all swollen and puffy, nipples erect, like fat pencil erasers. I captured the nub of her right breast and began to gently roll it between thumb and finger. As she began to moan, I pressed, in pulses, from tantalizingly soft to painfully hard. With that she began grinding herself against me in earnest. When I was younger, her uncontrolled rubbing had thrown me into a wild orgasmic frenzy. But I knew now that all I had to do was relax, move ever so gently to her strident rhythm. Sally could come three or four times in rapid succession. Me, well, with age, I was more like an old musket—one shot only and a long time to reload. So, I learned to make the most of my one shot.

I could tell when she was spent. With me still inside of her, Sally fell asleep on my chest. I gently stroked her back.

Outside, the daylight changed, becoming dark, with roiling black clouds. I remained in the reclined driver's seat of the big pickup, listening to Santana and the slowly increasing crescendo of raindrops. Sally shifted her weight ever so slightly. To my surprise, I felt myself getting hard again. I brought my hands down her back and my fingers cupped her buttocks. Then, I slid my right hand all the way down her backside and between her legs. Not trusting my imagination, I felt her and me for confirmation. I was firmly in place; we were sloppy wet. I brought my slickened index finger up and slid it deep along the crack of her ass. Still dozing, Sally moaned and then contracted in a series of tight spasms. I began to move under her.

She woke, saying, "Big Boy!"

The rain came down hard as we made love again in the dark of the day, amidst flashes of lightning and deep rumbling thunder. Carlos Santana sang, "*Oye Cómo Va.*"

THAT MEMORY, the reliving it, the writing it, leaves me feeling stunned and spent. I struggle to take the next step. Another sip of whiskey, but nothing comes to mind. Dr. McGaffen taught me that WET worked from the exposure of facts and feelings that come out anytime you journal. So, he said, when stuck, *don't stop writing*. Go to some beginning point, any beginning point, and then write from there.

I go now to my default. My WET starting place. When stuck, I use my very first memory, a memory from before I even had a sense of self. It is a recurring dream from my childhood that is like a life-long friend. In it I am a horse, an ebony-black stallion. At full gallop, my long legs and hard hooves propel me in vast strides. I fly across a sea of golden grass. The stallion energy surges through me, my great heart pounding. My mane, like a flag in a whirlwind, whips out behind. I rejoice in my strength, fearing nothing. In this dream my herd runs with me. I sense them all. The voices of a hundred horses thunder in my head.

chapter 2
Horse People

HORSES HAVE BEEN A PART OF MY LIFE from start to finish. My parents were both horse people—a rare breed these days. They were second cousins. My mother, Sarah Anne Pettigrew, grew up on a racehorse farm in Nashville, Tennessee. My father, Samuel Asa Montgomery, was a farm boy from the Allegheny River Valley, north of Pittsburgh, Pennsylvania. He came to Pettigrew Racing Stables as an exercise rider his first summer after high school and returned every summer thereafter until he graduated from college and married my mother. Under the tutelage of my Grandfather Pettigrew, Pa learned to train racehorses. When the United States entered World War II, my father joined the Army and served as commander of a Ranger battalion in Europe. He was a master of irregular warfare, from hand-to-hand combat to sniper-level marksmanship.

Post WWII, the racing game in Ocala was just getting started. My father's timing was perfect. Ocala grew at a rapid pace to become a world-renowned capital of the racehorse industry, and what became Montgomery Racing Stables grew with it.

My mother named all the foals and often did so with a sense of humor. The big bay colt born two hours before me, she named Breaking

Waters. Ma called him my twin. She proclaimed him a future champion the first time she saw the week-old colt run with his mother in the turnout pasture.

Breaking Waters won half a million dollars in his four-year racing career, a fortune in the early 1950s, and brought great prestige to our farm.

As an infant, I was strapped into a stroller parked in the foaling barn the rest of that spring while my mother delivered and cared for baby racehorses. My father hired an extra groom to help, but Ma insisted on working—we were a family farm. She refused to even consider what we now call "maternity leave."

My mother had me in the saddle at the age of two, riding two-up with her around the farm. By the time I was four, she'd taught me to ride on my own and gave me Geronimo, the horse she had ridden as a teenager in Tennessee. We rode together almost every day, me on Geronimo and Ma on one of the racing broodmares. She rotated riding each broodmare as a way of keeping in touch with their health and condition. From horseback, she taught me all about our farm, explaining the starting gate, the training track, the round pen, the training barn, the hot walkers, the breeding shed, and, in detail, the genetic characteristics of our two breeding stallions and sixteen broodmares.

Growing up on a horse farm wasn't easy, though. Farm boys know farm work. During school summer vacation, I worked with our team, eight, sometimes ten, hours a day, most of it in the saddle. We had a summer schedule. We started early to avoid Florida's brutal afternoon heat.

> ***5:00 a.m.*** *Breakfast at the long table in our poolside pavilion we called the "summer kitchen." There, Ma cooked up coffee, eggs, rye toast, bacon, and oatmeal for all the farm hands, grooms, and jockeys. My father gave us our daily briefing, so we were,*

as a team, on the same page. Every day, identical routine. (No one objected because the food was always delicious.)

I learned how to ride racehorses by first working as a "pony" rider. Izzie, our top jockey, would ride a two-year-old Thoroughbred in training hooked to me, on a big Spotted Saddle Horse gelding, working the lead rope. Montgomery Racing Stables also bred some of the finest Spotted Saddle Horses in the world. At Ma's urging, when my father brought her to the Ocala farm, he also imported her family's original racing "lead pony" bloodstock from Tennessee—three big Spotted Saddle Horse mares. A rare breed, originating with the Melungeon people of the Great Smoky Mountains, the typical Spotted Saddle Horse is comparable in size to most racehorses. They are unique, with spotted and pinto markings, and a four-beat, lateral, "single-foot" gait that is silky smooth to ride. The gait is called that because, as the horse moves, only one foot is in the air at a time. Most spotted horses have a super-calm disposition.

Along with the three mares came a gigantic black-and-white stallion named Ajax, on loan for breeding from the Pettigrew farm. A docile, well-gaited, half-Percheron and half-Spotted Saddle Horse, he was Grandfather Pettigrew's pride and joy. The stallion stood tall at seventeen hands—about six feet at his shoulders. He weighed close to two thousand pounds, all muscle. His size came from his black Percheron mother. The Percheron is a gray or black French draft horse, with an elegant look. They are huge, being among the largest of horse breeds, originally bred to pull heavy loads. Ajax's single-foot gait, refined conformation, and striking black-and-white pinto color came from a champion Spotted Saddle Horse stallion.

Through selective breeding over a dozen generations, all the pony horses at Montgomery Racing Stables would be descended from Ajax.

***5:30 a.m.** Go to the barn with Pa, Izzie, and our three top exercise riders, the Dolan brothers. Check on the horses, give instructions to the grooms on the schedule for training.*

Summer was Izzie's one big break in his Florida racing schedule. Florida tracks closed during this "mean" season, awaiting the cooler weather of fall and winter racing. Izzie lived with us all summer, every summer. From Ocala he traveled north, often with Pa, to race horses at specific tracks—Saratoga, Monmouth, and Belmont—in their big-money summer races.

When Izzie and I first met, I was a tall, gangly, pre-adolescent boy, surging through a growth spurt. Though I was half a head taller than Izzie, he was a *man*: five feet tall, compact, muscular, and graceful. He rose quickly to be the top jockey in Florida. But despite his stardom at the track and growing personal wealth, he always returned to live at our farm during breaks in the racing season. It became home for him, a place that grounded him at an age where sudden wealth and fame could have destroyed him. We were family. He often looked to my parents for guidance, and they gave him wise and loving counsel. I was lucky in that he did the same for me. Of course, my parents were a great influence in my life, but Izzie played an equal role. My parents loved me—I never doubted that—yet typically they talked at me. Izzie always talked *to* me.

***5:45 a.m.** Summer vacation, in the saddle, riding on the track with Izzie while the air was still fresh and cool.*

The race industry's use of the term "lead pony" is a little confusing to the uninitiated. "Pony," in common parlance, refers to a small breed of horse, and in horse training, the word "pony" is also a verb—"to pony" means to use one horse and rider to guide another horse-in-training or to lead a racehorse to the starting gate at the racetrack. The "pony rider" holds a lead line to the horse being "ponied." Racing lead ponies are always big horses, capable of pushing and bumping the young racehorses in line when needed. Lead ponies are also always gelded males, keeping sexual distractions off the racetrack. My family used our super-sized, extremely calm Spotted Saddle Horses to train our young, high-strung thoroughbred racehorses. And because a well-trained lead pony is often more valuable than a mediocre racehorse, we created a lucrative side business selling trained lead ponies to training farms and racetracks. When you turn on the television and see a big pinto lead pony at a Florida racetrack, he probably came from our farm.

Because the first horse my mom put me on, Geronimo, was a Spotted Saddle Horse, I have a special place in my heart for that breed. However, for racing, the pinnacle equine athlete is the Thoroughbred. They are the fastest and most athletic of the horse breeds, produced by selective breeding, beginning hundreds of years ago in England and Ireland, where the fastest local flat racing and jump racing mares were bred to one of three imported Arab racing stallions. Every, and I mean *every*, Thoroughbred racing horse today is descended from one or more of those three Arab stallions.

> ***11:45 a.m.*** *Finish riding. Izzie and I go to inspect the horses for soundness. Ensure the grooms cooled them down and bathed them before putting them back in the freshly cleaned barn.*

Ma taught me the basics of horsemanship and equitation. My father taught me the precepts of racehorse training. Both emphasized that a fast horse is only fast when he is healthy, and he is only going to stay healthy if properly cared for after a workout. I learned the ins and outs of cooling a horse down, checking ankles and tendons for swelling or soreness, and properly wrapping a horse's legs, from them. However, I learned the art of riding hot-blooded young racehorses from Izzie.

I was nine years old when Isadore Nieves came to our farm as a young apprentice jockey from Puerto Rico. Ma and Pa took him in as a favor to a friend from the island, and we all immediately took a liking to him. We treated him as part of our family from the start. Izzie reciprocated. He lived in our house until he was about twenty, then he bought a doublewide mobile home and installed it on the farm's far-west side.

Izzie was poetry in motion on a racehorse and an instant success at Florida's racetracks: Gulfstream Park, Hialeah Gardens, Calder Racecourse, and Tampa Bay Downs. Jockeys are paid ten percent of race winnings and Izzie earned almost $100,000 as an eighteen-year-old—big money in the 1960s. He was a talker, which was great for me because his nonstop dialog taught me *a lot*. When we rode together, he never shut up. He told stories from his life, everything from his harsh childhood in Puerto Rico to romantic adventures of the present, with zero filter. He spoke with intense detail and was a great storyteller.

For example, once, when I was twelve years old, he said to me, "Mary Margaret and I met after I won the Double Diamond Peanut Butter Grade-Three stakes race at Gulfstream. That put about six grand in my pocket, and I wanted to celebrate. I saw her for the first time at that bar, you know…"—he snapped his fingers twice as an aide-mémoire—"… Plaza Bar, near the racetrack. *Coño, ¡qué linda!* Fucking gorgeous! I bought her a drink. She asked for a Cosmo. It was cranberry red in a frosted martini glass with a little white floral print umbrella in it anchored to the bottom by a maraschino cherry. Her lipstick was red, almost a match to the red glow of the Cosmo. Then, thinking of those lips, I told Mary

Margaret that I would like to kiss her. Fact is, *chico*, I wanted to bang her like a loose screen door in a hurricane. I could tell from her eyes she knew what I was thinking. She looked down at me. She was beautiful, tall and blonde. I could read her mind. She was thinking, *You are only five feet tall but very, very handsome. Hmmm, might be fun.*"

At that, I started laughing. "Oh, yeah, Izzie, that's you! *El Guapo.*"

Izzie laughed too, and said, "Anyway, she did not know what to say to this *negrito*. She was speechless. So I said, 'I just bought a brand-new Porsche convertible. Why don't we finish these drinks, put the top down, and go for a ride to Hollywood Beach? I have a penthouse on the ocean. The view is magnificent.' See what I mean, Jake?"

I answered honestly, "No."

I had no real interest in sex at twelve. But, as I said, he was my mentor. Many of the stories he told me were imbued with some moral or life-enriching point he thought might aid my education, so Izzie made it clear. "Jake, when you grow up, remember this: You can't just rely on your good looks. Sometimes you need a Porsche to get laid."

> ***1:00*** *Lunch bell rings. Head back to the house for sweet tea and a sandwich from a tray Ma laid out on the kitchen counter, followed by a much-needed shower, a well-earned nap, and a bit of time spent reading whatever book I was devouring at the time.*

An avid reader, Izzie read every book he could find on horse training, equitation, and horse psychology. He was also a fan of the 1950s historical romance pulp fiction genre, and particularly fond of a now-forgotten author, Edison Marshall. The mid-century bestselling epics of James Michener were another of Izzie's favorites. I read every one of Izzie's hand-me-down paperbacks.

Though Izzie only went to school through sixth grade, being an avid reader, he was fully self-educated. Early on he shared his secret with me: "It's called a library card!" he exclaimed as he flashed a big-toothed smile and his Marion County Public Library card, with the word *COLORED* in all caps in the upper-left corner. He also carried a Marion County picture ID with a gold "VIP" star. This was issued by our county sheriff, a good friend of my father, and it identified Izzie as a jockey employed by Montgomery Racing Stables. The card, with its large gold star, prevented police harassment over Izzie's skin color. A similar star was attached to his rear bumper, near the license plate.

3:00 p.m *Izzie and I might take off on an outing together.*

We'd jump into Izzie's Porsche convertible at least once a week. It was a ritual. First, we went to Miss Jackie's Ice Cream Shoppe for takeout. It was always takeout because the screened-in sitting area had a flimsy unpainted plywood sign with *No Colored* scrawled in red and nailed at a slant onto the rickety whitewashed wood-frame door.

Then, we were off to the Marion County Library on Baseline Road. The library, back then, was racially segregated. Izzie, because he was cinnamon brown, had to use the "colored entrance" and "colored reading room." He always parked his lovingly waxed silver Porsche in front of the colored entrance. Being white, I wasn't allowed to use the colored entrance. I had to walk half-way around to the main entrance at the front of the building and meet him in the common area, where all the books were located. This, Izzie found hilarious, calling it my "white-boy walk" or "*camina chico blanco.*"

Izzie taught me Spanish. By the time I signed up for Spanish One in ninth grade, I was fluent, but with a strong accent. Almost all of Izzie's reading was in English, and as a result, with just a little concentration, he had no Spanish accent and a remarkable vocabulary. Not so in Spanish. He still spoke with his local dialect. When I was younger, before my formal Spanish classes began and I was introduced to the standard Castilian pronunciation, my Spanish carried Izzie's distinct Puerto Rican mountain twang.

***6:00 p.m.** Supper.*

Izzie often joined me, Ma, and Pa at the dinner table in the evening. Pa handled the business, so I didn't often spend much time with him during the workday. Probably a good thing. He was tough and stern. He was not a mean person; it was just his way. Asking a thoughtless question carried a chance of a smack on the head—his way of communicating, "Do not ask a question you can figure out yourself." His lessons in life, ethics, business, horses, riding, and martial arts often started with few words but, if needed, he could be "Mr. Professor," too.

With Izzie's example and my father's guidance, I was able to ride even the most challenging of the young racing stock by the time I was twelve. However, my path to manhood with my peers was much more difficult. My parents' excuse was that I spent far more time with horses than with children my age. In fact, the problem was me. As a boy, nothing about my preteen body was quite a proper fit: too tall, legs too long, wide shoulders but no chest, gigantic feet, and an aquiline nose disproportionate to my face. These were things I grew out of as I matured but not without being teased. Even my mother sometimes joked about my looks. She said, with a wink, that I reminded her of the children's story *The Ugly Duckling,* promising me that I would be handsome once the rest of my body had the chance to grow and catch up with my nose.

The bigger source of my issues was connecting with my peers: I am Autistic. I was diagnosed with early infantile autism as a child in the 1950s, an era when autism was sometimes called "childhood schizophrenia" and loaded with all the stigma and marginalization you might expect. It would be much later, in the 1990s, when I heard about Asperger's Syndrome, the former clinical term for autism without significant delays in language or cognition, and began self-identifying as such. (The term Asperger's has fallen out of favor since then, but I still find myself using it sometimes out of habit.) Over the years my autism became imperceptible to others around me, but it's always there—sometimes a blessing, sometimes a curse.

Later in life, I asked my mother to explain my initial diagnosis of autism. My father absolutely forbade any discussion of the sort, so she only talked about it that one time. In my mind, I captured forever that moment. When I pictured her afterward, I pictured her then. She was a truly beautiful woman, inside and out. Her pet-name for me was "Jakey," pronounced *Jay-Key*. "Jakey," she explained, "your grandma was astounded by the way you could memorize entire Bible passages."

My Grandma Pettigrew—a frequent visitor from Tennessee—was a stubbornly devout Catholic, and she loved the way I could memorize things. Even though Ma and Pa had become Presbyterian, my grandmother spent hours with me, memorizing Catholic tomes such as *Lives of the Saints,* and of course, the Bible. I've had the Old Testament and New Testament on tap since I was eight. I did not understand it all, but I remembered it, almost word for word.

"I know," I replied. "Twenty years later and I can still recite the entire *Catholic Book of Prayers*."

"Not bad for a lukewarm Presbyterian," Ma quipped with a smile. "Anyway, she thought you were a religious prodigy. Part of this, I think, deep, deep down, is because she never got over that I gave up Catholicism to get married. You can imagine what that was like."

"I can imagine!"

Ma and I laughed. Grandma Pettigrew had been relentless when it came to religion. Yet, parts of what Grandma schooled me in when I was a boy—sin...confession...reconciliation...redemption—they all fit perfectly into the underlying principles of WET journaling's therapeutic efficacy. It is a universal truth: confession is good for the soul.

Ma smiled. "One day, you had your first serious meltdown right in the living room. She'd had a tiff with you, demanding you repeat what she thought were the most important words of Jesus." Ma looked up, blinking a few times in the glare of the ceiling light, as if searching for words. "John 14:6, I think. 'I am the way, the truth and the life.' Except, instead of 'life,' you insisted upon saying 'light.' Your grandmother kept trying to get you to say 'life,' chastising you for not quoting Jesus correctly, but you refused to budge. You began chanting, 'The light, the light,' over and over. At that point, your grandma called out to me, and I came in from the laundry room. You were sitting on the living room floor, rocking back and forth. Your eyelids were fluttering, your hands were flapping up and down on your legs, and you were mumbling over and over 'The light, the light, the light,' for, I don't know, ten minutes. Nothing would snap you out of it. I thought it was an attack of epilepsy, so I rushed you to the hospital. But, as we drove up South Magnolia Avenue, you returned to normal. Acting as if nothing happened, you asked me, 'Why are we in the car?' It scared the hell out of me. Later, Doc Rodgers gave us the diagnosis, saying you had 'a manageable form of schizophrenia.'"

I think, probably for all of us, in life there are cataclysmic events that shape and define us. For me, my first such life-shaping cataclysm was not autism but rather a direct consequence of it. I was twisted—yes, twisted—by the extraordinary steps my father took to hide it from others. Back then, autism was considered a mental illness, and with it came a clear social stigma. From the first, my parents kept it secret. I think this hiding of who I was, and am, was and is at the heart my psychological issues.

There are three secrets about me, secrets imposed on me, that I've never shared. Autism is the first. Each of these hidden aspects of me created fear, or perhaps self-loathing. As a boy, I thought if I had to hide something from others, it must be "bad." But my autistic nature is as much a part of me as my sexuality, my service in the Phoenix Program and undercover work for SOCOM, or the nose (too big to be a secret) on my face. The act of hiding this part of who I was, well, it made me feel unworthy.

Nobody alive today knows about my autism. Some may guess but no one *knows*. In my youth, I knew I was different. Sometimes it was like the conscious part of me was floating above, observing the boy below, but not interacting. Sometimes, I was lost in a sea of words that I was unable to process. Like a horse, my preferred and natural communication channel was nonverbal. The slightest look, a hand sign, an expressive grunt, meant something to me, whereas a string of words did not. But I adapted and I learned to thrive in the world where others were comfortable. My mother worked with me every day from the time I was a toddler until I could speak clearly and read. She used flash cards. Effective and simple. For example, a card with the word "Dog" on one side had a picture of a dog on the other. Ma would show me both sides of the card, then say, "Dog," and "Woof woof," over and over until I responded. She mastered positive reinforcement, clapping and heaping praise as soon as I identified the word "Dog" on my own. As a result, I appeared to be a prodigy, reading by age four and reciting word for word things I'd read from memory.

As a child, I was uncomfortable with strange people and places. Any new place, any new person, was in and of itself a challenge to me. My mother worked hard, with love and kindness, to make me more sociable.

I think, with time, her efforts alone would have worked. My father, on the other hand, had standards he insisted upon. When meeting an adult, even someone I knew, I tended to avert my gaze and say nothing. Pa insisted I make eye contact, smile, shake hands, and utter a pleasant salutation. Starting when I was five years old, Pa would repeat these instructions to me two or three times before any social gathering. Afterward, once we were alone, he either commended me or, if I had failed to perform to his standards, out came the belt. He had a ritual to it. He would lay the wide leather work belt on the dining-room table for me to look at in apprehension and take out his pouch of papers and tobacco. Then, as he hand-rolled a cigarette, he'd explain why I was getting a whipping.

Even though it hurt, he never physically injured me—perhaps because he trained horses, where a properly applied whip is used to pressure not harm the animal. Emotionally, however, I grew to resent him. He shaped me into a different boy, one stinging welt at a time. It took a few years, but like a tiger whipped into civility for the circus ring, I learned to be not just polite but charming. At first it was just an act, but over time I wore the actor's mask more comfortably than my own awkward and halting countenance. I became socially adept.

My life was built on lies, and it all began with learning to keep secrets.

chapter 3
A Montgomery Man

"THE ONLY BAD THING ABOUT REINCARNATION is that you have to go through seventh grade over and over and over again." That's what an ex of mine told me once, anyways. I learned to have courage as a rider from Pa and Izzie, but in the *Lord of the Flies* jungle known to most as "junior high," I was to experience my first taste of bitter cowardice.

The ex was Chau Linh. We met at a pickup beach volleyball game our freshman year at University of Florida. It was the first week of school. We played on the same ragtag team, side by side. I was barefoot, having thrown my flip-flops and shirt to the sideline, and was wearing almost nothing, only too-tight cut-off jean shorts, a hippy headband, and my horse medallion. She, on the other hand, was dressed in sparkling white tennis shoes, white stretch slacks, and a long-sleeved, oversized, bright blue "Gator" football jersey, topped off with black Persol sunglasses and a floppy blue Woody Allen-style hat.

The sun was bright. I could feel the burn on my face and shoulders, and the resultant ruddy glow was immediate. At first, before she began barking volleyball orders at me in a clearly feminine voice, well, I thought she was a young man. Slender, athletic, and five feet seven inches tall, there was an androgyny in how she moved and dressed. As the volleyball game progressed, I was surprised at her athleticism and brilliant teamwork. (I learned later she had captained Lake Cheney Prep's women's volleyball team.) Together we scored point after point with her feeding me, at an athletic six feet four inches, perfect setups for spikes. It was great fun.

The "beach" was a big sand lot on campus, and the only waterfront was a lake—Lake Alice—filled with alligators...our school mascot. She came to me after the game, inviting me for pizza at Leonardo's. Intrigued by her, I responded without a second thought, "Great idea. Thanks, partner."

It dawned on me, as we found an umbrella-covered table on the outdoor wood patio deck of nearby Leonardo's Famous Pizza, that despite our afternoon as teammates, we had not been introduced, so I said, "I'm Jake Montgomery."

She said, "I'm Chau Linh."

It sounded to me like she said, "Jolene," and when I confirmed by asking, "Jolene?" she nodded yes. As we waited for a server in the shade of the umbrella, she removed her hat and a couple pins. Her hair, long and shimmering black, billowed forth. She shook her downturned head to jostle her casual coiffure into shape, then looked up at me with almond-shaped amber-brown eyes.

I blurted out, "You are beautiful."

"I know," she responded with a twitter of a laugh.

"You know at first," I said, "with the hat and pants, I thought you were a boy."

"Was that before or after that big chubby I saw in those tight shorts?" Apparently, she talked like a guy, too.

"Does it matter?" I asked, and at that she just laughed, then reached across the table and tapped me on my chest, where my horse medallion rested beneath my shirt. She told me that my medallion represented *Chi Tu*, the famous red horse of General *Guan Yu*.

With a chuckle, she declared, "Your face, red like *Guan Yu*."

I was mystified by her explanation of my talisman and had to ask, "Who is Guan Yu?"

"General Guan Yu is the Chinese god of war. My family gives him a special devotion."

I smiled at the unexpected quirkiness, reached into my Hawaiian shirt and took out the medallion. Between thumb and finger, I rubbed the reddish bronze horse for good luck. She smiled. I knew what that smile meant.

Chau Linh was from Vietnam, but ethnic Chinese, not Vietnamese, and was fluent in Vietnamese, Mandarin Chinese, French, and English. Saigon's Chinese had settled in as a respected community of merchants and soldiers hundreds of years before. Her father had a high-level US government job, Vietnam-related, at the Orlando Naval Base. Hers was a well-respected founding family in the growing Vietnamese immigrant community of Orlando's Little Saigon.

Ours was a relationship of convenience. It was her choice—a precondition, really. She told me young Vietnamese women were expected to be modest and chaste, virgins until marriage. She was sure her family would be appalled if they knew about us. So, it was secret sex. Love and commitment were out of bounds. Even though there was no future to it, even though it was just "casual sex," I loved Chau Linh but was smart enough to not say so. At the end of our sophomore year, she snagged a full scholarship and a transfer to Yale. She left...and my notice was what she called a "goodbye fuck." The words, "I'll miss you" never crossed her lips. I remember her face, her eyes, the afternoon we parted. I still believe she wanted to say, "I love you" and "I'll miss you," but her feelings were muted by devotion to her family, her culture, and her ambition.

How did I get from my seventh-grade disaster to Chau Linh?

Write Every Thought, that's how.

Truth be told, we talked far more than we fucked. Vietnam intrigued me, probably because I knew I'd be there soon—as soon as I finished college. The draft was in full force. The American presence in the war was growing rapidly, not ending. So, I learned from her something of life in Vietnam. I mastered simple conversations in her native tongue. Our meeting place, The Archer motel, had a big, bright blue, circular metal sign, flashing a yellow neon "$6" over and over, all night long. With a student ID came a discount on the price, from six dollars a night to three dollars for a six-hour stay. Students called it "Hotel Six," "Hotel Sex," and "The Fuck Hut." It was the only place we interacted. She made it crystal clear that if we met by chance anywhere else, she would act as if she barely knew me.

Hotel Six was built well before the era of air conditioning and elevators in North Florida. In the 1960s, it was a haven for students in search of privacy. One night, soaking wet in post-coital sweat, Chau Linh and I smoked a joint. In a marijuana-fueled dialogue, we talked about Buddhism and reincarnation. That's when she jokingly stated, "The only bad thing about reincarnation is that you have to go through seventh grade over and over and over again."

It was funny in the moment, but for me, there was a truth to it. I told her then about my seventh-grade nightmare. Except for my parents, she is the only one I ever shared it with because I think—*no,* I *know*—I am still embarrassed.

On the morning of my first day of junior high, I was putting books in my locker in the school's crowded hallway when Ronnie Tilton, a huge ninth-grade force of nature, rushed me from behind and slammed me face-first into the metal door. I fell to the floor, dazed, my face bleeding. I looked up, seeing double. Ronnie was standing over me with several of his friends. Wearing their red-and-gold football "letterman jackets," they laughed at me. They put their feet on me, nudging, delivering light kicks that weren't meant to hurt me—I was bleeding enough already. Their objective was to further humiliate me, and they did. I could do nothing. Frozen with shock and fear, tears began to flow, a flood fueled by shame and self-pity at my inability to respond.

"Look, the nigger-lover is crying like a baby," Ronnie crowed. And the more I wept, the more they laughed.

After school, when I told my parents, Pa asked, pointedly, "He called you 'nigger-lover'?"

"Yes, Pa," I replied, ashamed.

"This is Reverend Tilton's doing," Pa flatly stated. "The frigging Southern Baptists are going off the deep end with this racist bullshit. I know a lot of Baptists. Good people. But this 'Klan brand' perverts the Gospel."

He was getting emotional. Typically more rational than spiritual, he was now on a rare religious rant. I think he believed in Jesus, not so much as God but rather as a transformative historical figure and divinely inspired teacher. Even though Pa regularly went to church, and even though I knew he spent private time in prayer, I also felt he did not believe in theological concepts that were beyond his limits of fact-based reason. Maybe I'm wrong, but I think he was a practical and pragmatic man. Facts and history were all-important to my father.

Pa went to college to be a history teacher. This was his first love. So, as he was wont to do, he explained to me the history of the Southern Baptist denomination.

"In the mid-1800s, before the Civil War, the Baptist church expressly condemned slavery. Declared it to be an evil before God. With that declaration of the mother church, the Southern Baptists broke off from the Baptists. These Southern Baptists claimed slavery as a God-given right. In a way, the Southern Baptist denomination bears responsibility for the Civil War. That church convinced hundreds of thousands of poor white Southern sharecroppers that God was on their side. Poor white farmers—and any economist will tell you that their desperate poverty was induced by the availability of cheap slave labor—men who owned no slaves, fighting over slavery. Can you imagine?" He paused to catch his breath. "The whole thing makes no sense. Over the last two thousand years, Jesus has been the greatest advocate for the proposition that we are all equals, like brothers and sisters. The Roman Empire was a slave state. The teachings of Jesus, over time, broke its back. That a Christian religious denomination is in favor of slavery? Well, son, that is not a denomination, that is an abomination!"

Although his thinking then was well beyond my preteen ken, I nodded my agreement, and asked, "But why do they get you so het up?"

He pursed his lips and shook his head in a general expression of negativity.

"Son, I saw things in the war that come from this racist way of thinking, things you could never imagine," he said. "My Army Ranger unit was part of the advance team to take the concentration camp at Dachau. At a nearby railyard, almost fifty railroad cars were filled with bodies in various states of decomposition. Inside the camp...bodies were stacked in heaps, rotting. Survivors, mostly Russian POWs, said that all the surviving Jews were pulled out of the camp and marched south by SS guards the day before. My Ranger battalion was ordered to rescue them."

"Was this at the end of the war?" I asked.

"Yes, and what we found at Dachau, nobody could imagine. I still can't sleep sometimes if it comes back to me."

"Did you save them?"

"Yes. The Nazis left a trail of bodies in their wake as they headed due south. Any Jew who could not or would not march, well that person was shot. We chased them at a dogtrot—in the Army, we call it 'double-time'—and caught up in half a day. Once we started shooting, the Germans quickly surrendered. And as soon as the guards laid down their guns, the prisoners turned on them and killed them all.

"Afterward, there was a half-hearted inquiry—the Army wanted me to explain why all the enemy troops were killed, with no prisoners. I was under oath, so I just shrugged and said, 'It happened very fast.' Which was true, for it was over in minutes. But the whole truth? I just watched. Those prisoners did justice that day.

"Every dead body we had found on that road south, every Jew with a bullet to the back of the head, every stack of rotting corpses, spoke to me, crying out for justice. If the Jewish prisoners hadn't killed the guards, I swear to God I'd have shot every one of the SS sons-of-bitches myself."

"What's all that got to do with the Southern Baptists, Pa?"

My father was a man I could read from the look on his face. He gave me his "Is my son that stupid?" look and said, "Jake, the Christianizing of racism lets people join groups like the Klan. It lets them do bad things, thinking they do it with God's blessing. Nothing is more dangerous. This is the same thing as the goddamned Nazis! I'll be damned if I am going to let it go on here." He rubbed his furrowed brow. "You know, son, I think if Jesus H. Christ himself showed up at one of these KKK church rallies, they might lynch him by mistake. A long-haired, brown-skinned Jew talking 'love thy neighbor as thyself'?" Calming himself with a scratch to the back of his head in a gesture of rumination, Pa gave me a rueful smile, and said, "In fact, I am sure of it." Then, "Tilton's son is an ass, but, unlike you, he has become a man." My father looked me dead in the eyes and left no room for misunderstanding. "Montgomery men are warriors, not cowards. Today you acted like a boy, a scared little boy. That is understandable—you got ambushed—but next time, and there will be a next time, I expect you, Jacob Asa Montgomery, to act like a man—a Montgomery man."

After my seventh-grade beat-down, I was in training, three times a week. Pa gave me his old Army field manual entitled *Unarmed Combat*. It was a 400-page, step-by-step written explanation with pictorial examples on karate and judo techniques for soldiers. Of course, I memorized it. Pa would assign me a section to read, then, the next day we would spar in the backyard, but only after a half an hour of pushups, sit-ups, and jumping jacks to warm up. All he ever seemed to say was, "Watch this!" or "Pay attention," or "Watch well." When I didn't, he'd clock me with a punch or kick, combined with a curt "Pay attention!" Always hard enough to make the point clear, but without injuring me. If I lost my temper, he would hit me again harder, saying, "Keep a cool head!" If I started to cry, he popped me even harder, saying, "Now you have something to cry about!" or, another of his favorites, "Are you tearing up again? For Christ's sake, are you growing balls or tits?"

My father wielded threats and ridicule like a carpenter hammered nails. Izzie, however, was my confidant. His advice was rooted in the experience of one who had been bullied.

"Ronnie is bigger," I told Izzie. "I mean, *a lot* bigger."

"Sooner or later, you have to send a message," Izzie replied. "I encountered that kind of bullying a lot growing up." This came with a flourish of his hands to emphasize. "Everybody was bigger than me. You gotta even it out. Use a baseball bat."

"A bat? That's not a fair fight."

"A three-hundred-pound skunk-ape picking on a skinny kid isn't fair either, is it?" he shot back. "Sneak up on him if you have to. Do it so nobody but this guy knows it was you. Don't get caught—get even. But don't let this Ronnie get away with it. Never! *¡Nunca!*"

While I heard Izzie and my father loud and clear, my mother took me aside, as well, offering a different path. She loved paraphrasing Saint Augustine, and told me, "The path to a good life is not about being a better man than those around you; it is about accepting who you are and then being a better man than you were the day before, and the day before that. Son, with just a little bit of change each day, in time you will be the best man you can be."

She also told me, "Life is like a horse race. In a race, a lot of horses have a poor start, but win. It is not about how you start; it is about how you finish."

Sage advice.

Ma suggested that in many ways young people are like young horses; our spirits are wild but by learning self-control and accepting training, we, too, become useful and dependable. According to her, the secret for both boys and young horses was *to not break the spirit* in the process. She donned a Mona Lisa smile, tilted her head with an uplifted eyebrow, and as she often did when imparting advice, rolled back her hazel brown eyes for a moment, as if looking upward for heavenly guidance.

"Son, please don't pick a fight," she pleaded. "Avoid this Tilton boy. But prepare yourself. If trouble comes looking for you, be ready, as ready as possible—but do not start it."

I almost always did what my mother asked, so instead of fighting, I survived seventh grade by avoiding Ronnie Tilton. It was humiliating. I spent a year constantly retreating from any close contact and responding to insults by turning the other cheek. But every time I did so fueled a reservoir of resentment and rage. Even though I yearned to play football, I did not go out for the junior high team. Ronnie was a star lineman. As a teammate he was a sure recipe for disaster.

When Ronnie matriculated the following year to the senior high school campus, several miles away, I relaxed for the first time and stopped looking over my shoulder. While it seemed inevitable that I would have to deal with Ronnie Tilton, I was in no rush for that day of reckoning. Junior high without him around was like a drink of fresh spring water, wet and sweet, on a hot summer day.

chapter 4
Deep South

WHEN I WAS A YOUNG MAN, I was ashamed of the backward bigoted Florida of the 1950s and 60s. When we left Ocala in our family sedan for our annual vacation trips north, leaving the Deep South behind was like departing a third-world country. The culture, technology, and infrastructure became rapidly better as you headed north.

Florida was painfully backward then, competing annually with Mississippi for the worst public education in the country. However, we were first in a far more heinous category. Florida, per capita, led the nation in lynchings. “Lynching” is the term for death by hanging at the hands of a racist mob. Not everyone in Florida bought into this violent racism, but dissent was dangerous. There were many whites, including my parents, who were supportive of the Civil Rights Movement. But back then, north-central Florida was clearly more KKK than USA. Many of the worst human prejudices were legal, institutionalized, and socially acceptable, and it extended beyond the racism that permeated daily life. Women were second-class citizens. Jews and Catholics were openly vilified. Homosexuality was a license for beatings and rape.

Back then, we were strictly segregated. Whites were separated from anyone deemed “colored” at water fountains, schools, hotels, restaurants, and bathrooms. It was a time when the Ku Klux Klan regularly burned black churches and firebombed civil rights' workers. Florida's KKK was at the forefront of a violent and ruthless campaign of fear. Some Florida politicians, using gay bashing and race baiting as political currency, traded political expediency for morality. It was despicable.

Don't get me wrong, I love living in Ocala. I love our people. I love the land. The Florida that evolved after the 1970s was a different and far better place. I became proud to say, "I am from Florida." Why? Because Central Florida, beginning in the 1980s, was dramatically different from its sordid past. A massive influx of people have moved here from the Midwest and the North. Marion County's population has mushroomed from thirty-five thousand to four hundred thousand. Some want to pretend the ugly parts of our local history never happened. But I know that if we want the Florida of Disney resorts, beachfront hotels, sprawling senior citizen subdivisions, high-tech manufacturing facilities, supply-chain distribution hubs, and Fortune 500 businesses, we have to acknowledge those dark days. It is because I love my home that I refuse to go back to the "Deep South mentality" of racism and sexism, enforced by state-tolerated violence, without a fight.

As I've said, my family was in favor of the Civil Rights Movement. Pa came from Pennsylvania, and many on the Randolph side of his family were true Quakers. While no one would ever even dream my father was a Quaker pacifist, some of the Quaker values stuck with him. Quaker "melting pot" liberalism formed the ideological base for our family's view on civil rights. No exceptions. While, as a child, my parents' discourse related to social and political issues was often well above my pay grade, I listened. Ideas about how "tolerance of diversity is essential for a free society" were learned over the dinner table. As a boy, I was taught that all the racial laws of the time were wrong. My parents never wavered on that point.

Ma and Pa were not passive in their support of civil rights, either. They helped fund the legal fight for five young black men from Ocala whose court cases and appeals to get admitted to the University of Florida's Law, Pharmacy, and Engineering programs would help defeat segregation at the university level. Edward Dawson, Simuel "Sims" Harvey, Benson Vickers, John Matley, and Wilson Grant were known in press reports across the country as "The Ocala Five." Sims and John were our neighbors, living on generational family farms near us. I had known them both since I was a toddler. As a teenager John, who would become one of Ocala's preeminent architects, worked summers at our farm as a carpenter and roustabout. His sister, Janet, was Sims' girlfriend—and my babysitter until she moved to New York to go to college.

The Klan's Florida headquarters was a huge two-story wooden structure, painted white, on a wooded hillside overlooking Highway 301. In front of it stood a huge, whitewashed cross made from telephone poles. It was just eleven miles southeast of our farm, in a village called Oxford. In 1955, when I was seven, a dozen plus members came to our neighborhood. Dressed in hooded white robes, they burned crosses in front of the homes of both the Harvey and Matley families—typical Klan intimidation for Black people who "got out of line."

They showed up at our place a few days later. My parents' funding and public support of the lawsuits to integrate the University may have crossed a line with the KKK, but they hadn't a clue who they were dealing with. My father had become a respected part of the Ocala power structure. He knew how to pull strings and make people jump, and I'm pretty sure he could put a bullet in a miscreant's head without an upward blip in his blood pressure.

Pa got word from his friend, Sheriff T.J. "Bulldawg" Pugh, that the Klan was coming. Pa was waiting for them. Three pickup trucks, each with three Klansmen seated in front and a few more in the back, arrived with a dramatic flair. In an intimidation tactic they must have practiced, the trucks slid onto the threshold of our main entrance with military precision, stopping in a perfect line of Detroit iron, blocking our driveway. Moments later a big Ford diesel flatbed chugged to a stop behind the pickups, a disassembled cross strapped to it, and red cans of kerosene pinned under a cargo net behind the cab.

Men in white robes clambered out. Later, when I thought back on it, especially after my service as a Marine with two combat tours in Vietnam, I recognized the absurdity to their dress. They were like a troupe of malicious clowns armed with three-foot-long axe handles. But, as a young boy, I found the hoods and the white robes with ornate cross emblems and red Gothic symbols to be terrifying.

Pa met them with the three Dolan brothers—our exercise riders nicknamed "The IRA" by our other farm workers. My father recruited them after the war. They were from the North of Ireland. All three served in the the Commandos with my father in World War Two. The Dolans were excellent all-around racing grooms and exercise riders...but there was no doubt they were soldiers too.

Pa and the Dolan brothers stood, four across, blocking the entry road to our farm, each armed with a twelve-gauge pump-action shotgun. The brothers held their guns at "present arms," with the barrels pointed up. Pa, however, had his shotgun leveled at the Klansmen as they got out of the trucks. He also wore a holster with a big Colt revolver at his side.

I was there, too, sitting on the bench seat of our pickup truck with my mother. Ma had a nickel-plated Colt .45 Model 1911 semi-automatic pistol. It was uniquely hers, sporting white pearl Pachmayr grips with a dot of bright pink nail polish on the front sight. The pistol lay in her lap as she calmly watched. Two spare magazines filled with fat .45 bullets sat beside her on the seat. She knew how to use that .45, too—I'd seen her shoot the head off a rattlesnake at ten yards.

The truck had been parked, windows down, to give Ma a clear line of fire at the KKK from her open window. As more than a dozen men strode toward my father and the Dolans, she ordered me to get off the seat and onto the floor, but I wasn't going to miss a moment if I could help it. I ignored her and watched on, my eyes wide as saucers.

Pa minced no words as the Klansmen approached, their bright white robes flapping in the breeze. The light wind from the east blew across the highway toward our truck, carrying the clear smell of kerosene.

"There isn't going to be any cross burning here," Pa barked at the intruders. After a brief pause, he ordered, "Load!" The Dolans, with military precision, pumped and slammed twelve-gauge buckshot cartridges into their firing chambers. The metallic sound of the three pump-action shotguns chambering rounds in unison resounded like a clap of thunder. Then they too leveled their weapons at the Klansmen.

Pa's voice was deep and serious. "Looks like you boys brought axe handles to a gunfight. Big mistake! Now, you peckerheads listen very carefully. You get off Montgomery land. Now! If you don't go, if you make one wrong move, you need to make your peace with the Lord and ask yourselves which one of you hooded fuckers wants to die first."

With that, the driver of the flatbed carrying the cross pulled away. As the big truck lumbered off, the remaining Klansmen standing in our driveway seemed frozen.

"Aim!" Pa snapped, as if commanding a firing squad. The Dolans raised the guns that had been leveled off at the waist to a shoulder firing position. The targets were in their sights.

I thought Pa was going to shoot. From the tone of his voice alone, I thought he was going to kill them all. Apparently, so did the Klan. The costumed extremists quickly turned tail, loudly grousing, "Yankee!" "Mick scum!" and "Nigger lovers!" as they threw the axe handles into the back of the trucks, the wood clanging off the sheet metal floor. Then they drove off, a disharmonious screech of tires leaving behind a cloud of smoke and the acrid stench of burnt rubber.

BY THE EARLY 1960s, raw tension bubbled to the surface across North Central Florida. When I reached thirteen, race was *the* big issue. I'd been taught by my parents to believe in the Civil Rights Movement. My seventh-grade beat-down was because of it, I knew that, and other kids at school, including my friends, gave me a hard time. I was thick-skinned and simply ignored them. In all candor, as a "normal" white thirteen-year-old in a small southern town, support for the Civil Rights Movement would have been, at best, on the far horizon of my consciousness. But my parents' involvement made it my problem. With the short-sightedness of youth, I thought I had no skin in the game. I tried to talk with my father about our activism and the flack I was taking at school. He dismissed me abruptly, saying, "I told you, Jake, about the war. It is important we stand up for what's right here."

"I hope you can see that what your Pa and I are doing is an ideology, a belief in equality that he—that *we*—truly believe in," Ma said when I went to her and complained. "That is why your pa and I take a stand. Politically, spiritually, we believe Jesus' most important lesson is to love one another. Love, Jakey, not hate. The Klan, the Southern Baptist firebrand preachers, these George Wallace racist politicians, they are ruining Florida. Theirs is a politics based on hate. We must stand against it."

Such philosophizing was beyond my reach at that moment, but Ma did help me begin to form my own position on racism. I would begin to understand how Florida's very future would be dictated by whether we were a free, open, and progressive society or an oppressive, closed, and bigoted society. And by the time I showed up to Camp Oklawaha the summer after eighth grade, I knew that we all had skin in the game, no matter what our skin color.

The church camp was a rustic co-ed facility for children, nine through thirteen years of age, located deep in the Ocala National Forest on Lake Oklawaha. I had been a camper there every year since I was nine, and that summer before high school would be my last. It was a couple of weeks of bucolic camaraderie. My only vacation from our tough summer work schedule at the farm. I looked forward to canoeing, swimming, hiking, and campsite living with kids who had become my friends. Of course, there was daily Bible study, but I knew none of the kids were at camp for that part of the curriculum.

Consistent with Florida laws, the camp was strictly segregated. Whites only. Further, since a Protestant-based organization ran the camp, we had a mix of everything: strait-laced First Baptists, holy-roller Pentecostals, segregationist Southern Baptists, and me, a mild-mannered Presbyterian.

I was a Presbyterian because of a grand compromise fueled by true love. My Irish Catholic mother married my Quaker Schism-Methodist father. My parents were not zealots, they were pragmatists. They created for our family what they considered an ecumenical middle ground, one that served the long-term interests of our family and our business in Protestant-run Ocala. We became Presbyterians.

I knew all the kids at camp. The Ocala area had only one white junior high school in 1963. In addition to an all-white student body, it was also almost all Protestant. Black students went to George Washington Carver. Catholic kids, including Catholics of color, went to Holy Family Upper School near the Ocala Airport. That is how it was back then.

I was surprised to see Ronnie Tilton that year; he had never been a camper, and he was now in high school and well over the camp's age limit. Through his father's connections as a local minister, Ronnie had snagged a summer job as a junior camp counselor. As soon as I saw him, I wished I had never come. His presence had an immediate effect—I started breathing harder, my face flushing with emotion as I struggled to regain my composure.

Ronnie, at sixteen, was huge—a veritable mountain. Six feet, two inches tall, he was every bit of three-hundred-thirty pounds. The guy was twice the size of any of the other campers, except for me. He was athletic, in a lumbering way. He played first-string football and second-string basketball at Ocala Senior High. With close-cropped blond hair in a 1950s flat top, translucent blue eyes, and an odd-looking, exaggerated, pear-shaped body, he was menacing. His ass was so big he couldn't fit into the high school's basketball uniform, so he had to wear the uniform top and mismatched gigantic white gym shorts. At first glance, he looked out of shape, but I had watched him play football, and as a blocker, I knew he was like running into a brick wall.

I played football on the junior high team—wide-receiver and defensive end. I also ran track: high hurdles and all the sprint events, up to the four-hundred-forty-yard dash. Six feet tall already and growing, I was able to jump three feet in the air from a dead run. Since my altercation with Ronnie in seventh grade, I'd had thrice-weekly "combat" training sessions with my father, plus I spent every extra minute I could in the team weight room. I lifted weights with autistic intensity, and the results came quickly as I added bulk and muscle. My lanky adolescent frame was replaced by a thick-shouldered, V-shaped torso. Ronnie and I, as athletes, were polar opposites. He was built like a Sumo wrestler. I was more like an Olympic sprinter.

Our personalities were completely different, too. Because his father was the Southern Baptist minister in the tiny town of Oxford, Ronnie had a misplaced sense of privilege. He was loud and mean, a classic bully. As if that weren't enough, Ronnie was leader of a Klan youth group called the Young Knights. In contrast, I was enthralled by the Beatles and Rolling Stones, and imitating my musical heroes, was letting my hair grow. The year before, I'd bought an old Martin Dreadnought—a big-box, six-string, acoustic guitar—for thirty bucks at Joey's Pawn and Gun. Pa, with me in tow, used to stop at the pawnshop to buy racing saddles cheap. As soon as I saw the guitar, I knew I had to have it. I spent evenings teaching myself to play, mastering chord and scales until my fingers bled, and singing gospel, folk, and rock songs. I did not sing well, but I made up for it with enthusiasm. Thanks to autism, my ability to memorize both sheet music and lyrics was excellent and that camouflaged my otherwise mediocre vocal talent. I had a narrow range, enforced by an unpredictable squeakiness when I transgressed its boundaries—something Pa told me I would grow out of, although I didn't believe him.

The evenings at camp had always been my favorite part of the day. We would sit by the campfire, talking and singing, cooking hot dogs on sticks over the flames, eating roasted marshmallows and Hershey chocolate bar squares between graham crackers for dessert. That year, though, it was different. Ronnie's presence, and over a year of martial arts indoctrination by my father, meant it was time for my "coming of age." I knew I had to become a man.

I had my guitar at camp that year, wanting to show off the songs I'd mastered to my friends. However, as I looked across the campfire at

Ronnie Tilton, standing like a golem in the flickering shadows, I couldn't help cracking a wry smile as I thought, *Now* that *is no music lover*.

The integration of Florida's public schools, unimaginable to some, was on the horizon. I listened to an emotional fireside debate. Thirteen-year-old Meg McDougall passionately advocated the importance of working together to create a society where people were free to think and act on their conscience.

"A country where people are treated equal, without regard to sex, race, and religion. That's what Jesus would want," she implored with passion to a generally unreceptive audience.

Ronnie's response was terse: "What is wrong with you, girl, spouting that Jew commie hippy crap? And I know where it's coming from. It's coming from *him*." He pointed at me, fire in his eyes. "That nigger-lover."

That night by the campfire, other than playing an old church hymn "Morning Has Broken," I hadn't said a word about anything, including their civil rights debate, Ron's presence being the reason for my silence. In the back of my mind, I was trying to formulate a plan, a way to confront him, but on my terms. However, having been publicly branded "nigger-lover" meant everyone sat staring at me in expectation. In the Deep South, these were fighting words, and Ronnie Tilton was spoiling for a fight, whether I was ready or not.

We were of an age where my very manhood rested on what happened next. My father had told me this would happen. He had taught me what was expected of me. He had prepared me. I knew what had to be done, but honestly, at first, I did not want to do it. I sensed that it was a switch that, once turned on, could not be easily turned off.

"Ronnie..." I said, pausing to buy time. But, seeing no clear way out, I decided to speak my truth. I said it in a deeper voice, one that was new to me. "I want you to apologize, not just to me, not just to Meg, but to all of us." As the sentence ended, I recognized the altered timbre and tenor. I sounded like my father.

Ronnie's face took on a snarling grimace of disbelief and his skin tone showed shades of purple in the flickering light of the campfire. "Screw you, Montgomery, you hippy piece of shit."

I snapped back, "Think about what you are doing. This is a Christian camp. You are a junior camp counselor. You are supposed to be the teacher of our Bible class. Yet, all you do is talk hate. First and foremost, Jesus taught love, not hate. And...think about it. *Jesus was a Jew*. Not one of the people in the Gospel, *not one*, fit into your KKK definition of 'white.' What the heck is wrong with you?"

"Nigger-lover!" was his only response.

My boyish panic had passed. "That's right, Ron, I *am* a nigger-lover. I love Catholics and Jews, too. I am even making a real effort to love a vile ignorant piece of shit like you."

I felt something new rising within me. It was an irresistible desire, a strong and powerful bloodlust to begin the fight. *Lust.* I think it was the first time in my life I experienced a *lust* to do something. It was intoxicating. I laid my guitar against the log bench, and as if by second nature, my hands balled into fists and my legs tensed like coiled springs as the adrenalin flowed. I was ready. Just like my father taught me, I was thinking through the fight, planning my moves, assessing his weaknesses.

"Your mother is Catholic," Ronnie uttered with a venomous snarl. "You learn that BS from your 'Catlick' cocksuckin' mother?"

But I'd had an epiphany, for my father's indoctrination into the world of ritual male violence now required a 180-degree shift. He'd taught me to fight, but with a clear head—no anger. For me, and the desire rising within me, I somehow knew that keeping cool was not in my nature. I resolved to use everything Pa taught me but *also* this power rising within me. My desire to fight Ronnie was fueled by bloodlust. I had to fight...and fight to win. I wanted to kill this mean snarling turd, and I was no longer a circus animal doing tricks for an audience to the tune of a whip. Wild and fierce, my anger was a burning rage, getting hotter by the second, searing my face, as if I was too close to the campfire.

Fecklessly fearless, Ronnie walked in front of me, blocking the blaze of the fire, casting his shadow upon me. He taunted, "Get up and fight, you pussy!"

When I didn't move, he took one step closer, grabbed his crotch, goading, "Don't wanna fight? Okay, then—suck this, you 'Catlick' piece of shit. Suck this, nigger-lover. Pretend it's some big ole nigger dick!"

Several of the other guys—who I had thought were my friends—laughed.

My guitar was leaning beside me on the log bench. In what seemed like slow motion, Ronnie raised his left foot. Trying to save my guitar, I grabbed it by the neck, just not fast enough. Tilton's foot came down hard, targeting the sound hole and smashing the body. The old Martin blurted a death chord—B flat—as the big wood body was crushed by Tilton's enormous weight.

Something Izzie had told me a year earlier flashed to mind: *Use a baseball bat if you have to.*

I went berserk. Without a word, I leaped high into the air, broken guitar in hand. As I came down, I rained blows on Ronnie's head with the shattered Martin Dreadnaught. He covered himself, his arms protecting his face. As soon as he covered his face, I began kicking him, Army Ranger style, with the steel-toed Corcoran paratrooper boots I used for hiking at camp. I landed blow after blow. In seconds, Ronnie's tree-trunk legs buckled from well-placed kicks to the sides of his knees.

He dropped to the ground, whimpering. Then he was all mine. His pleading didn't even register with me, for I was lost in primal fury. I savaged him with endless kicks to the body. I might have even killed him had friends not pulled me away.

Our parents were called. In the 1960s, the police rarely got involved in such things. My father came. Ronnie's father came. Pa reacted when he heard from the camp director what he'd been told Ronnie had said about Ma. My father glared at Reverend Tilton. Pa always believed the man was one of the Klansmen who had come to our farm years earlier. Reverend Tilton saw the look and cringed. My father was respected in our community. He was President of the Thoroughbred Trainers, Breeders, and Owners Racing Guild (known in racing circles of the day as T-BORG), Worshipful Master of the local Masonic lodge, and on the board of directors of Marion State Bank. Pa was feared, too. Everyone seemed to know of his exploits as a decorated Army Ranger in the war. The Dolan brothers were mere icing on the cake.

Ronnie was fired for misconduct, and based upon my extreme violence, I was expelled. The camp's director specifically mentioned Ronnie's homosexual "Suck this..." comment, pointedly asking, "Reverend Tilton, where on earth did the boy even come up with such a thing?"

Reverend Tilton dropped his head for a moment, shaking it in a "No way" gesture, then stood up straight and looked right at his mauled son, his mouth set in a snarl. "Damn you, boy!" The angry minister jerked his injured son up from his chair, and Ronnie cried out in pain as his father pushed him out the door. The callous cruelty of it left the rest of us stunned. With that, the meeting was over.

On the way home, driving west with my father through the dark forest on Highway 40's two-lane blacktop, there was complete silence except for the rough rumble of the Chevy pickup's big inline-six motor and the rustle of warm summer air through the open windows. Then, his face lit by the dim yellow glow of the dashboard lights, Pa said, "You could've killed that kid."

"Could-a, but I didn't," I replied.

"Mind a little advice, son?"

"No, Pa, I don't mind."

"Next time, pick on somebody your own size." This came with a satisfied smile from Pa. Ronnie was gargantuan, so I couldn't help laughing.

We never spoke another word of the fight, but I knew he was pleased with me when he said, "I'd like you to come with me on my annual trip to sell yearlings to our customers in England."

"England! Wow, thanks, Pa."

My father cleared his throat and, with his left hand on the steering wheel, he used his right to remove the round amulet he always wore from his neck. It was thick, made of time-worn dark tarnished bronze, with the polished bas relief of a reddish bronze Chinese warhorse in the center. It was attached to a sweat-stained, black-leather cord. I had never seen him without it. The image of the horse glimmered in the cab's soft light, accentuated by the pitch black of the forest highway. He handed it to me and said, "Put it on, son."

"For me?"

"Yes, for you. It was always meant for you."

"But it's your good luck charm."

"No, it is an antiquity from the Tang Dynasty, fifteen-hundred years old. You can tell it's Tang era by the shape of the horse's head. It is a family heirloom. Not to say it didn't bring me good luck, because God knows I've had more than my share. My guess, it is probably from the days of our Norman ancestors. They traded all over West Asia. It was given to me by my father during the war. He told me it had been passed down generation to generation."

All I could do was nod as I slipped it over my head.

"By the time you turned thirteen, you were the best boy I'd ever seen on the back of a horse. But you were still a boy. Now, Jake, you are both a man and a warrior. More than anyone, I know you are the horseman meant to wear this."

I could feel the weight of the ancient medallion, not so much its heft in antique bronze but in the gravitas of the chain of ancestors who had worn it before me.

"Thanks, Pa."

"Be the best you can be, son. When the time comes, pass it on to the next generation."

With that we drove in silence. My mind drifted and I thought about the fight. I was no longer a boy, but was I man or monster? I had a sense I might have killed Ronnie if I hadn't been pulled away. Was this a metamorphosis, like some killer wasp emerging from a cocoon? I played the fight back in my mind, as if remote viewing from above. The savage I saw...it was me, but not the me I knew and understood. Perhaps, from the beginning, my father, with his stern and sometimes cruel efforts designed to help control my temper, had seen this dark passenger, this squatter on my psyche. With that, I put the incident out of my mind.

A few days later, our practice track was abuzz with news. The Klan's state meeting house in nearby Oxford had been firebombed the night before. The glow of the fireball could be seen for miles. By some ironic stroke of fate, the only vestige of the cross-burning hate-mongers left standing was the white-washed telephone-pole cross that stood at the peak of the hill on the front left side of the smoldering ruin.

I was with Izzie, listening to some of the old ranch hands and customers yak about it over coffee at the racetrack's viewing stand. One old timer theorized, "The radical Nigras are striking back." Another opined that one of the Klan's own firebombs they had been using on black churches had probably prematurely detonated. Izzie tapped me and nodded toward the three Dolan brothers, who were joking and laughing with one another as they washed down the horses they had just exercised on the racetrack.

"This sure smells like IRA to me," he whispered.

"Nah," I replied.

"Could be, Jake. I bet your Pa just sent Old Man Tilton a message: 'Don't ever fuck with my family again!'"

I FOUND OUT WHEN school started in late August that Ronnie had withdrawn from Ocala Senior High, his father having disowned him, refusing to even supply the boy needed medical attention.

Ronnie's mother had died when he was a young boy. His maternal aunt, a spinster high-school history teacher in Bushnell, Florida, intervened and took him in. It was there he recuperated from his injuries. She had no place for a man in her life but reveled in having a son. He missed a year of school to heal—he had a blown knee and fractured femur—and to adjust. Under the maternal wing of a cultured, well-educated, caring aunt, Ronnie flourished. He started a new life the next year at Bushnell High.

I've now known Ron—the *new* Ron—about forty years. He was changed through his aunt's love, and as hard as it may be to believe, as adults, we have become friends.

Just a few months after the fight at camp, in a hushed-toned scandal, it was announced that Reverend Tilton had been shot dead by an enraged father, a member of his congregation. Tilton was accused of molesting the man's twelve-year-old daughter. With that revelation, a few other cases, boys and girls, became grist for the rumor mill. The whole truth never became public, because, in an erroneously liberal interpretation of the laws of justifiable homicide, the county prosecutor refused to press charges against the aggrieved father who shot down Reverend Tilton.

At the time, the stories made me wonder what Ronnie must have experienced at his father's hands. *Explains a lot,* I said to myself.

Since childhood, my mother had taught me tolerance, saying, "Don't judge others if you haven't walked in their shoes." Perhaps that is why I was open later in life to a friendship with a man who could easily have been a lifelong enemy. However, I never regretted my decision that night at Camp Oklawaha. There are times you must fight for what is right and there are times you must fight to survive. That fateful night, I did both.

chapter 5

Past Is Prologue

IZZIE IS ON MY MIND, and for my journaling therapy, I guess it makes sense because I looked up to him, depended on him, and loved him as a brother for most of my life.

Izzie was the youngest in a family of six children. His father, taken aback by his child's unusually small size, would have disowned paternity but for the fact that Izzie had the Nieves' family wide-eyed, button-nose look stamped on his face. Nardo Nieves called Izzie *el enano*, which roughly translated to "the runt" or "the midget." His father's constant disparagement and physical abuse gave license to years of additional abuse at the hands of his older siblings. Izzie thought his name was "*Enano*" until his family sent him away for an apprenticeship at El Comandante, a racetrack near San Juan.

Izzie's backstory was quite remarkable—literally rags to riches. His was a poor family of Carib descent with just a splash of Spanish and African blood. They lived in a shanty on a muddy deforested mountainside just a mile from the lush and government-protected El Yunque National Forest in Puerto Rico. Except for the major landowners, who were of white Spanish descent, everyone from El Yunque had his cinnamon creole look flowing from their Carib heritage.

Izzie could ride almost from the time he could walk. As a young boy, he was inexplicably driven to it, riding donkeys and old nags—anything he could catch. Though small in stature, on a horse, Izzie became large, a force to be reckoned with. As he got older, it became apparent he had a special gift with horses. By the time he was twelve, rich neighbors would hire him to work off the excess energy of their hot-tempered Paso Fino horses in exchange for a good meal and a couple of dollars. The Paso was the pleasure horse of Puerto Rico, strong and smooth-riding, with a four-beat lateral "single-foot" gait.

Izzie would leap aboard a "problem horse" and take off into El Yunque for hours. After a few of those trips, even the fieriest Paso was grateful to calmly carry his pot-bellied middle-aged owner around the workout ring for a half an hour of entertainment.

One of the ranch owners Izzie worked for, Don Ernesto, was widely considered *El Patrón* of El Yunque. He became the key to Izzie's future. The rancher's first cousin owned the top racehorse on the island, an unbeaten stallion named Camarero. For a hundred dollars, cash in hand, Izzie was placed into an apprenticeship by his father. In Nardo Nieves' mind, he had "sold" his boy and was no longer responsible for him.

It was probably the best single thing that ever happened to Izzie.

It was raining when the black mud-splattered 1953 Cadillac factory-stretched limo pulled up in front of the Nieves' mountainside shanty. Izzie's mother was sobbing in a corner of the shack. His father, before pushing him out the door, twisted his ear and snarled, "No matter what they ask, you say '*Sí, señor*'...*¿entiendes?* And do not speak unless you are spoken to. Understand?"

All Izzie could manage, tears in his eyes as he looked at his mother for the last time, was, "*Sí, señor.*"

He never saw his family again.

His father handed over a sheaf of papers, including a birth certificate, baptismal certificate, and signed guardianship papers to Camarero's trainer, Pablo Suárez. Suárez had the build of a football linebacker; his mustachioed face, framed by close-cropped black hair, was swarthy and square. The driver opened the door and Izzie followed Suárez into the limousine's passenger cabin, which had two sofa-like bench seats facing each other. The interior was a work of art, dripping elegance in swaths of rich leather framed by burled walnut woodwork. In the back driver's-side corner sat a gentleman, Don—in the truest sense of the word—José Coll-Vidal, the owner of Camarero.

Izzie sat next to Suárez, who reached across to the owner and handed over the papers.

"Good morning, Isidoro," Don José said.

Izzie looked puzzled. Don José tilted his head and, with a quizzical arch of his left eyebrow, asked, "What is your name, young man?"

"*Enano*, Patron," Izzie answered.

At that, Suárez chuckled. Don José gave Suárez a stern glance, then turned to Izzie and said, with iron in his words, "We will have none of that. No more *Enano*. I never want to hear that again. Your name is Isidoro. We will call you Isidoro or Izzie from now on. Do you understand?"

"*Sí, señor.*"

"I am Señor Coll-Vidal."

"*Sí, señor.*"

"Do you know who I am?"

"*Sí, señor.*"

"My cousin, Don Ernesto, tells me you do magic with his horses. He also tells me you are very smart. Would you like to work with us, with my racehorses?"

"*Sí, señor.*"

"For the next few years, you will learn to be a horseman. This is a noble and ancient profession. You will be paid a man's wage. Day's pay for a day's work. You will work for Señor Suárez." He nodded toward the trainer. "You will be given a fair chance to learn everything about riding, training, and caring for racehorses. You will begin as a groom, and if you prove yourself, you will learn to be an exercise rider. Perhaps, one day, a jockey. Señor Suárez will be your teacher and your protector. You will be treated well, treated fairly, but only if you pay attention and work hard. If you don't, you are gone. Understand?"

"*Sí, señor.*"

Don José noted Izzie had nothing with him, only the ragged clothes on his back.

"Pablo, I like this boy," he said to the trainer. "Get him a kit, clothes, personal hygiene, whatever he needs." He looked out the window, then nodded to himself. "And I want you to tell those roughnecks in the stable dorm that if he is mistreated, I will have their balls."

For the rest of the trip, Don José and Suárez talked horses, and it was as if Izzie wasn't there. But Izzie listened, already soaking up knowledge like a sponge. On arrival at the Coll-Vidal facility near the racetrack, Suárez escorted him to a large dormitory-style bunkhouse bustling with grooms, exercise riders, and jockeys, young and old. Izzie looked about, and for the first time in his life, realized he was the same size as almost everyone else.

During the first few months he cleaned stalls, and fed, bathed, and brushed horses. After four months, he was allowed to exercise the worst of the worst in the stable, in island slang known as *los pencos*, or roughly translated, "the useless ones." With Izzie on board, one of them snapped awake and started running like a real racehorse. That's how he got his first ride as a jockey. The horse would only give one hundred percent for Izzie—no one else.

Izzie went on to score three wins in a row with the *penco* gelding in cheap money claiming races, races where any other horseman can put up the cash claim amount before the race, and after the race is over, the horse has a new owner. It wasn't long before the *penco* gelding was claimed. By then, Pablo Suárez had Izzie as race jockey for many of the better horses in the stable, and as exercise rider for the great Camarero. As a jockey, his apprentice racked up a winning streak that Puerto Rican racing aficionados still talk about.

The San Juan racetrack rumor mill worked overtime with speculation on how and when Izzie would leave for the big-time races in the United States. He was asked his plans often, but deflected the questions about his future, saying, "I like it here." Izzie was loyal to a fault. His career path to racing in the States was dictated more by a cruel course of events than ambition.

Camarero suffered an intestinal blockage in 1956, and after a week of suffering, he died. Don Ernesto came from El Yunque to be with his cousin after the passing of his prize racehorse, but he also had news for Izzie: his mother had died after being beaten by his drunken father.

Typically, spousal abuse among the poorest of the poor had no priority in the rural justice system—no autopsy, no investigation, just another dead *fleche* (the Spanish word for arrow, and derogatory slang for a person of Carib descent). Don Ernesto, however, never forgot the times Izzie, showing clear signs of brutal abuse, had shown up to work with his horses. And with his influence, Nardo Nieves was arrested.

Rural Puerto Rico in the 1950s was a vestige of colonial feudalism, and while there were police and even a judge for El Yunque, behind them all was the real law, the real power—*El Patrón*. All it took was a word from

Don Ernesto and Izzie's father's fate was sealed. In a way, it was Izzie who got justice for the one person in the world he loved, and for the only person in his family who had loved him. In just a week, Nardo was dead, beaten to death in a jail-yard fracas.

With the stallion Camarero dead, and his mother gone, Izzie felt few ties to Puerto Rico. Deep inside, his sense of loyalty struggled with an inchoate desire to leave. He asked Suárez for advice, and though Suárez wanted to keep the boy at El Comandante, he did the right thing. He said, "Izzie, a talent like yours is rare. Just like Camarero was a one in a million, that is you too—one in a million. You are the best I have ever seen. When God blesses a man with such talent, it creates a destiny, but only if you seize it. If you play your cards right, you are destined for a big future as a jockey. Don José and I agree, you need to go to Florida. Talent like yours deserves a shot."

"*Sí, señor*," Izzie quickly replied, his ties of gratitude and loyalty to Don Jose and Suarez released.

In a matter of only a few months, it was worked out. Izzie was given not just a blessing but a checkbook from Florida's Barnett Bank, Ocala Branch, an account in his name in the amount of $2,500, $500 in folding money, a one-way ticket via Pan Am Airlines to Miami, a Greyhound bus ticket from Miami to Ocala, and written instructions:

Mr. Montgomery will meet you at the bus station in Ocala. He will help you as a favor to me.

Izzie's tearful thank you to Suárez and Don José was sincere. These men had changed his life.

Pa sold horses to Don José Coll-Vidal, and over ten years of doing business, they had become good friends. When Don José came to Ocala for the big racehorse auction at Ocala Breeders Sales, he sometimes stayed in one of the three small bungalow-style cottages surrounding our swimming pool. He asked the favor of Pa when in Ocala shortly after Camarero's death. I was there when he said, "Sam, one of my boys, Izzie Nieves, is thinking of racing in Florida. He's a good boy, seventeen years old, with no family. If I introduce him to you, will you take him under your wing?"

Pa, ever practical, asked, "Does he speak English?"

"Some. Well enough to get around."

"Glad to help you then, José."

"I'll have to transfer his guardianship to you."

"Send me his papers, José, and after he's been here a while, if he and my missus agree, I'll have my lawyer handle it."

"Thank you, my friend. I will let the boy know and arrange his transport. You will like him, and I swear, he is very smart, with good common sense, and most of all, he has amazing talent. You know, I have been doing this for over thirty years, and I have never, *ever* seen a jockey as good as Izzie. Trust me, he'll make you a lot of money."

I OFTEN THINK BACK on Izzie and those days when I was first learning to ride racehorses. My entire life has been centered on horses, but when I rode as a young boy with my mother, the old gelding Geronimo was a gentle, accommodating soul, safe and predictable. Izzie took me to a different place. The two-year-old racehorses were untrained, high-energy, super athletic, and often wild-natured. Izzie taught me, and I tried to ride like him, but that was impossible. I was talented but his freakish genius was not in me. However, once I was trained, Montgomery Racing Stables never saw a two-year-old Thoroughbred I could not handle.

Just like many of the young racehorses we trained, when I found myself on the edge of manhood, self-control did not come naturally to me. So much was changing all at once. From my parents, I learned that it was through understanding our imperfections that we found our way to perfection. Pa never hesitated to use the belt or a smack on the head to drive his points home. My father was, at times, brutal with me. As I grew older, I confided in Izzie my anger and resentment, and he told me of his own abuse at his father's hands. The difference, he said, was that his father took pleasure in being cruel.

Mine was trying to teach me.

He then shared a story I hadn't yet heard.

"I was with your pa at the track in Monmouth, New Jersey," Izzie began. "I had just turned twenty and won a big race. I was celebrating, and by the end of the evening, I was drinking cheap whiskey with one of the grooms, a former jockey.

"Well, I was riding Montgomery horses in two races the next day. Past midnight, your pa found me and ordered, and I mean *ordered*, me to come with him. I was staggering drunk. He helped me back to my motel room, and as soon as the door closed behind us, he snatched me up and pinned—and I mean *slammed*—me against the wall. I was helpless as he said, 'Son—and Izzie, I do think of you as a son—I am only going to say this one time, so you'd better fucking listen: if I find you drunk like that again on the night before a race, I will kick the living shit out of you and that will be the last time you ever ride for me. Understand?'

"Of course, I was terrified—your pa is a strong guy—so I nodded, and he let me go. He sat me down on the bed and started pacing. Your pa doesn't have a great poker face, Jake. I could tell he was worried about me more than he was angry with me."

"What's the difference between anger and concern if they both lead to violence?" I asked Izzie flippantly. Had I posed such a question to my father, he would've smacked me and told me to figure it out myself. To tell the truth, had my dad tried to explain it to me at that age, I probably wouldn't have listened, because that's often the nature of the relationship between a teenage boy and his dad. Izzie, though, was more like an older brother, and I hung on every word that came out of his mouth.

"I'll tell you the difference, Jake," Izzie answered. "My dad beat me black and blue just 'cause he could. He did the same to *mi madre*. You know why my dad did it? Because he wanted to have absolute control, no matter the consequences. He was a sad man who failed at everything he did, so he took it out on his family, and—after all the crying and screaming—he'd just walk away. Your pa, though, Jake, he *never* walks away. He stayed with me in the motel room. He got me water and crackers to soak up the whiskey while he lectured me." Izzie stood up and mimicked my pa in that moment, adopting the swift dramatic gestures my pa makes and making his voice deeper while he acted the scene out for me: *"Do you want to end up like that drunken barn rat Benny Dipozito you were with? I don't think so. You know he used to be a jockey with a big future. But look at him now. Whiskey will do that to some men. But I'm not going to let it cripple you like that."*

I chuckled at the great impression of Pa—he captured him well—but Izzie wasn't laughing. He gave me a serious look and said, "You see, Jake, he was trying to teach me. Maybe he didn't know any other way to do it. But it worked. Maybe it worked because I knew he loved me. I never had a father that loved me, only your dad, and I know he loves you, too."

Izzie's life was hard, dangerous, and pain-filled. Racing was the most dangerous professional sport, measured in terms of fatalities and serious injury. When flying along on the back of a racehorse at forty-plus miles per hour, you have placed your life in God's hands. No matter how good you are, the danger is there. A horse breaks a leg and collapses in front of you, a horseshoe flies loose to clobber you, a girth strap breaks—

there are a hundred possible different disasters packed into a two-minute rush. Izzie had, over the course of his career, broken thirty-seven different bones. He'd suffered numerous concussions, and even fell into a coma twice. On more than one occasion he returned to our farm from the hospital for extended rehabilitation.

I loved Izzie, and despite all his hardships from his early life, he was the happiest man I ever knew. He even died happy. That was about twelve years ago. Izzie was never late for morning training, so one day when he hadn't shown up at the track, I went to his double wide and knocked. Sound from the TV filtered through the windows, but no one answered the door. I entered. There he was...gone. Sitting in his La-Z-Boy recliner, he wore only white boxer shorts. Oprah was on the TV. In his right hand, resting upright and unspilled on the arm of the chair, was a half-full can of his favorite Puerto Rican beer—Medalla. In that moment, a ray of sunlight landed on the golden beer can. It sparkled and I saw that Izzie was smiling. He died smiling.

I was called to his lawyer's office for the reading of the will. He'd written a letter for the lawyer to read, but wrote it to my parents, even though he knew they were both dead:

> *Sam and Sarah, I guess I am with you now. I am forever thankful to you for everything you have done for me. You took me in and guided me to a career where I became a man, a man that was respected and honored. I never really had the love of a family in my life before you. When you died so unexpectedly, I tried to be there for Jake. It was not my way, to marry or have children, but you know what Jake means to me. He has grown to be a fine man and your grandchildren, they are amazing. I have stories to tell you.*

Izzie left me everything he had: three banker boxes full of memorabilia, including two Eclipse Awards for Outstanding Jockey. The lawyer then handed me a checkbook for a joint account, in my name and Izzie's, with a balance of $532,678.94.

"This is your inheritance," the lawyer said.

Izzie had gone from being *El Enano*—the Runt—a nobody on the hardscrabble fringe of the El Yunque forest, with no future, to a jockey whose wins and awards are in the history books for all time. I took the checkbook, but no check was big enough to replace riding with him in the hour before dawn, ready to start a day of training. I missed his chatter, his running commentary on what he thought about almost everything under the sun. I missed his wisdom as well as his friendship. I relied on Izzie, and his advice, because I knew he loved me.

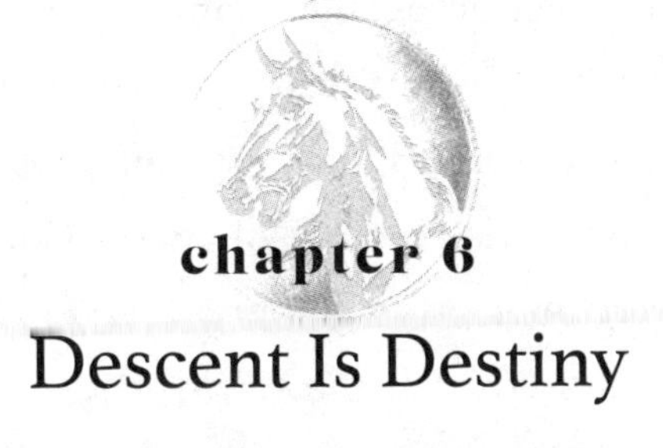

chapter 6
Descent Is Destiny

GOING TO ENGLAND! The unbridled excitement of a teenager is something I can describe but no longer feel. My traveling experience as a kid had been limited to long interstate car trips for obligatory annual summer visits to family. It had been the same every year during school break for as long as I could remember. We would load into the car and travel ten hours north to see Grandma and Grandpa Pettigrew in Tennessee. Then, after three or four days, we'd embark on another all-day drive north to the Montgomery and Mortimer farms in the mountain valleys of Western Pennsylvania, thirty miles north of Pittsburgh.

This summer was going to be different. Going to England became the most important thing in the world to me. I circled the departure date on the wall calendar above the antique tiger maple desk in my bedroom and crossed off each day that passed with a big blue "X." The desk had been my father's and a few more generations of Montgomery children before him. The tiger maple, with its naturally complex and intricate gold and black striping, became a source of autistic fascination as I frequently meditated on the maze of lines and swirls instead of doing homework.

Now, though, I was obsessed with the United Kingdom, and nothing distracted me from learning all I could about it. Our itinerary was

Ireland, then England, then across the Channel to Normandy, followed by a visit to Montgomery Castle in Wales. My spare time at night was spent reading Pa's written assignments from our Encyclopedia Britannica. He required I read specific entries about William the Conqueror and various members of the Mortimer, Montgomery, and FitzRandolph families. I was specifically obsessed with the town of Montgomery in Wales... learning everything I could about the town bearing my name, not just from the encyclopedia but also a deep dive into library resources. I was on a manic Anglophile high. A Roger Miller song, *England Swings*, was a big hit on the radio that year. One evening after dinner, I performed it, singing with my newly minted baritone voice and playing the more robust-toned Taylor acoustic guitar that my parents gifted me to replace my shattered Martin.

PA AND I FLEW, FIRST CLASS, on Pan Am from Miami to London. The First-Class cabin was luxurious, and the service was spectacular. Then, we caught a commuter flight into Dublin. Pa rented a car at the Dublin airport and our first stop was the Curragh in County Kildare. Ireland's flat-racing hub was just over an hour from the city. Jet-lagged, I slept in the car parked outside of the trackside training barns while Pa took care of business, which he wrapped up in just a few hours.

He woke me when he was done. "Stay awake until dark or your sleep is going to be screwed up," he cautioned.

From the Curragh, we drove to the Hill of Tara in County Meath. Hill of Tara was the political and spiritual center of the ancient Irish kingdoms. County Meath was the Irish epicenter for steeplechase racing. Our first stop was a pub where Pa met up with a cohort of Irish friends.

There I discovered that in Ireland I could legally drink a half-pint. (I suspected that was where the slang term "half-pint" for a youngster came from.) As I sipped my stout, I listened. It was a raucous never-ending flow of racing exploits and horse talk. I met Pa's best friend, Rory Darragh, Ireland's greatest jump race jockey in his day. His daughter Maureen Fitzgerald and her husband Gerry Fitzgerald were there too. Both were equestrian champions. For my benefit, the crew from the pub took us on a whirlwind tour of Golden Miller Stables and its training academy. From there it was off to the biggest house I'd ever seen, known simply as Kenwood, or Kenwood House, sitting halfway up the hill.

When we arrived at Kenwood it was as if a red carpet had been rolled out. An array of servants greeted us and helped us to our rooms. It felt like something more than just the hospitality extended to a business associate. It was clear to me we were honored guests. My father was persnickety with me, with instructions about cleanliness, dress, and manners, as we got ready for what would be my first formal dinner party. We were being honored by Gerry's mother, Lady Elizabeth Fitzgerald, and the dinner had all the trappings of the Biblical story of the prodigal son, complete with the finest wine and the fatted calf.

After dinner I snuck out to inspect Gerry's Jaguar XK120 convertible parked in front, top down. With the men embroiled in an emotion-charged, whiskey-fueled, political debate, only Lady Elizabeth noticed as I walked out. I had no interest in Irish politics, I didn't know the people or the issues the men were talking about, but that car was the most beautiful thing I had ever seen. As I sat in the driver's seat, I saw her watching me from a window. For just a moment, we were eye to eye—I could feel the intensity of her gaze—but I broke the connection to study the Jaguar's dash and gearshift, imagining myself driving through the Irish countryside.

The next day was spent with my father inspecting horses. Golden Miller was, according to Pa, "home to the greatest riders in the world, and the best of them is Rory Darragh." From the look of Rory, I did not doubt it. He was sinewy, with thick, well-defined arm muscles. Standing five feet, eight inches, he moved with the grace and balance of a big cat. He sported cropped reddish-brown hair, with a touch of steel-gray at the sides, and a trimmed copper beard. His tanned face, much like my own, even had a sun-kissed ruddy glow, not the more typical buttermilk-white Irish skin tone. Pa told me the meaning of his name in Gaelic: "Rory means 'red' and Darragh means 'oak.' Strong as oak, too. I've seen him whip a muscle-bound oaf twice his size at arm wrestling." Pa put his fists up and flexed his biceps for emphasis. I nodded in agreement. "By God, his name suits him well!" Pa exclaimed as he pounded his right fist into the palm of his left hand.

Rory trained both riders and horses in the art of the steeplechase, also called hunt racing or jump racing. Colonel Darragh, as he was known to his apprentices, also managed Ireland's finest stallion-breeding facility. The original part of the stable was four hundred years old, and the current operation was named after the great Golden Miller, a famous jump stallion from the 1930s, winner of the English Grand National, that had been foaled on the farm.

Rory was on a big black Irish Draught gelding when we drove up, and he dismounted to greet us. Pa had business to discuss with him but first, Rory looked at me, estimating the inseam of my leg, then lowered the stirrup straps on his saddle by several notches.

"You want to ride, Jake?" he asked, already knowing the answer.

"Yes, sir."

"This is my horse, Fitheach," he said.

"Never heard that name before. What does it mean, sir?"

He gave me a lopsided smile. "Ah, because he's coal black. *Fitheach* means 'raven' in the mother tongue. Now, take him out for an hour or two while your da and I work."

"Thank you, sir." I was itching to ride and explore the magnificent swale of a valley that unfolded before us.

The day before Pa and I left for Europe, Izzie had given me what he called a "coming-of-age" present. It was an Olympus camera with an adjustable zoom lens, in a leather camera case. A wide leather strap with black plastic cannisters of thirty-five-millimeter film attached like rifle cartridges in a Mexican bandolier secured the camera. Before mounting Fitheach, I strapped this gift across my chest.

"Jake, see that big hill?" Rory said, pointing to the prominent landmark a few miles away.

"Yes, sir."

"That is the Hill of Tara."

"Yes, sir."

"See that church steeple in between us and the hilltop?"

"Yes, sir.... Is that how I find my way back?"

It was a question that Rory didn't answer, but rather turned to my father and said, "Smart boy, Sam."

I was in the saddle in a heartbeat and slipped the big black gelding into a swift canter. Rory's horse was amazing, the epitome of harmony and power. Without a second thought, I headed for the hilltop and my first visit to the Stone of Destiny—*Lia Fáil* in Irish—which protruded straight up from the deep green hill known as Tara. This coronation stone for the ancient high kings of Ireland was a huge phallic monument. Ten feet of steel-gray granite protruding from the rich black soil at the apex of the hilltop, it reigned over an expansive vale. I had never seen a place so ancient or so naturally beautiful. I felt as if I were a part of this place. It wasn't just being part Irish, for I never thought myself Irish. I was American—red, white, and blue, through and through. It was a vibe, what some describe as a vortex, but whatever it was, I could feel it in my bones. From horseback, I framed the *Lia Fáil* with the scenic view beyond and clicked my first photo with the Olympus.

OUR NEXT STOP WAS LONDON. There we met a series of well-heeled French and English buyers. Today, a tremendous amount of vetting occurs in a big-dollar racehorse transaction—everything from workout times, to videos of the horse on the practice track, to X-rays. But the year of my first trip to England, we sold a little more than $250,000 in yearling racehorses based upon Pa's word alone, along with five-generation hand-drawn pedigrees. These young horses would often stay at our farm for training, some until they reached the age of two and a half and were ready to race, others for their entire racing career.

Pa's English customers were much more formal than his Irish friends. They were the *crème de la crème* of British society—typically "Sir" this and "His Lordship" that. To them, Pa was "Mister Montgomery." I was "Master Montgomery." I learned that in the British and Irish context, the terms were used differently than in the United States. "Mister" was the honorific used for those over eighteen and "Master" for a boy from a respected family under that age.

From Dover, we took a ferry across the English Channel to Normandy, France, and drove our rental car to the tomb of King William the Conqueror. We spent two days in Normandy, touring historical sites related to King William, and enjoyed a half-day excursion to an ancient stone warlord tower in Mortemer en Bray built by one of my Viking ancestors a thousand years before, when he'd first helped to conquer Normandy. It was reputed to be the oldest standing tower in France.

On the return trip, the ferry ploughed its way back to England through heavy seas, a thick foamy spray breaking over the broad bow. We stood on the ferry's top deck, and Pa explained to me how we were descended from King William. It prompted me to ask, "Does this mean we are somehow better than others because of it?"

He responded in a didactic tone, "First of all, a thousand years have passed. There are thousands upon thousands of descendants of King William out there. Almost thirty generations—you do the math. Second, being descended from Norman nobility is not necessarily something to brag about. Some of your ancestors have been great. Some have been depraved. When it comes to greatness, it's your actions that make the man." He paused before completing the moral point of his lesson: "A truly noble person is humble, and when circumstances allow, kind. Knowing about your ancestors, good and bad, provides life lessons. We train horses and it's very much the same. Why do I consider bloodlines before breeding? Because much of what that young horse is going to be is determined before he draws his first breath, by the bloodlines. Even a great trainer can't make a slow horse fast, but a bad trainer can make a fast horse slow. See what I mean, Jake?"

My honest response was, "No, Pa."

When I was slow on the uptake, my father could be sarcastic, so I had learned to just admit it, and perhaps because this subject matter was intangible to the point of being ethereal, his look was kind as he explained, "Jake, the man you are is a mosaic of hundreds of factors, some good and some, frankly, challenging." He paused, struggling for an example, then in a tone infused with affection, said, "You don't like it when people tease you about your nose, do you?"

"No, Pa."

"Neither your ma, nor I, have a nose like that, do we? Did you grow that nose on purpose, or even better, do you think your mother and I did something to make that nose?"

He knew I hated talking about my nose, and although I was silently fuming, he also had me thinking, as I responded once again with a shake of my head.

"My point, son, is that your nose, just like a hundred other things about the way you look and act, comes from ancestors you've never known or seen. And, just like the nose on your face, these factors are a part of you that I can't train, and you will learn to live with. Now think, Jake: maybe if you know where it comes from, you can better accept it as a part of you."

I nodded.

"Now, son, what did Laertes' father tell him before he left for France?" He knew my predilection for memorization, so he quickly caught himself and answered his own question to avoid my likely autism-driven recitation of the *hundreds* of words of advice bestowed, in Shakespeare's *Hamlet*, by a concerned father to his son, Laertes. Pa tapped me on the chest and said, "'To thine own self be true.'"

He waited for another head nod from me to confirm my understanding, and continued, "When you are challenged in life, remembering the accomplishments of those in the past can give confidence in the future. Remembering their failures can help avoid catastrophe. But remembering that who you are comes from them is just as important, because that is how you got here. You come by these traits honestly. So, be true to yourself in the best way possible.

"King William is a perfect example on the good side," he went on with a chuckle. "I'm not saying he was a saint, but he was a good king.

The illegitimate son of Robert, Duke of Normandy, rose to become Duke of Normandy, and eventually King of England. He did so over a host of others who had better blood claims. He did so not just by skill in combat but also by teaching himself from an early age to be the smartest and most politically astute guy in the room. William was a thinker and a diplomat. As a king, he became England's greatest. He unified England, and it has lasted as an unconquered nation for, ah...almost a thousand years."

"And on the bad side?" I asked.

"Son, you need look no further than King William's father, Duke Robert. First, remember Norman means 'north man.' He was Viking, and the greatest of Viking warriors were *berserkers*. Robert was a berserker."

"What is a berserker, Pa?"

"They were legendary Norse warriors who transformed in battle into a trance-like state, impervious to pain and having an insatiable fury. *Berserker* means something like 'bear men.'" He looked at me to assure himself I was getting it, then continued, "'Bear,' as in *ber*...ber...serk. But they were also sometimes referred to as 'men in wolf skin.' Anyway, this berserker gene is there, and it pops out in the stronger bloodlines every once in a while. Duke Robert was an extreme example. Do you know what he was called?"

"No, Pa."

"He was known far and wide as 'Robert the Devil,' even though he had dubbed himself 'Duke Robert the Magnificent.' He was a man of unimaginable violence and fury. They say he killed his older half-brother, Richard, to become duke. But here is what could be a little-known historical truth—the murder was not to claim the duchy, but a violent fit of anger over a stolen meat pie. *A meat pie*."

I pondered his condemnation of our ancestor Robert. I felt I understood the berserker firsthand. Indeed, I had been there in my fight with Ronnie Tilton. I did not accept my father's negative view of Duke Robert either, for I knew that without my berserker, I would have been Tilton's victim rather than the victor.

~

AFTER OUR RETURN TO LONDON, we spent a few days touring the countryside. We went to Ludlow Castle in Wigmore, on the edge of the border with Wales. Even though it was 1961, we were on an ancient-looking, smoke-belching, coal-fired steam train right out of a 1920s movie set. Ludlow Castle was an impressive sight—a massive, relatively intact, ancient Norman stone fortress. We visited the grave of Baron Roger Mortimer, the Lord of Ludlow and the Norman general who conquered Wales.

Baron Mortimer, according to Pa, was my great-grandfather, over twenty generations back. "The Montgomery and Mortimer families intermarried frequently because they were geographically close together," he said. "Montgomery Castle is just across the border in Wales, less than a day on horseback from here. Fragments of the two families even migrated to America together and eventually to far-western Pennsylvania."

I never questioned Pa on issues of genealogy. He often expounded with complete accuracy on horse bloodlines going back hundreds of years, so it made sense to me that he likely knew our own family bloodlines equally well.

The next day, we traveled by chauffeured car—an overstuffed two-tone 1958 Austin Princess—to the small town of Montgomery, Wales. The three-hour scenic trip included a lunch stop at the house of a distant cousin in the small Welsh border village of Newcastle. We traveled on narrow roads through beautiful hill country—sparsely populated because large areas were steep and rugged and not good for farming or livestock. On arrival in Montgomery, the quaint Welsh town that bore our family name, we left the driver behind and walked up the steep hill to the ruins of Montgomery Castle.

From the apex of the hill, where the castle once stood proud, Pa stretched out his right hand and pointed at the horizon. "Son, as far as you can see, your ancestors won these lands in battle. This is what has been given to yours."

I hesitated, thinking over the awkward ambiguity Pa created using "yours" in his statement. My high-masking autistic personality, having achieved a semblance of "normalcy" by listening carefully to every word and every nuance, caught the hidden subtext. Pa was a stickler for good grammar and not one to misspeak. I knew the solecism was intentional. But if Pa wanted to tell me clearly, he would have done so. So, I let it pass.

He came out of the pause with a vigorous "*Garde Bien*!"

Garde Bien, ancient Norman meaning "watch well," had been the Montgomery family motto for at least a thousand years.

I offered my well-trained Montgomery father-son response:

"*Garde Bien*."

chapter 7
The Awakening

IN JUNE OF '64, JUST AFTER my sixteenth birthday, I returned to Ireland. This time it was under protest. I traveled alone, having been told by my father that a summer as an apprentice stallion-handler to Rory Darragh, with special instruction at the nearby riding academy, was a "great opportunity for my future and not subject to debate." Pa was a lot of things, but not a liar.

My parents took me by car to the old Orlando Airport at McCoy Air Force Base. Back then Orlando had fewer than a hundred thousand people, with no tourists, and the airport was a small walk-through terminal on a small side apron attached to the military base. The ride to the airport was tense, with my mother and I both hushed, simmering with resentment at my involuntary summer deployment. They dropped me in the Eastern Airlines' parking lot. All I had was a suitcase filled with clothes, an Army backpack with my passport, tickets, English, Irish, and American currency, a book teaching conversational Gaelic to English speakers, and my guitar.

My mother was in tears as I turned away from the car. I squinted into the bright and brash Florida sun. In the background, the thunderous roar from the eight jet engines of a gigantic B-52 bomber taking off from the U.S. Air Force's long bomber runway sent shock waves rippling across the tarmac and into the parking area. Exhaust fumes of burnt JP-4 jet fuel made my eyes water. My mother's tears reminded me of Izzie's apprenticeship, and the last time he saw his mother. The thought made me stop and turn around.

I took a stride back toward the car, looked deep into her eyes, and said, "I love you, Ma. I'll be back. I promise."

Then, I was gone.

Upon my arrival in Ireland, there was no fanfare this time, no party at Kenwood. I was sent straight to the barracks and spent my first week training as "stallion handler," groom, exercise rider, and assistant in the breeding shed for only one horse, the great jump race stallion Peter Proper. Just two years earlier, Peter Proper, with Gerry Fitzgerald up, had won all the greatest jump races that England and Ireland had to offer. The stallion was called "Old Pete" by everyone at the stables, even though he was still in his prime. The apex of equine strength and athleticism, he approached everything from racing to breeding with an uncanny calm.

Horses exhibit wide ranges of physical diversity. The same goes for their personalities. Old Pete was unique in that he had a mind of his own, and unlike most horses, he used it. Great horses, like great humans, are born into this world every day. Pete was that kind of a horse—great.

Ridden. Most horses are ridden. One definition of "to ride" is "to forcefully persuade another to do what you want." For both horses and humans, it is much the same. We accept this subjugation. It fits our species' genetic profile as social animals. With horses in the wild, a herd of a hundred follows one or two leaders without question. In human hands, almost all horses follow, but some fight. Some horses connect with their human counterpart in what becomes a respectful, loving relationship. And then, once in a blue moon, there is a total outlier—a horse like Old

Pete. Among horses I have known, he was one in a million. Why? Because Pete's intelligence influenced the outcome. He was a thinker.

When I first saddled Pete, I started out slow, inspecting the place, jump by jump. As we progressed, I sensed he liked me. I relaxed as we rode around the campus. Darragh Equestrienne Center and Academy, known worldwide to female equine athletes as DECA, had ivy-covered stone, two stories, and an elegant portico entry flanked by academic classrooms and a meeting hall. The equestrian center, with stables, a full-size dressage arena called a *menage*, and a state-of-the-art stadium jumping facility, as well as several practice rings for dressage and show jumping, surrounded the rear of the school. The school was busy that summer, even though many of the full-time boarding students were away on vacation. I sat, relaxed on Pete, and watched as a gaggle of girls rode by on their way to the outdoor dressage ring. I caught their eye, which evoked a wave of giggles.

By then, I was six foot, three inches, one hundred eighty-five pounds, and still growing. I was almost always a head taller than anyone else around. In the barracks, the Irish stable hands and grooms called me *feckin a fathach* (loose translation: "the fucking giant") as often as Jake. A stroke of good luck brought me a mentor and protector. Rory, like my father, was close with the Dolan family. One of the senior grooms at Golden Miller was a nephew of our three Florida-based Dolan brothers. So, from the start, Danny Dolan took me under his wing.

As for the constant jabbering and insults, I soon realized this was how the young Irish muck savages talked to one another. Nary a sentence was uttered in the dorm that did not include *feck, shite, arse*, or *bollocks*. The Irish stable hands talked endlessly, I mean *on and on and on*, about four subjects: jump racing, Gaelic football, a stick sport called hurling, and what I suspected were highly fictionalized tales of sexual activity the prior weekend in Dublin. Listening to these exploits was instructive, as they covered ground I'd never even imagined. At the time, I thought this type of behavior was specific to Ireland. (As soon as I joined the Marines and lived in a military barracks with forty other young men, all officer candidates, I realized this behavior was more about group masculinity than nationality.)

As his apprentice, Rory took time with me, explaining in detail things about Irish racing and horsemanship. I'd helped at the Montgomery breeding shed since I was a boy, but Rory explained everything about his program to me anyway, so that I understood the "Golden Miller Way." A master instructor, he had his method. With precise detail, he outlined the three distinct groom functions in the breeding shed: mare handler, stallion handler, and entry man. The mare handler placed the straps called "hobbles" on the rear legs of the mare so she could not kick the stallion and wrapped her tail with an elastic bandage and tied it off to the side for ease of entry. My job as stallion handler was to lead the stud in, walking to the left of his head with two lead lines, one to a halter and the other to a "stud chain" of stainless steel that, given it was wrapped around the stallion's tender nose, with a snap got the horse's immediate attention. I had to keep the stallion moving forward and focused for breeding. Finally, the entry man was responsible for effective consummation, grabbing the stallion's extended penis with his right hand and guiding it into the mare as she was mounted from the rear. In his left hand, he often held a cup to collect spillover semen for sperm-count analysis.

Every first-class breeding operation had a small lab with a microscope. As a boy, my father taught me how to do the stallion sperm analysis, assessing not just count but also motility—a fancy word for "activity." Rory knew I'd been trained on the microscope and gave me that responsibility. At the end of every day, I went to the office with the microscope and the refrigerator to evaluate sperm samples. I'd then write a report to Rory with my assessment of sperm count and motility for each stallion bred that day.

I was in Rory's office with Gerry one morning and spied on the wall behind Rory's desk a photo of Rory, Gerry's father, and my father in British Army uniforms. I asked, "During the war?" and Rory explained that the three men served together on secondment as officers in a British unit, the Eighth Commandos. The three of them, along with several British counterparts, specialized in behind-enemy-lines horse-mounted commando missions. I knew Pa had served in England and fought from D-Day through the German surrender, but seeing him in a British uniform was a surprise. I had mistakenly assumed he always served as a U.S. Army Ranger.

Gerry's father died at Kenwood, a year and a half after Gerry was born. Unresolved complications due to severe wounds incurred on a commando raid near Wangen, Germany, finally took their toll. However, Rory and Pa stayed in close contact after the war. When you saw them together, you would think they were brothers, not from looks but from the way they moved and interacted.

Rory pointed at the photo. "Jake, you look like your father, except you're about a head taller and, well, you obviously got that big feckin' conk from somewhere else."

"What's a conk?" I asked.

"Your nose, boy, your nose." He motioned toward my face. I grimaced, still sensitive about that specific characteristic being the butt of humor. Rory rolled on, oblivious to my discomfort. "You are right up there with 'Old Conky,' the long-passed Duke of Wellington himself. First Irishman to run England, you know." He nodded at me once, his brows arched, as if to ensure I understood as I stewed in my embarrassment. "Lady Elizabeth claims him as one of her own. His granddaughter married into the FitzRandolphs. Gerry, she was your great-grandmother. Check the painting of the old Duke in Kenwood House." Then Rory paused before going on. "I tell you, I see your da in you, Jake, especially in the way you ride. I remember watching you ride away on Fitheach the first time we met. You are a natural."

"Thank you, sir."

"Your da, well, Jake, he is just about the finest man I've had the privilege to know."

"Mother always speaks very highly of him," Gerry chimed in. "Says Major Montgomery saved my father's life."

"That he did, Gerry, let me tell you," Rory responded.

Pa had a shoebox full of medals on a shelf behind his desk. Curious about soldiering, I'd asked him about them when I was a boy, but he always brushed me off with vague answers. All these years later, I can still hear him say, "The War, that was a hard time, Jake. I served in the European Theater." He rarely spoke of that time of his life, yet I pried it out of him that he had been awarded the United States' Purple Heart, two Silver Stars, and a Bronze Star. From England, the king had personally presented him the Victoria Cross. He was one of the few Americans to ever sport the royal post-nominal Victoria Cross, Britain's equivalent to our Medal of Honor.

Spurred into nostalgic reminiscence, Rory began telling his war story.

"We boyos, Fitz and I, had been palling around since we could walk. Made sense we'd go off to war together. We were called the 'Irish Volunteers.' Not the smartest thing I've ever done, that," he exclaimed. "Nobody here respected it, but during 'The Emergency'—Jake, that's what we called the War—some of us were ordered by our government to join the British ranks. The Taoiseach—that's Ireland's equivalent of Prime Minister—was Eamon de Valera. He met with us over a dinner hosted by Gerry's grandparents."

Gerry nodded. "He was close with my grandfather, right?"

"Aye, Gerry, your granddad was a hero in the War of Independence. And they were close friends," Rory explained. "The Taoiseach sent Fitz and me on our way to England with instructions to come back alive and with an encyclopedic knowledge of British strategy and tactics. I only met the Taoiseach that one time but, because de Valera was Ireland's greatest statesman, it made a big impression on me."

Gerry folded his arms, then raised a finger for emphasis, and said to me, "Kids today study him in school in Ireland just like you do with George Washington."

"Jake, did you know de Valera was born in America? New York City," Rory interjected. I shook my head.

"Irish mother. Cuban father. His father left them, and she returned with her son to Ireland when he was just a wee lad," Rory said, then continued with the war story. "As de Valera ordered, Fitz and I were seconded into the British Eighth Commandos with commissions as British Army captains. We were already Irish Army officers, but that was a bit of a joke. The Irish National Equestrian Team was all military, based at McKee Barracks in Dublin. It was the way our government funded our great national sport. All the riders were salaried officers. Even the grooms were Army noncoms. Truth be told, we were more playboys than soldiers. But,"—he uttered a heartfelt sigh—"the British Commandos changed all that. When it comes to slaughter, boys, no one is more heartless than an Englishman. After three months of intensive commando training, we were stone-cold killers."

Rory paused to collect his thoughts. "Jake, your da arrived at the Eighth, stationed near Glastonbury, just a few months after Pearl Harbor. Somebody high up in England had to have pulled strings to bring him over. He was one of the first Americans deployed there. We were the only other officers in the Eighth that weren't British. As soon as he arrived, Fitz pulled him aside with, 'Welcome to England, cousin...' Turns out we three were all related, and on various tangled branches of the family trees, we were second and third cousins...every which way. Because of that, we became a tight team, like brothers."

Rory took a bottle of Tullamore Dew from the credenza behind his desk, along with three coffee mugs. He looked me over and asked, "You drink whiskey, lad?"

"No," I said, but he poured each of us a drink anyway.

"We were on a mission in Germany's Black Forest. We had a squad of noncoms, Eamon being the top sergeant. After we parachuted into a clearing in the Black Forest, near the pre-war French border, we were met by German anti-Nazi resistance fighters. They supplied us with horses, which allowed us to approach the target swiftly, but quietly. They knew the mountain trails across the steep and rugged forest terrain. The target was a medical research facility disguised as a farm. They were using large animals, goats and horses, for nerve gas experiments." He took a swig from his cup. "Gerry, your da was in charge. We were sent to kill or capture a top German scientist, the Nazi's top biological and chemical warfare specialist, grab his documents, and blow up his lab. The place was guarded by a platoon of SS. With no moon, it was dark as the back of a stag-beetle."

He raised his glass in a toast to no one particular, then took another sip of whiskey.

"Fitz, Sam, and Eamon went in for the hit. It was supposed to be done silently, but shots were fired, the alarm was raised, and the night lit up with German flares. Fitz had killed the target but was gut-shot in the fracas. It was like we moved in just one moment from the blackest of nights to the midday sun. Sam, pistol blazing, was shooting Germans left and right as he ran, with Fitz clinging to his back. Eamon ran behind, providing covering fire from his semi-automatic carbine. The mission was successful, but at a big price." Rory looked at me intently. "Jake, your da got took a bullet in the shoulder as they made their escape, but he never broke stride as he ran to us, carrying Fitz on his back. Then, we all escaped on horseback."

"Damn!" I exclaimed. The story excited me. Fighting, war, combat—it all stirred something inside me. When Vietnam cranked up later, when my friends and even my parents had concerns about the propriety of the war, I deflected judgment because with the military draft, I had no choice but to serve. But the "real me," the teenager with a whiskey buzz who was excited to hear a story where a man was killed and his own father was wounded, *that* was the me that wanted to go to war.

Rory went on, telling me the part of the story I already knew. "Sam was awarded the Victoria Cross, presented by King George himself. I tell ya, lad, your da is a hero."

All I could think to say was a low, barely uttered, "Wow."

"Because of his wounds," Rory continued, "Fitz was sent home to Ireland, so he didn't attend the royal ceremony. Given my family's Irish nationalist roots and their service in the War of Independence, it's hard to understand, but I was proud to be a part of the ceremony. I felt like a feckin' 'West Brit' for the first and only time in my life. I won't deny it, meeting Ole King George was a big deal for me. The Victoria Cross is the highest royal military honor. Press made a big deal of it.

"From the reception at Windsor Castle, Sam and I left for Ireland. We camped out as honored guests at Kenwood for a month. Good thing your family is stinking rich, Gerry. We would have eaten and drunk a normal Irish family out of house and home."

"Speaking of eating," Gerry chimed in, "we are having dinner tomorrow at Kenwood House. Could you join us, Jake? You'll be seeing Maureen this afternoon for your first day of formal schooling, so I'll confirm with her and get it arranged."

"Sure, Gerry," I replied, "I can check with Maureen for the details."

Rory chuckled. "Boy, you mind your tongue's respectful when you show up at the Academy. That is *Máistreás Maureen* to you. Call her Maureen, and you'll be running back here with a riding crop shoved up your arse."

Gerry laughed. "I almost forgot, Jake, my mother has been asking me about you. She doesn't like you living in the workers' barracks. Everything okay there?"

"Yes, I'm learning a lot of Irish culture," I said with a grin, then finished off my whiskey.

As Rory and Gerry chatted on, I silently repeated "Máistreás Maureen" to myself beneath my breath, mildly stimming with the alliteration, preparing to depart. Before I could go, Rory poured a splash of the Tullamore Dew into each of our cups and proposed a toast honoring long-dead Fitz, shouting, "To the lost!" The final dram of whiskey was smooth and warm. I left with a glow.

~

A TWO-MILE-LONG GRASS OVAL near the breeding shed contained a practice track with three- to four-foot-tall jumps every furlong, which was an eighth of a mile. The infield of the track was a practice area for cross-country—hunt-style jumps, like banks and ditches. I walked and jogged Pete the entire time. We didn't take a single jump. He was eager to go but I relaxed him, as my mother taught me to do when on a new horse. Pete and I had all summer to jump and run, but today was one more chance to get to know one another, to make a good impression.

This stallion was a natural, responding to the slightest leg cues and any shift of my balance, needing only a touch of rein. He was so responsive that I felt awkward—clumsy, even. After an hour we ambled back to the stallion barn and Rory nodded at me with approval.

Once unsaddled, I took Pete on foot for a long cool-down walk, then washed him and put him in his stall. When I returned to the shed, Denny Mayo was bringing in a young chestnut stallion to service a flashy bay mare. The owner of the mare was there, wide-eyed at the sight. The stallion was wide-eyed, too, with flared nostrils, snorting as if breathing fire. His penis was fully extended, an inflamed red and white, two-foot-long appendage, bouncing around with what seemed like a life of its own.

The stallion, screaming and snorting, walked in powered by his rear legs, coiled and ready to mount. Denny was short and slight, and the horse on occasion lifted him off the ground as he ploughed forward toward the mare. The harsh stud chain across his nose was snapping to get control but with no effect. Ahead of it, the mare was just as eager, flashing pink, squirting and squealing with excitement.

I approached to tell Rory that I was done with Pete but, not wanting to interrupt, I stood off to the side, waiting to be recognized by the older men.

"I tell you, Rory," the customer said, "that big chestnut stallion is giving me an inferiority complex."

"Oi, Bart, you say, mate, now that you're an old man, you don't get quite so excited?"

"To be sure, I cannot bring the missus here. She'll call me out as a slacker."

Rory chuckled. "No worries, Bart. Just explain the facts to her."

"The facts, them's what worries me. That stallion can do that every day, all week long." He shrugged. "And he's a fire-breathin' dragon every time to boot."

"Big difference here, Bart, big difference," Rory said with mock sobriety.

"I'll say," Bart replied. "About a feckin' yard difference." He held his right arm out, stretched upward, with a clenched fist.

"Shite, no, Bart, no. It's quite simple. Unlike you, and no disrespect to your missus, that big chestnut stud hasn't been mounting the same old nag for twenty-five feckin' years."

Rory's customer laughed so hard that he doubled over. At sixteen, I did not really understand their joking, but as I remember it now for the first time in almost sixty years, I am laughing.

I WAS SUMMONED into the office over an intercom to the antechamber, "Susan, bring in Master Montgomery."

"Máistreás Fitzgerald is ready for you," the assistant said. She walked to the door. "Go on in. And stand at attention in front of her desk."

I entered, noticing straight off the riding crop on the desk near her right hand. "Good afternoon, Máistreás."

"Good day, Jake. Please call me Maureen."

"Yes, Maureen."

"You are a family friend, but if I'm going to give you special instruction, I need to go over our ground rules. Your parents said you're intelligent and capable of following directions," she said. "Therefore, I am going to assume when I speak, you understand me. If not, I expect you to say so."

She was condescending, and I was sixteen, so I replied with a clear hint of sarcasm, "Yes, ma'am. I understand English."

Instantly her eyes lit up. She slapped her riding crop on the desk. Then she rose and came closer. "I caution you, Master Montgomery, do not become impertinent with me."

With an effort to convey a humility I did not feel, eyes downcast, I whispered, "Yes, ma'am."

"Now, young man, tell me why you wanted to come here for the summer?"

I gave the question careful consideration. She expected honesty, and she was my host. Ma would not think well of me if I told Maureen that my father pushed the trip over Ma's tempestuous objections and my repeated statements that I didn't want to go.

"Ma'am, I confess I did not want to come. I had plans at home for the summer. I just finished rebuilding a high-power performance car, a 1961 Chevy Impala SS. I worked on it all last year and had hoped to enjoy it during summer break. However, my father thought my time was better spent here."

"Hmm," she murmured. "You like cars, auto racing?"

"Yes, ma'am," I replied with enthusiasm. "I sure do."

"Is that what you want to be, a race car driver?"

"Wish I could, ma'am, but I think I will be a racehorse trainer."

"I watched you riding Old Pete earlier. Who taught you to ride?"

"My mother, mostly." For some reason I did not want to mention Izzie.

"No formal instruction?"

"No, ma'am. For the first few years, from two to four years old, I rode with her around our farm. She set me in front of her and taught me straight from the saddle. Got my own horse at four, an old gelding. I've been riding horses ever since, almost every day, mostly helping bring young horses to our practice track, working as an exercise rider for the young racing horses, also bringing in cattle and hunting deer and boar in the forest. My father and one of our jockeys taught me to ride the racehorses." I made a gesture I'd learned from Izzie, pointing with my right hand from my feet to my head. "Just for training, of course, because of my size."

She chuckled at my reference to size. It was true; I was almost as heavy as two American race jockeys combined. She made a gesture for me to stand up straight, saying, "Your posture in the saddle is wrong—we do not ride here at a slouch. Balance is the most important part of what we do. You must be upright and balanced on the flat before we begin to jump. We have at least a week of schooling on the flat before I teach you to jump. You cannot have good balance without good posture. Also, you need to better understand how to use your legs and hands. The first thing we work on tomorrow is balance and advanced equitation."

"Yes, ma'am."

"Next thing, in order of importance, is strength. Not brutish strength"—she tapped her riding crop against her leg—"but core strength. Do you know what I mean by that?"

"No, ma'am."

She stood just two feet in front of me, so close I could smell her: bacon, dark chocolate, and lavender. It was the best thing I had smelled in my life. She gave me an upward nod. "Please pull up your shirt, to your rib cage."

I was confused, and she could see it on my face. With her riding crop, she poked at my beltline, using the flat flap of the whip to tug up on my shirt, signaling me to pull it up. "Come on, boy."

I complied.

"This," she said, poking me in the navel with the crop, "this is your core. Front and back, it is the center of strength for riding. A great rider must have strength at the core." She took a moment to make direct eye contact, her eyes a sparkling emerald green. Next, she traced an X across my bare abdomen with the crop. "Hmm, you seem very well muscled there." The caress of the short leather whip went like an SOS radio message, first up to my brain and then straight down to my loins.

"The rider's next most important asset is leg strength, principally the thighs." As if it were the most natural thing to do, she tapped the tip of the crop between my legs, right at my upper thighs, signaling for me to widen my stance. I complied. Then, she bent her knee and leaned forward, her head less than a foot away from my belt buckle. She put her hand on my upper right thigh, and I stifled a gasp as she squeezed hard. Then she looked up at me. "Flex this muscle."

I complied, my thigh muscles bulging.

"Excellent leg strength," she said as she rose from her inspection.

Her touch was more than I could bear without a visible sexual response, and she stared, clearly focused on the throbbing bulge in my pants.

"Master Montgomery, I do not think I have ever asked this of a student." The corners of her mouth curled up in a wry smile. "Of course, I only teach girls here, but, purely in the interest of safety, I feel I must inquire: Are you wearing underwear?"

"No, ma'am."

"And why not?"

"I forgot to pack them."

"Boys!" she harrumphed. "Do you use athletic supporters in Florida sports?"

"Yes, ma'am. We call them jock straps."

"Well, now," she said, "Would that be 'jock,' as in, let's say, 'jockey'?" She struggled to mask her amusement. "I trust somebody informed you before now that we train riders in the sports of stadium jumping and jump racing, which can involve very strong impacts." She made direct eye contact again, searching for understanding. "Do you know what I mean? Do you understand me?"

I was taken aback, and stammered, "Y-ya-yes, yes, ma'am."

My protruding enthusiasm had wilted, like a flower after a hard frost. I was red-faced with embarrassment but knew she was telling the truth. As if acknowledging that we had crossed a threshold from professional to personal, she uttered in a sultry voice, "You may call me Maureen," then reverted to her didactic tone as if nothing happened. "The third important component of being a good rider is presence of mind. Please bring it with you tomorrow for your lesson. And, for goodness' sake, walk into town, go to the chemist's shop, and buy an athletic supporter. Get your other protective equipment—helmet and body pads—from my father. Show up tomorrow,"—she pointed at my crotch, touching me there with the riding crop— "with your privates flopping around like laundry in the wind and I will break those bollocks myself."

Many boys would have been reduced to tears by her cutting comment, but not me. I looked her straight in the eye. Fixated. Such an intense green, flecked with brown and gold. She was the one who broke the stare, blinking then casting a glance toward the floor.

"Yes, ma'am," I said once more.

"Maureen, *not* ma'am," she replied sternly. "I'm not some old lady."

Just for fun, I replied, "Yes, ma'am."

My grin was matched by her bubbling laughter. With that, she gave a slight nod of dismissal and said, "Please join us for dinner tomorrow night. We will fetch you around seven. Do you have a tie and sports coat?"

"Yes, Maureen."

"Wear them for dinner, please."

"Will do. Thank you."

I did an about-face, left the room, and walked straight to the village chemist. It was both a pharmacy and a dry-goods store. The cashier was a cute young lady, maybe eighteen, with milk-white skin, long dark-red hair, a perfect splash of freckles, and eyes as blue as the sky. Of course, I couldn't find the athletic supporters. I thought of asking but looked at her and couldn't bring myself to speak the words. Something about the sexual awakening that had just occurred left me tongue-tied. I fumbled around the pharmacy section of the shop, looking aimlessly from section to section, not knowing jock straps, feminine hygiene products, and condoms were all kept hidden behind the counter so as not to cause public affront, with the sale of condoms requiring a doctor's prescription. The clerk recognized my confused teenage look, and mercifully, interceded.

"Can I help you?" she asked. I told her what I wanted, and she responded with, "What size?" Once again, I was tongue-tied. She looked me up and down, gauging my height, and with an impish grin said, "Well, let's see, you are quite big, so let us just go with a large." Then, in a moment ever-etched in my memory, she winked and said, "For now."

I handed over the cash and thanked her by name, which was on her tag: Colleen.

She smiled. “And, young sir, what might your name be?”

“Uh, uh… Jake,” I stammered, almost as if I didn’t know my own name. “I’m working this summer at DECA.”

Her nod affirmed she knew of DECA, the Darragh Equestrian Center, and then she asked, “Are you an American, Jake?”

“Yes.”

“Come back soon,” she said.

I looked at Colleen. She looked back at me intently. The moment was charged with what I now suspected was a strong sexual energy. Prior to this point in my life I had told myself, and others, “I am a man now.” I was so enamored with the concept that I had ignored the facts. Two months before, if given the choice of a date with a beautiful young lady or a drive in a Ferrari, it was no choice at all. Cars were everything to me; women meant nothing. But in just one hour, I had gone from a state of naïve asexuality to feeling sexual with every fiber of my being.

chapter 8

Never Let the Horse Make the Decisions

AS I SAT ASTRIDE PETE, trotting toward Maureen's office, the only thing on my mind was Maureen Aideen Darragh Fitzgerald. My new equitation teacher was ten years older than I was. Her hair showed reddish auburn in the sun and yet, by some strange alchemy, seemed black as night in the shade. She shared, but with sublime femininity, her father's muscular athleticism, not an ounce of spare fat.

I don't know if what happened next was caused by my mental reverie, or perhaps Pete just had enough of my schoolboy crush, but with no warning he went from a lazy walk to a fast canter. The horse was a powerhouse, and he surprised me. The acceleration was so abrupt, I almost fell off his back. He was running headlong toward the two-meter-high privacy hedge surrounding the schooling arena. I had no idea what was on the other side. Disaster loomed as I struggled to regain my seat and secure purchase through my stirrups. I tried to rein him in, pulling back hard, but had no control as we plunged headlong into the landscaped thick green wall. As he went up and over, I loosened the reins and grabbed his mane with both hands. My elbows extended out like wings. I leaned forward, my face touching his corded neck. We were flying, barely clearing the hedge. We landed with a thump, followed by a couple of hops, and skidded to a stop in the schooling arena.

It was amazing, exhilarating, and left my heart going so fast I could hardly breathe. I could hear it pounding in my head, like an Irish bodhran drum with a profundo bass line at a hundred beats per minute. Then, as I struggled to regain my composure, Pete, with insouciant nonchalance, trotted to the front porch of the school's administrative office where Maureen stood wide-eyed, in disbelief.

"What kind of a crazy wanker are you?" she shrieked at me. "That horse is worth over a million quid. For Christ's sake, you could have injured him, and killed yourself to boot. I cannot *believe* Elizabeth insists on you riding Pete! I damn well told you—feckin' told you—*no jumping* until we achieve a good balanced posture. You looked like a big feckin' bird, half in the saddle with your elbows out flapping around like wings, and that big feckin' beak of yours buried in the horse's neck!"

I was shocked by her *ad hominem* attack. In a faltering response to her screeching, I responded, "Ma'am I, ah, um...I didn't think—"

"Think?" she roared again. "You are too ignorant to even presume to think. You, young man, need to follow my instructions!"

Then, in a theatrical change of character, she laughed. It wasn't a normal laugh. It had a frantic edge to it.

"You should have seen yourself," she said in a more moderated manner. "Eyes wide with fear, arms flapping in the wind, like some absurd big bird. 'Big Bird'! Yes, that's what I'm going to call you—Big Bird—until you show me something better." She nodded to herself. With that, her approach became even more condescending, as if she were dealing with a child. "Come now, Big Bird, let's go over to the arena and do some figure eights." She started walking. "Remember, Big Bird, today's lesson is about posture. Stop sitting like a stooped-over Neanderthal. Get upright, perpendicular to the horse's back." She looked up at me. "Back straight, Big Bird, back straight!"

This went on for twenty minutes, with her nagging me at every turn about my posture, hand position, leg position, or the angle of my foot in the stirrup, often poking at me with the riding crop like I was a cow. For a "normal" person, this might have been overwhelming or mortifying or both. For me, the mild abuse was irrelevant static. She was my first crush, my fixation. Maureen played me like a virtuoso plays a violin. But I wasn't just reacting to her, I was learning. Equitation was an art I intended to master.

Once she realized her gruff sarcasm left me undeterred, she changed her tactics and blew my mind. "Your mother taught you to ride from the saddle?"

"Yes."

"I'm coming up."

Before I processed her words, she reached across my thigh and crotch, grabbed the buckle of my belt, and vaulted, catlike, without effort, into position behind me. I sensed great amusement from Pete, who snorted and gave a little scoot of excitement.

"How did Mommy hold you when you rode together? Like this, Big Bird?" She reached around me and interlocked her fingers over my navel.

I couldn't form a response—the words simply wouldn't come out.

"Answer me. Did your mommy do it like this?"

"Yes, ma'am."

Thinking back on this, I consider now how things have changed over fifty years. Today, there are virtual classes and exams that focus on preventing the very kind of interaction I had with Maureen. Organizations focus sharply on the impropriety of a riding instructor making sexual advances toward any student when there is an imbalance of power, and in particular when that student is a minor. In the sixties, such activity—especially when the "innocent" was male and the sexual instigator female—was, at most, the basis for a bawdy congratulatory toast when all was said and done. Today, though, we expel and criminally sanction individuals who behave in ways exactly as Maureen did.

This fact doesn't change what happened then or how I felt about it. Then was then and now is now. Fact is, her actions rendered me mute; my sexual inexperience was no match for her. She sensed it and manipulated that energy. I knew on some level what was happening was wrong. I think she did too. But my moral hesitation was instantly dashed by my lust. I was not forced. I let her control me. She was the first woman who really seemed to "want" me. I could not refuse.

As we trotted, performing figure eights around the arena, Maureen pushed and poked to get my body position correct. I think I would have been even more aroused but for her constant references to my mother and use of the obnoxious appellation "Big Bird."

"Is this how Mommy did it, Big Bird?" she asked as she pulled both my shoulders back and forced an erect posture by pressing her breasts against my back.

Her hands then dropped, one to the center of my lower belly, pulling me tighter to her, the other slipping all the way down, her heat enveloping me.

"This is something most people do not know. This is where your core energy comes from, your root chakra. Feel it rise. Use it."

I was dizzy with excitement. Then, she dismounted as abruptly as she'd mounted.

"Gerry and I will pick you up tonight. Walk over to the school office, there." She pointed. "Seven sharp. Please dress correctly. Lady Elizabeth has no tolerance for slovenliness."

She snapped her finger with a loud pop, turned, and walked away. Like the day before, when I was mesmerized as I stared into her eyes, it was now her tight rounded bottom that fascinated me. Sitting stupefied in the saddle, I stared, unblinking, my mouth gaping open, as she sashayed away, her ass swinging, as if to the beat of a metronome. Just the sight of her made me rock hard.

On an impulse, I tweaked Pete's right rein, squaring him up toward the hedge.

"Okay, boy, let's see you do that again."

As I nudged him with my heels, he didn't budge, but rather turned his head all the way around to stare at me. We were eye to eye and, because of his contorted pose, his were bulging. He snorted, spewing a fine mist of mucus over me, then laid his ears back and curled his upper lip, fully exposing his red gums and grain-stained teeth in what can only be described as a big smile. Pete's not-so-subtle message was: "You must be joking!"

Then, on his own, Pete decided to walk back to the stallion barn as if I were a brainless bag of potatoes strapped to his back. I tried to stop him, tried to turn him, but to no avail. Returning to the stable was a good idea, just not my idea. I gave up and thereby violated one of my father's oft-imparted rules of horsemanship: *Never let the horse make the decisions.*

Having given Pete his head, I went back to daydreaming about Maureen. I was intensely aroused. Every small shift of the horse's ambling walk evoked erotic impulses. I'd never even masturbated before, but my raging hard-on fought an epic battle for living space with my now far-too-small jock strap. Embarrassingly, my first orgasm was on Old Pete. When I ejaculated, I knew what had happened. A flood of good feelings washed over me and left me in an empty mental space, bereft of thought or constructs. Frankly, I didn't care where the horse went. It was as if I opened my eyes, and we were at the stable wash rack.

With Pete put away and fed, I rushed to clean up and dress for dinner. My navy-blue sport coat and slate-gray slacks were wrinkled—victims of my transatlantic trip. I dutifully pressed them in the dorm laundry room and ironed a clean white dress shirt. Then I touched up my black Oxford shoes with a quick spit shine until the toes sparkled. Preparations finished, I went to my bunk and took a nap, dreaming of Maureen.

At six o'clock, I showered and put on my dinner attire. A maroon tie, a gift from Grandma and Grandpa Pettigrew, twisted into a simple, but neat, four-in-hand knot topped off my outfit. Another of my Autistic quirks—unlike my classmates who dressed in ripped jeans and ratty T-shirts as a fashion statement, I enjoyed formal dress. It gave me a feeling of peace and security, like a hug. A suit and tie, even a military uniform—such clothes locked me in the comforting embrace of knowing *I looked the way I was supposed to look.*

Promptly at seven, Gerry arrived in his new car, a two-seater Aston Martin coupe. Gerry, but no Maureen. He got out.

"Cheers, cousin."

I was dismayed. The look on my face was enough to communicate, *Where is Maureen?* But that look was quickly displaced by my admiration of his car.

"Maureen is feeling a bit under the weather." With an expression of nonchalance and a flick of the wrist, he tossed me the keys. "She says you love sport cars. Want to give 'er a go?" In the distance, a stallion squealed. "Old Pete," Gerry quipped. "He always knows if I'm nearby, even a half-mile away. Uncanny."

"No shit, 'uncanny.' I think he was riding me instead of me

riding him today. The horse ignored me and jumped into the schooling arena over that high hedge." I pointed at it. "Then, after, when I tried to make him jump again, he ignored me and walked, pretty as you please, back to the wash rack."

"If you can jump that big feckin' hedge, you can handle this bad bitch. Remember, we drive on the left."

The silver 1961 DB4 GT with the aluminum Zagato body was the most beautiful car I'd ever seen.

"Can I really push it?"

"Do you know how?" he asked. "This isn't some old milk wagon."

"I have a Chevy Impala SS Turbofire 409, with dual quads, four on the floor, and a race-tuned suspension."

"Fast?"

"You bet!"

He shrugged. "Then go for it!"

The Aston Martin's brutal 330 horsepower inline six throbbed to life. I shoved it into first gear, clutch to the floor. "Where to?"

"To the left, cousin. Go left. Down the road about three miles and then you take the left fork and go halfway up the hill. You've been there—once you're on the road up, you can't miss that huge Georgian white hat-box monstrosity we lovingly call Kenwood. It must have been all the rage when my grandparents got married."

"You keep calling me cousin. Are we related?"

"My mother said we were cousins. Let her explain. I don't pay attention to these family-tree things so important to her."

"My father is the same way. Always talking about the Randolph, Mortimer, and Montgomery families."

"Truth be told, Jake, we are an incestuous lot. Maureen is my second cousin, twice over on the Fitzgerald side, and a second cousin once removed on the FitzRandolph-Spennithorne line. Spennithorne, near York, is the FitzRandolph's ancient fiefdom. They've held it near a thousand years. But, as to the 'cousins' thing, in my opinion, it is a form of familial genetic arrogance, where we only marry relatives. By the way, I'm a Montgomery, too, the fourteenth Lord Montgomery. It's an English title that passed to me when my father died."

"No shit," was all I could say.

"I have no use for titles. Unlike my mother, I think Irish, not English. Just like you have Vietnam, we are—despite the formal peace—really at war with England over the occupied counties of Ulster. It is a long-term guerilla war for the Northeast of Ireland. That will change only when the British Crown leaves this land and we come to peace with the ethnic British among us. The ethnic Brits are far more Irish than they are British anyways. Plus, we've been so saturated with English culture that we will never really be free of it. My mother, in a way, is the true enemy. She controls almost all the English and Euro brands sold in Ireland. Every radio and TV commercial she does for Marmite, Jaguar, or Golden Syrup makes England a part of our daily life." He laughed at himself. "Of course, like almost everyone in Ireland, I love Golden Syrup and Jaguars."

For just a moment I flashed back to a few weeks earlier, when my father ordered me to go to Ireland—my long-awaited summer vacation with my restored Chevy 409 ruined. Even though I had been furious, I'd known better than to direct my ire at my father. I could not count the times as a child he'd whipped my ass with his belt in response to the slightest temper tantrum or sign of disrespect. I thought of myself as a man at sixteen, just not enough of a man for that battle. Without a word, I had turned and walked across to the equipment garage, cranked up the Chevy 409, and gone straight for the interstate highway, I-75. I drove south fifteen miles to the Bushnell exit, watching for highway patrol speed traps along the return northbound route. On heading back home, I'd hit the gas at the northbound on-ramp, and in just a few seconds, taken the car to its top end, somewhere well over the one hundred twenty miles per hour capacity of the speedometer. The speed had tried to tear the car apart—I'd been able to feel, in the screaming of the motor and the groaning of the torque twisted chassis, the threat of impending doom—but a demon had possessed me. I could not slow down. The roar and rumble had washed my anger away. I could think of nothing but driving and driving fast.

So, just like then, I took my surging emotions to the road. The Aston Martin was already warm, so I revved the motor to 2,500 rpm, popped the clutch, and floored the accelerator, throwing a shower of gravel ten yards to the rear. I'd had a monthly subscription to *Car and Driver* magazine since I was twelve, and the DB4 GT had been a featured car when it came out. I remembered its impressive stats. It had what was for the time, the early 1960s, massive acceleration, zero to sixty in less than six seconds. Just under six seconds sounds puny today, but then it was supercar territory. Just a few cars, my Chevy 409 included, were a part of that club. But, unlike the Chevy Impala, this Aston Martin had the handling of a Grand Prix race car. I intended to squeeze out every drop of that promised performance.

Without braking, I entered the corner, pushed the clutch partway in, slipping it as I revved up, then popped it out, setting up a sliding turn as the resulting shock load of torque broke loose the rear wheels. Then I downshifted and slammed on the accelerator, doing a drift turn to the left. The smell of burnt rubber from the Dunlop tires hit my nostrils as I shifted into fourth gear. We hit "ton up"—over a hundred miles per hour—on the straightaway a few seconds later. The engine was screaming at just below redline after I downshifted and braked to swerve into the switchback at the base of the Hill of Tara before shifting to third and shooting upward at full blast.

"Feck, boy!" Gerry yelled over the engine noise. "I had my doubts about this cousins BS, but with driving like that, we might actually be related. Now slow the feck down! We're here."

"Thanks, man, this car is something special," I said as I pulled to a stop, cut the engine, and we got out. I couldn't wipe the big smile off my face.

I offered him the keys, but he demurred.

"Keep them. You drive back."

With that, he took out his silver flask and had a generous swig. He didn't offer me any.

"Let's go." He led the way up the grand front steps of the palatial entrance. The butler—he must have been waiting for us—opened the front door from the inside as we approached.

"Good evening, sir," he said to Gerry.

Then an older man approached. "Hello, Gerry!" He glanced at me before turning back to Gerry. "Jake, I presume?"

"Yes, it is." Gerry gestured toward me. "Jake, meet Eamon Cavanaugh. He served in the war with our fathers. Eamon runs our home and the houses in Dublin and London. He also oversees several of the manufacturing facilities in Shannon and Sligo, as well as our farming businesses here in County Meath."

"Hello, Mister Cavanaugh," I said, hand outstretched. His grip was firm, containing a strength not to be underestimated.

"Good evening, Master Montgomery. Your father, a fine man, the major." He then turned to Gerry. "Your mother will meet you in the drawing room."

The atrium was as opulent as I remembered from my trip two years before with my father, with an inlaid marble floor and a grand double staircase to the second story. The drawing room, in the left ground-floor wing, was equally graceful and sophisticated. Portraits, some hundreds of years old, hung on the walls. An elegant dining table in the next room over was set for four. I paused to inspect a painting of a British soldier, perhaps from the Napoleonic War era. The portrait caught my eye. I could not place it, but something about him was familiar.

"Hello, my love," Gerry's mother said to him with a lilting accent.

I turned to see him kiss her before he gestured at me. "Major Montgomery's son, Jake."

"Jake, welcome," she said. "I have so looked forward to seeing you again. My goodness, I think you have grown more than a foot since last we met, and look at those broad shoulders." She extended her hands, one on each shoulder.

"The pleasure is mine, Lady Elizabeth." I looked up with a direct gaze and a smile. She was in her forties—tall, trim, and elegant. As Gerry and Eamon discussed a personnel problem at one of their factories, she took me aside.

"Jake, your father is one of my favorite people. I saw you looking at that portrait of your, and Gerry's, great-great-great-grandfather, Sir Ralph FitzRandolph, Viscount Spennithorne." She paused to appreciate the painting. "He strongly resembles your father, don't you think?"

"Indeed, I was thinking he looked like my father. Is that why Gerry says we are cousins?"

"Look there." Without answering my question, she pointed to another portrait across the hall. "My father." I nodded as she added, "He has your nose. We call it the Wellesley nose, inherited from him..."—she pointed to a different portrait— "the First Duke of Wellington, Sir Arthur Wellesley."

Then she answered my question: "Your father is related to me through the FitzRandolphs of Spennithorne and the American Randolphs in Pennsylvania. These Randolphs are all direct descendants of Charlemagne. Your Grandmother Montgomery is a Randolph, as is your Great-Grandmother Mortimer. Your mother, through her Irish-born mother, is also a second cousin to Gerry's father, twice over, on the Cullane and FitzAlan lines."

"My father taught me some things about my heritage but never told me we were all related."

She smiled. "We are. In fact, you and I share many strong family connections. Later, when we have some time, I will explain them all to you. We even share a few unique family traits. So, to me, you are always going to be very special."

"Why, ma'am?" I asked, taking care not to seem impertinent.

"Because, of all the cousins around today, only you and I share the FitzRandolph birthmark. Legend has it that it comes down to us from Charlemagne."

"What birthmark?"

"On your neck, just above the breastbone."

I knew immediately what she was talking about—a golden-brown splotch that, with a little imagination, resembled a lily. I remembered the old women at my great-grandmother's farm fawning over me and inspecting the mark when I was a youngster.

"You have one too?"

"Me, too," she said, and, after brushing her hair back, she pointed with her left hand to a light but distinct golden *fleur de lis* on her neck below her right ear. Almost identical. "That isn't all, Jake. I hear you have autism."

I froze, wondering how she could know something my father kept so well hidden.

"I do, too," she continued, "but when I was young, it was a just part of growing up a little different. It runs in our family, so my parents dealt with it at home. So, maybe better than anybody, I know what you are going through. Instead of it being a problem, with the help of my family, I turned it into an asset. You can too. You should also know that special inherited trait is one shared over the last thousand years by several of the greatest lords and ladies of our house."

I wasn't sure what to say. No one had ever talked about my autism in a positive way. It was always something to be dealt with, corrected, or hidden. It struck an unanticipated emotional chord. So, I changed the subject.

"Your stable is beautiful. It is a well-run operation, ma'am."

She smiled at my obvious redirection. "I hear you've been riding my horse, Peter Proper?"

I grinned as Gerry rejoined us. "Great horse! But I'm not sure who is in charge yet."

"Well, that is Pete," she replied. "Gerry always said, once the race started, he just gave Pete his head and settled in for the ride." Gerry nodded in agreement, mouth full of an *hors d'oeuvre*.

The food was exquisite. Through dinner, Lady Elizabeth kept me talking by skillfully asking question after question in a way that made for good table conversation. We talked about my parents, our farm, our horses, my aspirations, and even my Chevy Impala.

She went particularly deep on the topic of religion, as if she were looking for something. First, she talked about Ireland being a Catholic country but a tolerant one, too. Then she told me about her upbringing under the Church of England and her conversion to Catholicism to marry Gerry's father. Gerry opined that the problems all started with Henry the Eighth breaking from the Roman Catholics, who held a claim flowing from Jesus to the divine right to anoint kings. The newly formed Church of England had no such claim, so Henry, and the generations of English aristocracy that followed, actively sought to destroy Catholicism by brutally persecuting the faithful in England and Ireland.

Lady Elizabeth wasted no time in repartee, saying with a complaining tone, "Keep in mind my son is neither Church of England nor Catholic. I think 'agnostic libertine' is the proper label."

"Mother, I have told you repeatedly that *my* beliefs are *my* business. Please stop misrepresenting them." It was the only time I'd seen him resist her in any way. She rolled her eyes, then she set her sights on me and pressed for me to answer.

"We are Presbyterians, ma'am, but just because of my parents. I hold my own beliefs."

Her eyes widened in surprise. "Please, Jake, tell us then, what are these beliefs you hold?"

"I know I'm young but...so, umm, well...I believe in God...well, not just *believe* it...I *know* it. I feel it. But I just can't find words for it. To tell the truth, I believe in God, but really can't explain why. I suppose I'm just not that smart. But, I am smart enough to not allow some other man tell me what God is or isn't."

Gerry looked at me. "Jake, that is one of the most honest and intelligent opinions I've heard. Here, Protestants and Catholics spew hate-filled things against each other, ministers from the pulpit, their parishioners on the street. What kind of God would promote this insane fratricide among Christians?"

With an impertinent wink and grin, I answered his question with a query of my own: "Perhaps an Irish God?" The table erupted in laughter. Eamon raised his glass and toasted: "To the Irish Gods!"

Lady Elizabeth looked at me and smiled. "My, oh my, such an impish grin!" Then she turned to her son. "Gerry, I do love this boy, don't you?"

Gerry chuckled. "Yes, but enough talk about religion. Remember, Mother, you taught me, 'No religion at the table.'"

With another toast, glasses raised, Gerry exclaimed, "Welcome to the family, Cousin Jake! And, Mother, I do approve. He's fun. He drives like Sterling Moss. And, unlike our tosser cousins from York, he feels like family."

With that Eamon barked, "Here, here!"

"I knew he would," Elizabeth replied, for all to hear.

At her discreet direction, much of the remaining dinner conversation was about me. I glowed in the spotlight of her attention. By the dessert course, I think she may have had the most comprehensive understanding of sixteen-year-old Jake Montgomery of anyone on the planet, me included.

Her parting words as we prepared to leave were really an order: "Eamon, please arrange to have Master Montgomery's things moved up from the barracks to Kenwood, Gerry's old room. Move in tomorrow. I trust that is fine with you, Jake?"

Eamon nodded, and I could only agree, saying, "Yes, ma'am. Thank you very much."

"We still have Gerry's first car in the garage out back, an old Jaguar." When Gerry had showed up to get me in the Aston Martin, I'd wondered briefly about the XK120 I'd so admired years before. "By coincidence," —she smiled at Eamon—"the chauffeur just had it serviced. Eamon, would you please make sure it is available for Master Montgomery in the morning?"

"Of course, Elizabeth."

"It is an XK120, 1953 drop-head coupe," Gerry said. "My first love! Just like you and your Chevy 409. In its day, the XK120 was reputed to be the fastest production car in the world, though when compared to my Aston or your Impala SS, it will feel underpowered. Modest acceleration, geared for top-end speed, but it handles like a dream."

"I do look forward to having a boy in the house again," Elizabeth said. "Eamon, please give Master Montgomery a weekly allowance—two hundred quid should do." She looked to Gerry for approval, and as he nodded in the affirmative, she exclaimed, "I feel we are going to have a wonderful summer!"

Gerry laughed. "Careful, Jake, a couple months as the pet of Kenwood House, and she'll turn you into a Little Lord Fauntleroy."

I smiled, recognizing his reference to the famous nineteenth-century book about an American boy being groomed to inherit his English uncle's estate and aristocratic titles.

As I drove the Aston Martin back, much slower this time, we traveled in silence—that phenomenon where comfort exists when there is nothing material to say. As we neared the dormitory, Gerry broke our quietude.

"Tomorrow, I am going to teach you to jump. Maureen has a doctor's visit in Dublin and will be out a few days." Disappointment must have been written on my face, because he then said, "Don't look so glum, boy. While I am not Maureen"—he delivered this with a knowing smile—"I guarantee you, this will be a riding lesson you will never forget. Have Pete ready in the breeding shed at half-past ten. We are going to do a practice race to the top of the Hill of Tara, Irish style."

"Irish style?" I asked.

"Yes, Jake, Irish style. From here to King's Seat, there are ten jumps, a double-ditch Irish bank, and a water jump, and from there a sprint to the big stone. No rules, except we go around nothing and over everything."

"I know it," I said. "I walked that course, inspecting the jumps as I hiked my way up to the Stone of Destiny from the dorm a few days ago."

"Excellent," he responded.

The three-and-a-half-mile serpentine course led to King's Seat, two stone pillars, not quite three yards apart. Legend had it that a true king of Ireland could drive his chariot between them at full speed without any contact. The Stone of Destiny, what Gerry called the "Big Stone," was the massive granite protrusion at the top of the hill—a powerful monument from prehistory, the site of druidic human and animal sacrifices and the ancient rituals for crowning a king.

It was clear to me that Gerry planned on winning this race he masked as a lesson. As I lay in bed on my last night in the barracks, my thoughts were of the coming race, picturing it jump by jump. Then it came to me. Gerry picked the final points for a reason: only one horse could pass through King's Seat at a time. First through King Seat, first to the Stone of Destiny, and I knew what I had to do. I had to beat him at his own game. First to the bottleneck, slow down to break the other horse's stride, then haul ass to the Stone of Destiny. With that clear in my mind, I slipped into a deep sleep.

chapter 9
Lessons Learned

THE MOVE TO KENWOOD HOUSE had me excited; I arrived at the stable early, my travel kit in hand. As I approached, Eamon and Conrad also showed up—Eamon driving the silver XK120, top down. Conrad had in tow a scrawny, freckled, bright-eyed blonde housekeeper to assist him. After an exchange of "Hiyas," I entered with them, Eamon and I turning toward Rory's office, where Rory focused on me with exaggerated cheer.

"Top o' the morning to you, young Master Montgomery. Looks like you are moving up to the manor house, and riding in style!" He pointed out to the courtyard at the pristine silver Jaguar convertible—the Irish call it a "drop-head coupe"—sitting beside a big gunmetal-gray, chauffeur-driven Bentley sedan. The uniformed driver leaned against the Bentley's fender, enjoying a smoke.

"Is that really for me?"

"Seems so, young man," he replied.

"Then, top o' the morning it is, Colonel Darragh!" I said with an ear-to-ear grin and my best Irish accent. I snapped my fingers and asked, "Eamon, my man, what do we need to do to make this happen?"

"Well, Jake," Eamon said as he abruptly rose from the chair he'd just sat down in and stood facing me. "First, let's dispense with this

'His Lordship Montgomery' foolishness, which is only compounded by Colonel Darragh's 'Top o' the morning' silliness. Second, I *run* the Kenwood estate, several hundred hectares of farm holdings, our poultry plant, our slaughterhouse, and our manufacturing facility and operations. In case I'm not being clear, I am *not* your manservant, and you, young man, are *not* 'Lord Montgomery.'" With an eye roll and raised brows, he snapped his fingers in an exaggerated manner to make his point clear. "I served with Colonel Darragh, Captain Fitzgerald, and your father through the war as a top sergeant. Now understand this, young Master Montgomery, we at Kenwood House are first and foremost an Irish Republican household, based on the strong principles of Irish nationalism and social equality. Your da has instructed me to act in his stead during your secondment to Kenwood House. In the event you need discipline, I have been given full authority to do so from your father. Back in the day, the Commandos, you wouldn't be the first young whelp Major Montgomery had me tune up. So, if you keep putting on airs, I'll box your ears myself, same as your da would if he caught you."

I was embarrassed, but I also felt my temper rising, a piece of me ready to test this challenge. Probably a big berserker-induced mistake on my part if he was even half the fighter Pa was. Rory, sensing my teenage temper, and perhaps my lack of control, placed his hand on my shoulder, establishing his authority and calming the situation. Then, turning us all toward humor, he began to laugh.

"Bollocks, Eamon, you old feckin' hypocrite. You talk like a bleeding socialist but when Lady Elizabeth whistles, you come running like a well-trained hound. Nay, worse, a bootlicking lap dog!"

"True, Rory, but that is personal, not politics."

"By God, Eamon," Rory said as he gestured with a mock theatrical flourish, his right hand skyward. "You surely were a fine commando, and no man could ask for a better top sergeant, but I never would have thought you'd become a heinous West Brit bootlicker in your old age."

Eamon guffawed. "Aye, Colonel, but you must admit she has such lovely boots."

The culture of County Meath was steeped in humor, often sharper than a knife. Eamon, true to his home culture, was no exception. He appreciated good humor, even if at his own expense. The man was known to be Lady Elizabeth's closest companion; it was one of those unspoken truths. Everyone respected his status as the lover of Widow Fitzgerald, yet because she refused to remarry, and unmarried union violated both church and civil laws of the times, their relationship would remain as it was, an open, but respected, secret.

THE BEAUTY OF THE DAY registered with me. It was a bright sunny morning. A light, cool breeze from the northeast danced across the hills and valleys, bringing with it the faint smell of pine and jasmine. All in all, it was a perfect day for a race.

Gerry rode Trigger—a magnificent golden gelding and his champion stadium jumper. Pete was a proven steeplechase racer. For a moment Gerry's choice brought to mind Pa saying to the Klan, "You boys brought ax handles to a gunfight." But I also knew there was more here, as Gerry was a seasoned competitor and I was a novice. I mounted Pete as they approached, calling out, "Hey, cousin."

"Hiya, Jake."

"Trigger's a beauty," I said to him.

"Finest stadium jump horse in Ireland. Perfect combination of beauty, brains, and athleticism." With that, he moved right into the lesson.

"Maureen insisted I give you instruction on jumping before we begin."

"Maureen said I had to work on posture and balance first."

"Bah! She has dressage as her first love and trains her students to ride like they wear a back brace. I've watched you. You certainly don't have a classic dressage seat but yours is as naturally balanced a hunt seat as any rider I have ever seen," he said as we entered the schooling arena. "Now, in a stadium competition, you have time to think through and plan your jumps. In a race, it's not so easy. Things move fast. But you can't let the speed of events deter you from essential basics. My first step is that 'we'—always remember you and the horse are equal partners—focus on the jump. I call it 'approach.' As we approach, I want the horse to target the jump with me. Most horses, as you approach, have a 'tell' and will let you know that they have the jump in focus. Trigger dips his head just a tad. Pete has a head bob. You and your horse must become one, centered on the fence, accepting the jump. Once on approach, and your horse lets you know he has accepted the jump and has it in focus, almost every time you will have a good jump. Do you understand?"

"Yes, I have it."

"Now, Maureen was correct when she taught you that posture is critical. Why? Because balance is king here. Coming in on approach, you adopt a comfortable, flexible posture, not stiff or forced, but always with your weight, your center of gravity, in balance."

"Does it come naturally?" I asked.

"For some. However, you will feel it if you're out of position. Maureen told me you were out of balance when Pete jumped that hedge yesterday. You could feel it, right?"

"Yes, but what do I do about it?"

"Adjust yourself in advance. Remember, yesterday Pete was taking *you* for a ride. You were surprised and unprepared. Just focus, relax, and keep those elbows in, Big Bird." He laughed as he said it, but I sensed he was benevolent, not hurling a mocking dig. I wondered, though, how much about our lesson Maureen had told him.

Gerry motioned toward a small cross-rail set up along one side of the schooling area. Pete and I cantered over it, the big stallion barely trying as he took the fence in stride and my body moved easily along with him.

"Now the vertical!" Gerry called, pointing to a bigger jump with red-and-white poles—well over two feet high. Pete and I did the practice jump successfully three times—no more flapping of the wings—then Gerry gave a shout. "You got it!"

"Right-o!"

After Gerry warmed up Trigger over the same small fences he'd used for me to find my position, he nodded toward the arena exit.

"You know the course?" he asked.

"Yep."

"Then, tally ho!" he shouted as Trigger moved out, with Pete and me following, leaving the schooling area at a canter.

The Hill of Tara in summer was a place of unimaginable beauty. I once again sensed its palpable, spiritual energy. I relaxed on Pete as we followed Gerry and Trigger. It was an easy pace, with modest jumps at the foot of the hill. But, as we ascended in a dragon's tail of switchbacks, going from jump to jump, the course became ever more challenging. As we followed Gerry and Trigger, I let Pete set the pace. Just as Gerry said, Pete had a clear tell when we approached a jump, giving a slight bob of his head several times. I would never have noticed had my mentor not taken the time to explain. I improvised, squeezing my fingers on the reins in response to tell Pete that I, too, had accepted the jump.

When we cleared the last jump before King's Seat, Pete began an all-out sprint to overtake Trigger. As we came alongside them, Gerry, in a remarkable display of balance and flexibility, pulled his foot from the stirrup and kicked me just below the ribs. Surprised, I was almost unseated. Pete slowed until I could collect myself. It seemed clear Trigger would reach King's Seat first and block our path to victory. However, as I regained my balance, I lost my composure. I was fuming. Pete was in concert with me, and we rocketed into an all-out sprint. I was ready to tear Gerry from his saddle if I could catch him. Pete was game. I had been on a lot of fine racehorses in my life but, I swear, that last eighth of a mile to King's Seat on Old Pete was as fast as I had ever ridden. We ran that furlong in under ten seconds.

Gerry, seeing us at full gallop, slowed, then stopped in King's Seat, blocking us. I started pulling back on the reins to avoid a collision, but Pete was beyond control. He picked up more speed, and acquiescing, I relaxed the reins. The stone pillars were filling my vision when his head bobbed three times. He was going to jump Gerry and Trigger. I squeezed the reins to let him know I'd accepted his choice, then prepared myself.

Pete launched like a rocket. We flew over my stunned cousin and his horse, between the two stone pillars. Lucky for all of us, Trigger dropped his back slightly as if in supplication, and Gerry ducked. Pete, flying high, landed on the other side of King's Seat in full stride. Another quarter mile to the finish, but there was no way for Gerry and Trigger to recover the lost ground.

We reached the Stone of Destiny first, and I was ecstatic with our win. But, when Gerry trotted up, my temper erupted, as we both dismounted

"You kicked me!"

He had an innocent look on his face. "You weren't expecting that?"

"Of course not!"

"Well, that's your first jump-racing lesson: expecteth the

unexpected. Nobody plays fair in jump races. Expect anything. Plus, I was testing you. You didn't give up. You've got grit. Then, you caught me by complete surprise, jumping over us at King's Seat. I thought you would stop."

"I would have stopped but for Pete. It was his idea. He bobbed his head a few times and over we went full-tilt Irish style—go over, not around."

"Aye, well, here endeth the lesson—expecteth the unexpected." He pulled out his silver flask, engraved with the Fitzgerald coat of arms, and offered the whiskey to me, with a toasting gesture. "Great ride, cousin."

The horses, ground tied, ate the lush grass and rested. We sat, side by side, our backs against the Stone of Destiny. Gerry took a swig of the whiskey.

"Jake, I told you that you would never forget this lesson. Well, this race, for me, anyway, was simply unforgettable. But there's more. What I'm going to tell you is the part I thought you'd remember always. Maybe you will."

I accepted the flask from him. "What?"

"Do you have any clue why you're really here?"

"To learn to ride, I guess."

"No." He laughed. "You obviously know how to ride. You just beat a world champion at his own game. The truth of it is, you and I are part of a big and ancient family. We're here because our parents are moving us around like chess pieces, for their concept of what is best for the family. You and I play a part in the game." He looked down the hill for a moment. "It is very hard for me to say this..." He sighed. "But I insisted I be the one to talk to you, not my mother."

"Come on," I said, giving his arm a friendly slap. "What are you blathering about?"

He shifted his weight, his personal discomfort clear. "Jake, this is serious. I'm not joking around. Please listen before reacting. Maureen and I want to have a child. However, I am sterile. I can't father a child. Mumps."

I was clueless. Instead of saying something comforting or supportive, I said, "Huh?"

"That's why you're here, Jake. That's why Maureen was flirting you up. To make sure you were interested."

"Huh?" Again, it was the only sound that would come out of my mouth.

Gerry took a long swig from the flask. "Look, Jake, Maureen and I are not your typical straitlaced couple. We've both had other lovers and still love each other. But when it came to having children, and the sterility issue, I asked my mother for advice, about adoption—that kind of thing. But I lost control of the conversation. She came up with this entire plan in a flash, must have been thinking about it all along. I knew she would never allow the Spennithorne title to pass to her cousins in York. She despises them. At first, it seemed she was bullying me into it. Then it dawned on me. She was absolutely right. Some anonymous sperm donor was ridiculous. Why not find for our child a father who is an excellent physical specimen, highly intelligent, with qualities I share, and with bloodlines that make the child truly part of my family as well as Maureen's? It was clear to me, once I put all the pieces together. Made sense. Also, I could see, before I even brought the issue up, that Mother, in her role as Lady Elizabeth, Viscountess Spennithorne, had selected you."

I swallowed a ball of spit. "Huh?"

He looked at me, his brows furrowed. "If you say 'huh' again, I'm going to withdraw the part about high intelligence." He snorted a laugh and took another swig. "Maureen has agreed and is returning this afternoon from Dublin. To ensure success, she has been receiving fertility treatments."

"Gerry, this is crazy. I have never even been with a woman."

"I know...I know, this is probably not how you visualized your first time. Most of us have some romantic delusion about what it will be like. I've got news for you, though, it's not Romeo and Juliet. My first time was a half-drunk, hurried, guilt-ridden spasm in the front seat of the family sedan. Believe me, as weird as it sounds, this is a better opportunity. I'd be proud to have you sire my child. Maureen will, too. And, most importantly, if you agree, I want you to know that we will be excellent parents."

"I don't understand. Do we do it and then pretend it never happened?"

"No, Jake. You will go on to live your life, fall in love, get married, and have children. Even though separated by an ocean, we will still be family."

"Our parents? Does my mother know?"

"Ya, Jake."

"No wonder she was throwing a fit about me leaving."

"My mother talked to Sarah, and she eventually agreed. Yours knows how important children are to a family."

"Who else knows?"

"Rory."

"Why?"

"He's Maureen's father and going to be a grandfather, but my guess is that it's because my mother never even breeds a horse without consulting with him. She probably wanted his opinion on how the kid would turn out."

Pete stepped over and lowered his head to nuzzle me. A feeling came over me and I knew it was going to be all right. I scratched his head. "Good stallion."

"That's at the heart of it," Gerry said, his smile lighting his eyes. "We think you'll be a good stallion, eh, cousin?"

"You aren't jealous?"

"Jake, I have loved Maureen since we were children. If I were able to get her pregnant myself, I'd do that. You're the next best option, and I'm perfectly happy with that."

I was unsure of myself. There were so many questions.

"When?" I asked.

"Evening and morning for the next four days. Doc says twice a day is best. I'll drop you both off at our townhouse in Dublin tonight. Maureen will stay with you. Rory will get someone to care for Pete. I've told everyone that we're giving you an educational tour of Dublin."

"Educational. Funny. Uh...where will you be? I mean, I don't know if I'm comfortable with you watch—"

Before I could finish my sentence, he firmly stated, "I will be in Dublin, but *not* with you, rest assured. I have a lover in the city. Maureen knows. There will be no regrets on our end so long as you are okay with it. Can you do it, Jake?"

"Of course," I said with forced false bravado.

"It is settled, then," he affirmed. "You'll be our favorite cousin from across the pond. And, if something should happen to us, you'll be the guardian. The child will want for nothing, and of course, she will get to see 'Uncle Jake' often."

I leaned away to stare at him. "She?"

"Ha-ha, yes, *She*, with a capital 'S.' My mother has even picked out her name: Elizabeth Marie."

"Do you even get a say?"

"Of course I do. I'll be the kid's father! Why argue now? Save it for later. For all we know, it will be a boy."

"Has she got a boy's name picked?"

"No, but I'll start the negotiations with 'Rufus' after one of our illustrious ancestors, and she'll be grateful to agree to Gerald," he said. His posture shifted and he began to stand up. I began to do the same, and he stopped me. "You hang back here for a bit. I'll take a ride, let you think on it by yourself for half an hour, and you let me know when I get back, all right?"

"Thank you, that sounds good."

Gerry handed me his flask. "Here, it helps with the thinking," he said with a wink. He got back on Trigger and rode off.

The bottom line was, as inexperienced as I was, I knew that I *wanted* Maureen. What I felt for her was desire—raw, untrained, and unrestrained. At first, I'd thought how she made me feel was just a schoolboy crush, but now the stakes were so much higher. Like any sixteen-year-old, overwhelmed by a flood of hormones, I asked myself, *Is this love?* I was torn. Gerry was right, what was being proposed wasn't how I'd imagined my first time, but I also hadn't imagined it drunk in the front seat of a car either. Maybe he was right. Maybe it would be better this way.

At the same time, it was bizarre to have my family so intertwined like this. My father had *never* spoken to me about sex, except for his brief discourse on "...the birds do it, the bees do it, and you've seen the horses do it. It is a part of people's nature, too." Of course, now, Pa was doling out my sperm like one of his prize stallions without even telling me! Who was he to decide what my first time would be like?

Looking back as a grown man with my own kids, I can't imagine even asking my children to do something like I was asked that day. At the time, part of me wanted to say no—it was a crazy plan, after all! "No strings attached"—just the creation of a human child! The implications were obvious to me. But, in the middle of my teen angst and discomfort, I was also beseiged by fantasies of what it might be like to have sex with Maureen. What teenager refuses when presented with the opportunity to fuck the object of his fantasy?

In the end I quelled my fears and my frustrations with a simple goal, a goal that was rapidly dominating my autism-driven consciousness. *I am sixteen and need to have sex!* With that in mind, there was only one possible answer to Gerry's query, a resounding, "Yes!" Even now, decades later, I know I made the right decision...perhaps for the wrong reasons, but the right decision, nonetheless.

Just as I'd come to this conclusion, Gerry reappeared on Trigger. Before he could speak, I stood up, raised the flask, and announced, "To Baby Gerald!" I took a swig and passed the flask to him.

"To Gerald," he responded, drinking deep.

The deal was sealed.

THAT NIGHT, Gerry dropped us off at their "townhouse" on Raglan Road, Ballsbridge, Dublin. I was awed by the huge, two-story, ivy-covered, red-brick Edwardian manse, located in one of Dublin's most exclusive enclaves. A townhouse in Ireland was *not* the same as a townhouse in North Central Florida, that's for sure. As I exited from the rear seat, Gerry came round to get Maureen's front passenger door. He extended a hand and she rose with catlike grace into a gentle embrace. I stood watching, feeling awkward, not knowing what to say or do. I felt out of place in a world of sophisticated adults, so different from me.

The car drove off at a slow pace. I watched the Rolls disappear around a corner, but Maureen never looked back. She led me up the broad stone entry stairs bordered by exotic floral shrubs in full fuchsia bloom. She opened the gray-green door, with its shiny brass knob at its center. Without a word being spoken, we crossed the formal atrium. The first floor was an antique-laden throwback to an ornate and formal era. Then we ascended the grand staircase to the top floor. The upper floor master suite was a dramatic fusion design, the impact driven by the surprising shift in aesthetic. Without disturbing the original Edwardian frontal view, they'd opened the entire second floor and converted it into a contemporary space, lit by large picture windows facing the rear gardens. Scandinavian simplicity in design, furnishings, and wall coverings, with the rear walls of expansive glass framing the Irish summer's flowering trees in the garden, created an impressionistic explosion of color. The foot of a king-size bed faced windows open to the garden, giving the sense of a portal into a floral dimension. The adjacent bath was huge, with a walk-in Jacuzzi tub, a sauna, and a spacious, glass-enclosed shower.

Hand in hand, we walked to a chrome-and-white leather settee where Maureen sat and slipped off her shoes. Then she stood, took off her coat, and laid it on the settee. Underneath, she wore a silk shift with an Oriental floral design. With no undergarment, it was more a negligee than a dress. I stood gawking as she walked into the bathroom and turned on the shower. Steam, like dense fog, soon spilled over the top of the glass shower enclosure, spreading into the rest of the bathroom as a fine mist.

Without a word, she undressed me. I tried to help but she smacked my hand away. It wasn't long before I stood naked. She caressed me everywhere with a light floating stroke—everywhere but where I ached for her touch. Then, she gave just a tug on the strap of her dress. It fell to the floor, leaving her standing naked opposite me. *Playboy* photos aside, I had never seen a woman naked, nevermind been undressed with one before. It filled me with awe. I started to tell her how beautiful she was, but she placed her index finger on my lips to silence me. She reached in to moderate the water temperature then led me in. I stood, as if helpless, like a toddler getting bathed by his mother. Caressing every nook and cranny, she took my excitement to an excruciating place. She moved behind me and administered the soapy washcloth to my nether region with one hand, while reaching around and grasping my hard-on with the other. Instantly, I came in her hand. Laughing, she said, "Whoa, boy!" The orgasm left me dazed, but Maureen was undeterred as she continued to squeeze and stroke me. "This is your first time, isn't it?"

I turned my head to look at her and in a raspy voice replied, "Yes, but I think I know what to do."

She laughed again, this time a soft melodious chuckle. "Don't think," she whispered. "Your job is to relax and enjoy—to learn. I am going to teach you how to make love to a woman."

With her continued ministrations and the energy of youth, once more I was ready. "Relax..." she said as she moved in front of me, wrapped her arms around my neck, and effortlessly lifted herself up. Maureen's sexual athleticism was something never surpassed in all my later years of experience. For a moment, her breasts were in my face and her legs around my waist. As she positioned herself, I hungrily kissed her body. Then she slid down and held on to my neck with one arm and my back with the other, while I gripped her buttocks with both hands. I slid right in, then pushed her against the wall and began moving in a frenzy. She moaned, "Come, Jake, come..." over and over.

My pace was ferocious and out of control. Her voice in my ear was driving me on and on, but unlike before I did not ejaculate. Her right arm rose and when it came down, she slapped the shower wall, crying out, "Come, Jake, come!" She wanted her baby.

Then I came. It was overwhelming. My whole torso twitched in body-racking spasms, pressing her hard against the shower wall. Dizzy and shaking from excitement, I felt my knees buckle. But I caught myself. Her legs released me. She hung from my neck for a moment, six inches off the floor, then dropped down with the balance of a cat. She stood before me and grabbed my hair, pushing me to my knees. She twisted the knot of hair, forcing me to look up at her. I tried to focus as the hot shower pelted my face. She seemed another woman, her green eyes darkened by the foggy steam. Displaying a leering smile devoid of innocence, she opened herself to me and shoved my face into her. By some basic instinct, as if by nature, I began to figure out what to do. Her response awakened a whole new sense of power.

THAT WEEKEND I LEARNED THINGS I might never have discovered in a lifetime of groping around for clues in Ocala. Maureen taught me, and in doing so, gave me a gift of sexual edification. But for her guidance, I'd have perhaps always been a "taker," focused only on my own gratification. However, under her tutelage, I became a "giver." Everything we shared was done with passion, but she refused to interject love into the equation, and I had an autistic intuition to stay emotionally disconnected, instincts that protected me from what clearly would have been my first heartbreak.

On Sunday night, Maureen helped me pack my backpack, signaling our tryst was ending. Then she shoved me back onto the bed for one last climactic go. Afterward, lying abed and sharing a cigarette, she said, "Weekend is over, Big Bird. It's been super—really, super—but it is time to go."

With that, we dressed in silence. Arm in arm, she escorted me to the front door. The chauffeur in the grey Bentley was waiting for me out front. I turned to look back at her, one last glance, but the door to the townhouse was closed. It was just that simple.

chapter 10
Free Love

THE FOLLOWING THURSDAY, I pulled up in front of the local pharmacy in the Jaguar, top down, motor rumbling. Colleen looked out the window. I smiled. She smiled.

We were together the rest of the summer. I miss that teenage ability to go from zero to one hundred in a flash, for that is how quickly I went from being a nervous virgin to having my first real relationship. Such is youth.

I found Colleen irresistible. She met my awkwardness with confidence, my American naiveté with a European worldliness, my still boy-girl social awkwardness with a remarkable grace. Colleen quickly became my libertine guide to a lifestyle previously unimaginable to a mildly autistic sixteen-year-old farm boy from Ocala. She was nothing short of ingenious in finding things to do: in quick order and around my riding and horsemanship education we made our way to a student beer-bash at Maynooth; an art exhibit at UCD, University College Dublin; and burgers and pints at a pub named after James Joyce.

All of this was against the backdrop of the 1960s tsunami of "free love" called the sexual revolution. It soon flooded my thinking. Just as I was searching to find my sexual self, as we all must do during the second decade of life, the world around me was turned upside down as the youth of Europe and America searched for a new moral center. We were at the vanguard of a cultural shift, akin to emerging from the Dark Ages into the Renaissance. I was in Ireland for the awakening of this brave new world, excited to see it hand-in-hand with Colleen.

She was a leader of the young art-crowd's social scene in Dublin, where she appeared to be a star in every sense of the word. Her reputation as a sexually adventurous and avant-garde artist wasn't diminished in the least by her having a compliant boy-toy in tow. I had cash to burn, and we spent the weekends I could get away from the stables at a cheap hotel near Old Town and St. Stephen's Green. My weekends were often free, as I was "family" at Kenwood now, and that came with perks. Grooms took care of Pete, and Lady Elizabeth seemed to accept my suddenly active social life, no explanation required.

Colleen loved to dance all the latest dances. From her, I learned the Twist, the Pony, and the Watutsi. My favorite, though, was an emerging dance craze centered in one of Dublin's all-night "underground" dance clubs—illegal unlicensed venues in urban basements that reeked of booze, marijuana, and ether. The music, Jamaican ska, came with a walking bass line and off-beat rhythm. It touched a primal chord within me. We'd dance, then find a dark corner of the club and make out.

Colleen was quirky when it came to sex. She wanted an audience, or at least the potential for one. We had sex the first time I took her for a ride in the Jag.

"Stop here!" she commanded.

Thinking she'd noticed a problem, I pulled over. Colleen got out and stood by the front tire. I followed. She shoved me against the flared front fender and began kissing me. Then, we proceeded to have sex, her on top, on the "bonnet" (as she called it), in the middle of the day, parked alongside a country road. I will never forget the sheet metal of the bonnet creaking. I had trouble concentrating, thinking we were going to damage the car.

When Colleen invited me to her family's beach cottage on Ireland's wild Atlantic coast, next to the Cliffs of Kilkee in County Clare, I couldn't help but be excited. I missed the ocean and looked forward to a couple days alone with her at the beach. My feelings for Colleen had quickly become different than the ones I'd harbored for Maureen merely a few weeks earlier. I was a hormone-driven teenager, but the time Colleen and I were spending together overcame the Autistic instinct I had for distance and turned me into a bit of a hopeless romantic. I hadn't yet become attuned to Colleen's propensity to omit major details. I fantasized about us holding hands, taking long romantic walks along the coast.

Our weekend at the Kilkee beach house was not my girlfriend's romantic overture but rather a master stroke of misdirection. First, her father and mother knew nothing of me, as she'd kept our relationship a secret. I don't know why this surprised me. She wasn't allowed to go to the beach house alone, but any such trip with her girlfriends or family would leave no room for me. It was only the day before our departure that she broke the news to me that, to resolve this predicament, "Uncle" Mike, a longtime family friend, would be going with us.

Her father gave her permission to go to the beach with Mike without a second thought. I met Mike and Colleen, stopped at an off-ramp of the Shannon motorway. They were in his light-blue English Ford Anglia econobox. I was in the Jaguar with the top down. As I got out of my car to fetch Colleen, she shouted, "Follow us!" and the Anglia pulled away. Perplexed, I followed them for over an hour to an old house near the Cliffs of Kilkee. It was a traditionally designed Irish cottage—a single-story high-ceilinged rectangle, with a white-plastered exterior and a steep red-shingle roof. It stood on a rock-strewn knoll set above dune and beach. Though safe from waves and tide, the relentless sea breeze gave the cottage a deeply weathered patina. The secluded section of beach, a crescent sandy strand isolated by wild rock outcroppings to the left and cliffs to the right, formed a tiny tidal lagoon.

Colleen didn't lie so much as allow me to misunderstand things. In some ways, this was cruel, but in other ways it helped me learn to be discerning with my relationships. My impression, on arriving at the seaside retreat, was that Mike would just facilitate the promised weekend tryst—that is: drop Colleen off and leave. That wasn't her plan at all, and I remember my consternation as I watched Mike bring his travel bag into the cottage.

I often think back on that moment, the moment I first saw Mike. Svelte, with tight jeans, a navy blue windbreaker, and Ray-Ban Wayfarer sunglasses, he was about five feet nine, with a slim athletic build. What was truly unique, however, was his face. It was striking in its androgynous facial symmetry and ivory-white complexion. Mike had captivating bright blue eyes, made even more striking by dark purple limbal rings—Elizabeth Taylor eyes. He wore his jet-black hair in the long mid-1960s Beatles' style of George Harrison. Not merely handsome, he was beautiful. There was no other way to describe him.

Michael James Colton had a master's in literature, with honors, from University College Dublin. Through the recommendation of his parish priest and the intervention of the local bishop, Mike secured a teaching position at Maynooth University, the national undergraduate Catholic college. Despite Irish Catholicism, Maynooth is, and always has been, known for a culture open to and tolerant of homosexuality. Mike fit right in. His role as an effeminate gay man was key to Colleen's plan. A plan which she kept from her father and from me.

Twenty-nine-year-old "Uncle" Mike and Colleen were both artists. He gave her painting lessons starting when she was ten. They were frequent participants in art shows in Dublin, and both had paintings for sale in many of the city's galleries. Colleen's father collected Mike's watercolor landscapes, having several of them framed and hung in his business office in a building next to the pharmacy. He paid big money for the paintings. At sixteen, I was naïve about homosexuality, but once I had a better understanding of things, I always thought there might be more to the relationship between Mike and Colleen's father than just "patron of the arts." Colleen said as much when, with a wink, she relayed that her father trusted Mike with her "without reservation." I just didn't understand the wink at the time.

Mike brought three bottles of whiskey and a bottle of absinthe. Colleen brought several grams of pharmaceutical-grade cocaine pilfered from the family pharmacy. I had no experience with drugs, and no real parental warnings, so I followed along. We began by drinking the absinthe, not with its ceremonial spoon and sugar ceremony, but neat, straight-up, its fierce and burning sour licorice taste preparing the palate for what was to come. Then we shared line after line of coke. It seemed it was the summer of firsts: I sucked it up. In that moment, cocaine's amoral anything-goes mood was the perfect prescription, filled by the chemist's daughter.

With the clarity that feels like truth through a first-time drug user's eyes, I suddenly could see Colleen had a crush on Michael. As I watched her faux flirtation with him, I was jealous, both angry and surprised at having a rival for her affections. However, as the buzz from the cocaine and absinthe settled in, a compliant voyeuristic passivity quelled my green-eyed monster, and I suddenly sensed a physical reaction, not only to watching Colleen, but also to Mike. From my armchair in a corner of the dining room, the drugs induced a skewed perspective. It was like looking at them through a tunnel with me in a corner, a far corner, of the room.

And I was aroused by them both.

Hours later, as Colleen slept off all that we had imbibed, Mike and I sat on lawn chairs in front of the cottage. We were perfectly positioned to enjoy the sun setting over the Atlantic in glorious, layered hues of yellow, coral, purple, quicksilver, smoke-gray, and pink. The glassy water, from shore to the sunburst horizon, was laid out in long clearly outlined rose-gold black-framed panels parallel to the skyline, each frame defined by the fine, shimmering lines created by small swells of calf-high waves approaching shore. We smoked Lucky Strike cigarettes. Between the coke and the absinthe, I was in a world of my own, enthralled by the red ball logo on the Lucky Strike cigarette pack.

"Magnificent, isn't it?" Mike said.

"Huh, what?" I replied.

He gave me a stern look, and gestured to the ocean, saying, "The sunset."

"Yes, amazing colors."

Mike said, "People do not stop to see the beauty that surrounds us. If I painted that, just as it is, it would be called impressionism. With those freakishly well-defined golden layers across the water, perhaps even an abstract. Yet it is real. It is a glimpse of paradise that no artist can fully capture, nor author fully describe. You must learn to enjoy such moments, for that, really, is beauty. I think that is what I live for."

Without waiting for my response, he asked, off-topic, "Have you ever been with a man?"

The drugs still in my system softened the shock of the question. I shifted in my seat, wondering if he had sensed me watching him with Colleen, and said, "This summer is the first time I've been with anyone *ever*."

He laughed. "Clever cunt, that Colleen." He gave me a coquettish look. "Maybe next time?"

My face blushed, but after a moment's hesitation, I murmured, "Maybe next time."

FOR THE NEXT TWO YEARS, I worked summers in Ireland. With time, I grew to love Colleen...and Mike. Loving them came naturally to me. By that, I mean it was consistent with my nature. I know many may say I was exploited by Gerry and Maureen, and by Mike and Colleen—that I was "just a boy"—but that's never been how I felt. I did my work with the horses and spent time with my Kenwood House family, but all I could think about was Mike and Colleen. Over those years we became inseparable. Every free minute was filled attending lectures on art and literature, going to the cinema, enjoying a weekend picnic at the city park on River Liffey, taking ambling trail rides across the Tara vale, and yes, there was sex, great sex. But I'm not just talking about sex, I'm talking love, the kind of love that makes us human.

As I had time, we would wander together on excursions—a weekend here, a weekend there: Paris, Amsterdam, the Greek islands, Marrakech—drifting as bit players across the 1960s European scene while the world changed from the black-and-white monochrome of the staid Ozzie and Harriet family-values' TV sit-com to the psychedelic hues of the Beatles' *Sgt. Pepper's Lonely Hearts Club Band* album cover. Free love was our mantra, no strings attached. If it felt right, it was right. We three lived by a code: "It's your thing, do what you want to do."

Among friends, Mike was openly and unashamedly gay, and Colleen was equally open as bisexual. I was their protégé. Such openness among trusted friends was not the same as coming out publicly because in those times homosexuality was a felony, with a penalty of prison time, and in England, even castration. Because of that, no one then was "out" the way we would eventually (thankfully) come to think of as normal.

While in many ways 1960s Irish society was permissive, it all happened in private. People were open about who and how they loved only among friends. Permissiveness as to personal conduct was imbued in Irish culture, without regard to the draconian church and civil legal prohibitions of the day. The Irish had spent so many years ignoring colonial English laws that they often had little personal regard for the laws of their own Irish government or the rules of the Catholic Church. Nevertheless, display gay sex or affection in a public place and the Gardaí—the Irish police force—would arrest you in a heartbeat.

Throughout Europe it was much the same; openness had to be avoided except in gay-friendly clubs. In many ways, our threesome relationship was our pretextual passport to togetherness: two teenage lovers, engaged to be married, on vacation from school, strictly chaperoned by "Uncle" Mike. This allowed us access to the finest hotels—checking in to a hotel suite for a weekend was as simple as showing passports and laying out the cash. We rehearsed our roles and played them well. Everyone accepted us as normal.

I knew then that my emerging sexuality was divergent. I was not straight, but I wasn't gay either. Bisexual didn't quite fit because in those early years I had many opportunities for sex with men that others found attractive, but I felt nothing. My sexuality was, and still is, driven by some quirky laws of attraction I have never fully understood. I knew, even if no one else did, that I was an outlier that fit into none of the boxes. I don't even know if there is a word for it now—maybe pansexuality. But I don't really think that pansexuality is a fair description. My laws of attraction were fluid, unpredictable. I look back at my lovers and know that who I was and who I am just doesn't fit in a box with a label for sexual orientation.

From the time I was thirteen, I knew I was different. When all my friends were already looking at pictures in *Playboy*, I was asexual. From my sexual awakening at sixteen, I've lived my life as a heterosexual—except for my experiences with Mike and Colleen. Now, sitting here in my seventies, I'm back to where I started, asexual. But I lived my life, for the most part, without sharing my sexual preferences, not even needing to lie about them. From the start, I believed, and still believe, who I love and how I love them is no one else's business.

LADY ELIZABETH GAVE ME A PRESENT just after Maureen's pregnancy with twins was confirmed: $150,000 was placed in an account in my name at Bank of Ireland. It facilitated the "playboy" excursions with Mike and Colleen during my later summer trips abroad. Today, it would be worth...maybe a million. She told me to consider the money as part of something that was our secret.

My "stud fee"—that was the first thing that came to my mind.

I think she sensed that I felt the gift somehow cheapened the relationship. She looked at me intently, then asked if I could keep another secret, a very important secret, a secret she had shared only with my father, and something she promised my father she'd tell me when the time was right. I assured her I could with a nod of my head.

Lady Elizabeth then told me the gift of the money was to allow me to live like an important part of her family—she made it clear it was *family money*.

"Jake," she said. "I deeply appreciate the gift you have given us. It is even more important because *we* are family. I am your aunt, your father's half-sister..."

I responded with shock, "What?"

She took a deep breath to compose herself. "It happened with my father. He is your biological grandfather. He had a teenage love affair with your Grandmother Montgomery. She was on a vacation with her mother, a summer vacation at Spennithorne. Maggie Mortimer was my father's first true love. I am certain that sentiment was reciprocated. However, my parents' marriage had been prearranged; it was a merger of aristocratic families and business interests that could not be undone. It was all very hush-hush. After Maggie returned home to Pennsylvania, she discovered she was pregnant. The family matriarchs, in England and Pennsylvania, came up with a secret solution. She was quickly married to your Grandfather Montgomery. The viscount, your great-grandfather, funded a 'family' wedding gift of a beautiful farm for the young couple. Later that same year, my parents married, as planned."

I must have had a look of sheer disbelief on my face. I simply could not imagine my Grandmother Montgomery having a torrid teen affair with her second cousin.

"Don't look so surprised, Jake, such things happen all the time... your father is my half-brother. I am your aunt."

I was stunned, as so often happened in the company of the Kenwood clan, but for the first time this whole seemingly mad scenario made sense. Gerry and Maureen's children would carry the bloodline of Lady Elizabeth, through her father, and my father, into the future.

Seven months after I returned home from my rendezvous with paternity, as I was leaving the house for a tennis match with friends, my mother shared the news.

"Cousin Elizabeth called. She is a grandmother! Twins! Gerald Rory Fitzgerald and Montgomery Randolph Fitzgerald. Two healthy baby boys."

My father sat at the kitchen counter sipping black coffee and reading the racing form. He barely grunted acknowledgment. Nothing about my mother's conduct even remotely suggested she knew these were *my* sons, *her* grandsons. I wondered, had they separated what they had agreed to when they sent me to Ireland from their reality, as I'd been trying to do?

I looked at Ma with a snarky sardonic smile, the kind only a smart-ass seventeen-year-old can muster, and said, "Well, just call me Uncle Jake."

I heard Pa harrumph, "Teenagers!" as I left the house, twirling my tennis racket.

WHILE I DID PUT IN ENOUGH TIME at Golden Miller to avoid a total fabrication to my parents, my extracurricular activities were the real reason I went back to Ireland the two following summers. Not only did a world of experimentation with Colleen and Mike beckon, but Lady Elizabeth treated me like a son after the birth of the twins, not a glorified stableboy. She took me to London with her on Fitzgerald Industries business trips. We traveled in her jet. Dressed in a business suit, I carried her briefcase and watched her negotiate deals. The way she worked a room fascinated me. In adapting to autism, she had learned to interact with others by plan, but all the while making it look as if it were the most spontaneous and natural thing in the world.

While in London, she always took time to take me shopping at the best boutiques. She would drop a thousand pounds sterling buying clothes, shoes, and jewelry for me at the hottest shops on Carnaby Street. Gerry had aged out as her "baby," and he had no interest in going shopping with his mother, but I loved every minute of it.

Elizabeth and I also shared a form of telepathy. She seemed to sense what I wanted with uncanny regularity. On our return from one such trip, a gleaming Norton Atlas motorcycle was parked in front of Kenwood House. How she knew I lusted after one, I'm not sure. My guess, was she saw the look on my face when I first saw a Norton parked curbside just off St. James Street, near Green Park in London. I never even mentioned it to her, but somehow, she knew.

Like I said, nothing was denied me.

I thought back to Gerry's cautionary warning when Elizabeth first "adopted" me. It rang true. I had become the Little Lord Fauntleroy of Kenwood House, but one distinctly of my generation. Instead of the curled locks, velveteen coats, and preening Victorian manners made famous in the novel, I played my role with drink, drugs, wild sex, fast cars, and rock and roll. What a difference a hundred years makes! But the twentieth-century Lord Fauntleroy was not my destiny. After three summers in Ireland, I knew it. I wanted to be home, home with my horses. I clearly saw the man I would become if I followed Lady Elizabeth and Mike and Colleen further, and I knew, despite my love for all of them, that was not the man I was meant to be.

chapter 11
Number 19

During the Vietnam War, America conducted a military draft lottery based on date of birth. At stake, based on the luck of the draw, was freedom from the draft or mandatory military service. It was held the year before young men turned eighteen. My birthday drew number "19," which guaranteed being drafted. Number "19" was a one-way government-paid ticket to the war. The return trip was in God's hands.

Because I had a full academic scholarship to the University of Florida, the draft board gave me a temporary deferment, but "19" out of "365" meant I had to report for military service upon graduation.

Vietnam was different than other wars. It was a TV war. We'd all seen the news clips showing the severely wounded and dead American soldiers and the devastation caused to the Vietnamese by napalm and bombing. I would like to say my military service was based only on patriotic ideals, but that would be a half truth. It was complicated. Most young people in the late 1960s were dead set against the Vietnam War. Not me. While "Hell, no, we won't go!" was the popular sentiment, I was different. It was a difference I hid from my friends at the university just to get along. I *wanted* to go. There was something in me that yearned to be a soldier. I sold myself on the idea that soldiering was in my genes.

But I also knew that leaving my family and dodging the draft was impossible for me. For the same reasons I kept my libertine lifestyle in Ireland secret from family and friends in Ocala, I simply could not dodge the draft and destroy in scandal all that my parents had built for me. I had been brainwashed from the beginning. When push came to shove, I would never tarnish the Montgomery name. Shaming my family by cutting and running to Canada, or back to Ireland, was never a real option.

Love had something to do with it too. Sally and I met at a party in October of our senior year at the University of Florida. It was a beer bash on The Commons after an afternoon of Gators' football. Deenette Orville, a high school friend of mine, had a cute, tall, strawberry-blonde sorority sister in tow. I guess it was what people call love at first sight. I say we fell in love. In all fairness, at first it was more of an out-of-control physical reaction. It was instantaneous and palpable; a first for me, her presence left me thunderstruck. I took Sally's hand to say hello, and at her touch, my knees went weak. I felt hot, like the fever that comes from eating too many jalapeño peppers.

After flashing a cute smile, her first words to me were, "My goodness, you are tall." At the age of nineteen, I had reached my full height, well over six feet. I was speechless, so in response I just smiled, but then, after the wave of emotion passed, we talked and talked: horses, music, the war.

When the dancing started, we danced without touching, sixties rock, for almost half an hour. I wanted to grab her. Then, a slow dance came, with Marvin Gaye singing his chartbuster "How Sweet It Is To Be Loved By You." I pulled Sally close and held her tight, swaying, lost in the music.

When I realized I was crushing her against me, one hand on her back, the other on her buttocks, I eased away, apologizing, "Sorry, I got carried away."

Sally, on tiptoes, pulled herself back into my embrace and whispered in my ear, "I feel it too, Big Boy. Don't stop dancing."

That was her name for me for the next forty-plus years: Big Boy.

We became lovers that night, and for the first time in my life I sensed both commitment and unconditional acceptance from a woman. For that reason, Sally was the only one to whom I could tell the truth, the whole truth. After a few weeks together, in an impulsive autism-charged moment, I blurted it all out with no filter. We were at The Archer, not just for sex, but as had been the case with Chau Linh three years earlier, also for privacy. In the 1960s, it was not easy for unmarried young adults on campus to be alone together. She lived at a sorority house where male visitors were forbidden except in the common areas and before nine at night. I lived in a men's dormitory, with a strict "no female visitors" policy. Co-ed dorms did not exist back then.

Sally was alerted to the fact that something new and unusual was coming because the timber and cadence of my voice changed. I began with an Autistic person's tone of forced formality: "Sally Ann Johansson,"—I had never addressed her like that before—"I have something very important to tell you about me, before we can become *us*, before I can marry you."

Her eyes widened at what literally was a proposal, or at least a clear expression of intent. She stared at me in shock as I said, "I value you because: One, you are kind. Two, you are good in bed. Three, you are beautiful. Four, you want children. Five, you like horses...."

I went on and on with a list of thirty-three attributes nonstop. Her jaw dropped slightly after the first five and, by the end, especially after a few of the more graphic sexual comments, I could see on her face what she was too kind to verbalize. But, undeterred, I continued, "Before we go any further together, and I want very much to go further, I must tell you who I am and what I am. You must know me, the real Jacob Asa Montgomery."

With that I blurted it all out in extreme detail, starting with my autism, which at this point of the conversation was crystal clear. Then, I told her everything: from my teenage sexcapades, including my bisexual experiences, to my brutal uncontrolled violence with Ronnie Tilton, to my secret family in Ireland—including the two children.

She was taken aback by the scope of it all and kept repeating, grasping for normalcy, "This is crazy, Jake, crazy." Then she paused, her face congested with emotion, close to tears. "Please tell me you are kidding. You're pulling my leg, aren't you?"

I assured her it was all true then said, "But wait, there is one last thing."

The look on her face was reinforced by her pantomime, eyes rolled back and hands up in an "I surrender" gesture. But I had to finish what I had started, so I blurted out, "And I'm number '19.' Draft number '19.' I am going to Vietnam."

With that, Sally started crying. Why? Because the man, the soulmate she'd envisioned, was not what she imagined him to be. That "Jake" had just been shattered.

She wanted to go back to the sorority house and think. We had come to the motel on my motorcycle so, as she walked toward the door, I offered her a ride home. She curtly rejected me, saying, "I'll walk. I need to walk."

Even though fifty years have passed, in my mind's eye I can see that scene, every word, every gesture, and every expression. Having such an uncanny memory is cruel—it prevents the sugarcoating of fiction, the lies and half-truths most people live by and use to doctor their pasts to make life palatable in the recollection. I too have those lies and rationalizations that paint the public picture of me, but I cannot forget *who* I really am and *what* I really am. Eidetic memory is cruel and unforgiving.

The way I "confessed" to Sally was not simply thoughtless, it was ridiculously brutish. I seemed to have no common sense, and therefore no compassion, for how she would perceive it. I loved her...and I hurt her. It was one of those moments you replay over and over again in your head, late at night, humiliated every time.

Three days later—three anxious days for me—she called.

"Jake, please get us a room at Hotel 6. Come pick me up."

My response was immediate, almost desperate, telling her that I loved her and would be there, FAST. Once in our hotel room, we drank Canadian Club from a pint bottle, smoked a joint, then made love. Afterward, sitting in bed, we were propped up against the headboard. We shared a Lucky Strike, passing the one cigarette back and forth. The window was open but there was no wind to ameliorate the room's warm and stagnant air, which smelled like sex and cigarettes. We played as we smoked, blowing rings that hung above the bed. She looked me in the eyes. I wanted to look away but forced myself to hold her gaze.

She said, "Jake, I think I know who you are, what you are, and some of that does not even remotely fit into what I thought I wanted in a man. I also know that you probably are not going to change." I flinched at those words, but relief came quickly. "But for the very first time in my life I feel, *really feel*, like a woman in love. I know, without a doubt, that I'm in love with you, and I mean it, for the long haul. I'm hoping you love me the same way. So, I know what I want and—" She paused. "I mean for the rest of my life...*I want you*. I WANT YOU, Big Boy."

Sally knew everything, and she still wanted me. She had only two requests. They were simple and fair.

"Please don't hurt me, and if we stay together, have a family, please take care of us."

She made me verbalize it with, "I promise."

Next, she said, "I can't depend on you to be faithful, can I?"

I had known this was coming, so with eyes downcast and feeling dread, I replied, "I'll do my best."

"Your best? Is that a two-way street?"

It was tough to say, but I knew the answer, and nodded, saying, "I know, I know. But I will always love you."

She had tears in her eyes. Then, she came to my open arms, and we held each other as if life itself depended upon it.

With Sally, I found a partner with whom I wanted to live the well-planned life path charted by my parents—the role I had played ninety-five percent of my life. The rich-kid playboy hipster that made up the other five percent, well, I chalked it up as summer-vacation craziness. That lifestyle was not the version of destiny I wanted.

I remember the moment when I picked between the two. With Sally, my parents, and the horse farm, I could clearly see a future. When I looked at life in Ireland, I couldn't. For me, it was a dead end that went nowhere because it would have cut me apart from my family. I simply chose a future for me, for us, that I could see. I chose a future I could live with. Pragmatic.

WHILE SALLY BECAME A TRUE confidant, I lied to everyone else. I lied on the Marine Corps enlistment questionnaire about my autism, homosexual activity, and drug use. Why lie? Because I was certain the Marines would have rejected me otherwise. I wanted to get married and have children. I wanted to be a good husband and father. I wanted to be a good Marine. I wanted to be respected in our hometown. I wanted to play my role and work at Montgomery Racing to support my parents and my family and build a future for us. And, without doubt, I wanted my parents, and Sally, to be proud of me.

While at first our love was like a fever, with more heat than common sense, it lasted. My parents loved Sally and encouraged me to marry her. Izzie, forever my "big brother," told me his life, filled with casual relationships, was not the right example for me. He knew my dreams and aspirations. He proclaimed that I *could*, with emphasis on the uncertainty of "could," be a good husband and father if I worked at it, saying, "Just remember, Jake, once you start having kids, they deserve your life-long love and attention. I had a horrible father. I know how that goes. Just follow your parents' example."

The only people I did not consult were Mike and Colleen. I think I was embarrassed to explain it to them. We had spouted the dogma of free love like a religion. My new direction seemingly betrayed that doctrine. So, without even a word to them, I moved toward marriage. Teaching me the precepts of free love, they had always said, "No strings attached," with a tone of religious righteousness. Avoiding the emotional entanglement, I simply took them at their word.

Sally and I prepared to start a life together. College graduation, something for celebration in normal times, for us was bittersweet. The Vietnam War was a controlling factor in our lives. Newly graduated, just married, already with a baby on the way, and holding a draft notice requiring me to report for duty, I volunteered for the Marines. By volunteering, I could pick my branch of service and specialty. I chose

Marine Corps, asking for Officer Candidate School.

They accepted me.

The hardest thing during my first six months as a Marine was separation from Sally. James, our baby boy, was born while I was in training. I didn't see him until my leave between Officer Candidate School graduation and advanced training, and then we had only two weeks together. It was also my first time not in the company of horses for an extended period. Several weeks into my basic officer training at Quantico, I felt a depression settle on me like a dense fog. I could not shake it off, so as soon as training ended for the day I went for a run. As I fought to burn away the blues with exercise, I came upon a sign that read *Quantico Stables* and altered my course, jogging up a narrow winding tree-lined road on the perimeter of the Quantico base. There I discovered a horse stable, providing mounts for Marines to ride for a small service charge to offset the costs. Trail rides into the Virginia countryside...it was just the fix I needed.

After Quantico, I was commissioned a second lieutenant. My commissioning ceremony was attended by my parents, Sally's parents, and Sally and baby James. With graduation came another two weeks leave, and vacation with the family at the nearby Johansson farm. Then I was off to California for parachute, underwater demolition, and Recon training before a final pre-deployment leave at home with my family, and then my first year in Vietnam.

As I think back to my early days in the Corps, for Lieutenant Jake Montgomery, the red-hot crucible that tempered me, that formed me, was Vietnam. I was a Recon platoon leader during the three-month siege of Khe Sahn. The big Marine base near the Laotian border was surrounded by several North Vietnamese Army divisions, massed artillery, and even tank battalions. The NVA arrived in force and planned a humiliating defeat for America, like France's catastrophic defeat at Dien Bien Phu, ending the French Vietnamese War years earlier. I came in by helicopter as a platoon leader, a replacement for a recently deceased second lieutenant. By some cruel irony, men from my new platoon loaded his body bag onto the chopper as I exited. This notion that "the last guy with this job got killed" was ever-present in the back of my mind, setting the tone for my service.

The base was surrounded by the North Vietnamese Army. We were under an almost constant artillery barrage. My company commander, Rudy Nicks, assigned me the platoon, and gave me a tactical briefing and my orders for a rapidly approaching night mission. I didn't even have time to learn the names of my men before I was ordering them to sneak out through the perimeter defenses, cross NVA lines, and target entrenched and bunkered enemy positions for airstrikes. Everyone had a nickname..."Booger," "Surfer," "Grease Monkey," "Cowboy"...like the barn names for the horses back home on our farm. They called me "Shavetail" at first. "Shavetail Louie" was what *all* young lieutenants (called "LT" or "Louie") with no combat experience were called. I spent a month with that nickname. The men knew my family was involved in horse racing and that I could ride, and so when I lifted a heavy wall locker—debris from an NVA artillery strike—trapping Grease Monkey, one of the guys declared, "LT's strong as a fucking horse!"

I became "Horseman."

My platoon had fifteen men. We bonded quickly. I learned fast. In some sense, they were leading me at first; these Recon Marines were highly trained and battle-hardened. Much of our work was done at night, setting up ambushes or observation stations. We even ambushed, hit-and-run style, lightly defended NVA positions from behind their lines, designed to keep the main NVA force distracted. I lost many brothers-in-arms and true friends, and I killed many enemy soldiers in return. I never kept a body count, but it was high. The pain and horror were constant and often overwhelming. However, where others were emotionally destroyed, I thrived. I responded—not by shrinking back into myself, but by flourishing with that berserker brutality that seemed natural and instinctive.

Shortly after the siege of Khe Sahn was lifted, I was promoted from second to first lieutenant and assigned as a platoon leader: Second Platoon, Charlie Company, 3rd Recon Battalion. I was based at Camp Carrol, a Marine fire base near Dong Ha, located just south of the Demilitarized Zone between North and South Vietnam. I made a point of being on every mission possible. I never asked anything of my men that I wouldn't do myself.

This day-to-day combat led to an inevitable cataclysm. I was leading a squad-sized patrol into NVA territory when we encountered a North Vietnamese Army recon platoon, also on patrol. We were outnumbered three to one, outflanked, and because we were behind enemy lines, we were trapped. I radioed for emergency close air support and a helicopter extraction, but the end of the battle came before the airpower arrived. Recon patrols travel light. In a short time, we all, the NVA platoon and my squad both, were out of ammunition. We fought in close combat, fixed bayonets and hand-to-hand. I also had on me my weapon of choice for close combat, a government-issue E-tool—a folding, sharp, spade-head shovel with a thirty-inch handle.

My memories of the battle are only fleeting fragments. I still clearly remember the feeling of an NVA soldier bayonetting me in the shoulder as I lay on the ground, stunned by a bullet that had gone into the front of my helmet, spinning it off and creasing my forehead. Thinking me dead, he kneeled over me and was tugging at the leather cord to my horsehead amulet. My blood-drenched eyes were like slits, but I could see enough—just his outline against the backlight of the sun. I reached to my belt and unsheathed my KA-BAR fighting knife. In a swift skilled move, I stabbed him, opening major blood vessels as I pushed the knife all the way in and across his abdomen, then up until I was stopped by his ribcage. He died on top of me, expiring so fast his hand never left the red horse talisman as he crumpled. The berserker in me then got up and smashed his head repeatedly with the shovel.

Only three NVA were left, me versus three, and my last recollection is of me looking at them, their AK-47s with fixed bayonets pointed at me, and of them looking at me, but not shooting. Not shooting told me they had no ammunition left. The enemy soldiers seemed frozen. I saw the fear in their eyes. Yes, it was three against one, but it was not so simple. By comparison, I was a blood-encrusted Goliath wielding a shovel. I charged them.

But after that, I remember nothing.

When the flight of rescue helicopters landed to take us out, I was passed out in a bloodied grove of trees populated only by the dead. I was the only survivor. All my men were dead, with almost three times that number of NVA slain. Several of the enemy had met their end by shovel.

That was the rub.

I was flown by U.S. Army helicopter to the 95th Evacuation Hospital on Da Nang's China Beach, and then by jet transport to the big Navy hospital in Yokosuka, Japan. After ten days in the hospital, an official board of inquiry was formed. The rescue team reported that many of the dead NVA soldiers appeared to have been mutilated, by a shovel—my shovel. Photos were also taken by one of the aircrew members who had helped gather and return our dead. Those pictures were sent up the chain of command.

I was in a hospital bed when I first learned of the inquiry. A clerk from the Judge Advocate's office came to my room and read me my rights under the Uniform Code of Military Justice. I was provided counsel: Marine Corps lawyer Major Zachary Zoberman. He was easy-going and calmed me down from the first. He noted we were both from Central Florida and said, "My friends call me ZZ." That set the tone for what would become a lifelong relationship with ZZ, both as my friend and my lawyer. His advice, "I see here a concussion, and you were found unconscious. The clinical notes reflect no clear memory of the battle. I will operate under the assumption that you cannot remember what happened, unless you tell me right now that you clearly, and I mean clearly, remember. No speculation or conjecture, okay?"

My recall was reduced to flashes of violence, like some blurred cinematic flashback effect from a bad slasher movie—I duly responded with, "Yes, sir. I can't clearly remember much."

At the hearing, I did not testify and my lawyer's closing to the board was powerful.

"Overwhelmed by an enemy force, First Lieutenant Montgomery's squad fought with the enemy until they had no ammunition left. The NVA, also out of ammo but trusting in their superior numbers, attacked with fixed bayonets. First Lieutenant Montgomery and his men fought valiantly, to the death. Due to his head injury, a bullet to the forehead, First Lieutenant Montgomery cannot clearly remember what happened. Nevertheless, the report and especially the photos at the scene of the battle make what happened quite evident. The last of the NVA charged the Marines, and at the end there was only one Marine left. In brutal close combat, the remaining NVA were killed by Lieutenant Montgomery. He used the only weapon remaining to him, his entrenching tool. Yes, a Marine Corps-issue E-tool. A shovel! This inquiry was convened based on the Army evacuation team's after-action report, raising concerns as to the mutilated condition of the bodies of some of the enemy soldiers. This victory, as costly as it was, was won by this brave Marine and his valiant squad, fighting to the bitter end. The last American standing, he fought with the only weapon he had left. Death by shovel is not pretty, but fighting to the end with everything and anything at your disposal.... Well, gentlemen, I respectfully submit that is what being a Marine is all about."

After the inquiry, there were no criminal charges filed. Instead, the report of the board became a recommendation for both commendation—the Navy Cross—and early promotion. I had another two weeks of recovery in the hospital, and then a choice: I could go home early due to the severity of my injuries or go back to Vietnam.

I had five months left on my tour of duty, and I requested to return to my unit.

My request to return to Vietnam was met with surprise at the Navy base. Perhaps in response, a Navy chaplain was sent to talk with me. He told me he understood what I had been through and asked if I would like to seek "reconciliation and forgiveness." But I was filled with a new and deep bitterness and a virulent anger. I asked him—challenged him, really—"Are you saying *you* can forgive me?"

"No, son, it is God who forgives. I am here as his representative."

My eyes were averted as I suddenly thought through God's role in putting me in such hellish circumstances. The God I had always so intuitively believed in. Then I turned my head and glared at him. "God's representative?" I snapped. I venomously spat out, "*You* are God's representative?" I sat up like a shot in the hospital bed. The abrupt movement carried a violent surge of energy, clear and palpable.

The chaplain flinched and stumbled back a step, but then he nodded.

"Then, *Padre*, you need to get down on your fucking knees and beg *me* for forgiveness. You beg my forgiveness for the hell I've gone through. Or get the fuck out of my room."

I remember the minister backing toward the door, struggling to regain his composure. I had revealed to him the demon within me. It was something I'd so long hidden, even from myself. "Son," the chaplain said, "that is the devil talking."

"Could be," I mumbled as I recalled my father's tale years ago about Duke Robert "the Devil," my long dead ancestor. "Could be."

In a way, the chaplain's visit helped me. Thanks to him, in one fell swoop, I emptied myself of the venom. Still, I knew I couldn't return to my family in my state of mind. I needed time. Even if I couldn't change a piece of my nature, I could learn new ways to better control it, as I had in the past.

Upon my return to Vietnam, I was promoted early to captain and given command of Echo Company, 3rd Recon Battalion. Command of a recon company was an honor for a junior captain. As company commander, I spent most of my time directing our three recon platoons from the operations center. Even though I was now playing a more administrative role, the men of Echo Company reveled in my story. Just a week after my arrival, my first sergeant came to me with a new battle flag, a bright blue banner with a well-embroidered golden "E" and a silver-embossed entrenching tool. It became our unit battle flag. As "E" Company 3rd Battalion, it was only natural that the men adopted the name "The E-Tools." And once the E-tool sigil became well known, we were also called the "Shovelheads," a name the unit bears to this day.

And in combat, my men were ferocious.

The brutality of the battle for Khe Sahn and my follow-up duty along the DMZ did not destroy me—it *made* me, and the change could be seen clearly on my face. Photos from when I first arrived in "I" Corps—the area along the border between South and North Vietnam—show a fresh-faced smiling young man. A photo taken just a year later shows a face hard and grim. I was tempered in the rage of battle, coming out of that forge sharp and pitiless. Growing up, I usually didn't feel things in the ways other people seemed to. After Vietnam, often I didn't feel anything at all.

AFTER ALMOST THIRTEEN months away, I returned to the States. That last month in Vietnam was tough, not just because of the combat environment, but also because I couldn't come to grips with the idea of returning home. It is hard to explain, even now, looking back. In combat, I was thought to be fearless. I was lauded for courage under fire. The hard-to-explain part is that I was afraid...afraid to go home. Sounds crazy, but it is true. Maybe it was the communication, or rather, the lack thereof. Soldiers fighting overseas today keep in constant touch with their loved ones, usually through frequent cell-phone video conversations. In Vietnam, there was nothing like that. The technology didn't exist. A wall of silence separated me from my family for a year. Yes, there were letters, but it wasn't enough to keep the silence from ripping at the very fabric of my relationships. In 'Nam, we called the United States "the World," as if we were on some other planet.

I think there was something else at the heart of my fear. I saw men who stayed in Vietnam, in front-line combat units, for years. After the first year, they voluntarily extended their tours in six-month increments. Why? I think some of us, me included, were meant for war. It was our place. Compared to it, a tailgate party before the big football game, dinner and a movie with friends, or after-school soccer with the kids all seemed bland, like food without salt and spice.

Sally and James had lived at her parents' farm while I was in Vietnam. Sally was an only child, and her parents had lavished them with love and attention. During my initial homecoming, I stayed in their South Carolina, Great Smoky Mountain hideaway for the mandatory two-week change of station leave; then Sally, James, and I loaded up our car and reported to Camp Lejeune on the North Carolina coast, a six-hour drive. We were given an unairconditioned two-bedroom, one-bath duplex located in the junior officers housing area, 245-A, Tarawa Terrace.

My remaining sixteen months of active duty as a Marine were planned to be as commander of a unit, teaching jungle warfare techniques to advanced infantry trainees. But my first mission, an essential one, was to install window air conditioners in the duplex. Camp Lejeune was hotter and more humid that summer than either Florida *or* Vietnam.

At Lejeune, I was in heaven with my son James. He was a toddler, walking and talking. And he loved his daddy. At first, Sally and I were fine, like old times, but after a few months at Lejeune, she became depressed. Back then, because I had changed so much, I assumed it was all because of me. I hadn't repeated my pre-deployment mistake of telling her too much. I relayed very little about my time in Vietnam. Now I wonder if that lack of communication, that retraction of my earlier impulse to share who I really was with my soulmate, caused her sadness. Or perhaps it was already the bad water taking its toll. Depression is one of the symptoms traced to the contaminants at the base. Anyway, it was never the same for us after Vietnam. The depression drove a gap between us that could not be bridged.

Though I sensed a loss of emotional intimacy, we still had sex. I needed it. Sally did too. Even so, I knew we had changed the game. It wasn't the kind of lovemaking our relationship was based on, but for me it was fierce and satisfying. Then she got pregnant. The new baby coming seemed to help lift the depression, our awkwardness with each other shifting, the joy of the coming child serving as hope, a meaningful replacement for the silent void—and for me a diversion from my deep well of war horrors. We explored baby names. Sally had a grandfather named Geoffrey Andrew. We agreed on that, if a boy, and Abigail Elyse, if a girl.

Sally dutifully went to the base hospital for her prenatal checkups. We found out well before the baby's due date that there was a serious heart problem, a congenital birth defect requiring surgery as soon as the baby was healthy enough. Sally, usually my mainstay for advice, was stunned by the news. I remember her telling me, "I knew there was something wrong, Jake, something wrong inside of me. I knew it."

Then, at birth, our baby boy's heart defect turned out to be far worse than anticipated. He also had serious neurological defects. Our doctor said nothing could be done.

Watching that baby die, a little bit each day for two weeks, as he turned black and shriveled before my eyes, was one of the hardest things I've ever experienced. I think it was the feeling of sheer helplessness. There was nothing I could do but suffer.

My parents, her parents, even Izzie came to be with us. The family was awash in suffering. However, I began to distance myself emotionally. It was imperceptible to others, but I knew how to deal with death. Vietnam had taught me that. I walled myself off from the pain.

Sally simply snapped. She slipped from a depression into a near-catatonic state. She was hospitalized for two months in a psych ward at Lejeune; the diagnosis was post-partum depression. James and I visited every day. Her parents came and her mother practically lived at the hospital. But it was as if Sally didn't know us.

The whole scenario forced me to do a gut check. Though I told no one, I could feel the cruel entity I had tried to leave behind in Vietnam still inside me, a parasite of the psyche that fed and flourished on my worst emotions. My anger was simmering and on the verge of boiling over. Sally's derangement and our baby's death fed this dark passenger. Had I known then that the government and its contractors knowingly disposed of benzine and other solvents improperly, contaminating my family's drinking water, leading to our baby's death and my wife's lifelong battle with depression, then Parkinson's, and finally cancer, there would have been a fucking massacre, a bloody fucking massacre. Then and there, I'd have extracted my justice in blood.

But I didn't know, and it was all just too much. Three years into our marriage, I felt like Sally was lost, as well as our baby. Her near-catatonic state left me with little hope. I could have spun completely out of control, but I remembered my promise to Sally before we were married. I had promised her from the very beginning that, no matter what, I would take care of her and our children.

A successful life is often reduced to a two-step equation: accept bad things as they are, then work hard to make things better. The death of our newborn son contorted grief into painful Gordian knots, but with Sally unhinged, I was the only one with the ability to realize that we still had a two-year-old boy to raise. I had to reach deep within, no matter how brutalized and battered I felt, and come up with a plan. I sensed our lives, as a family, depended upon it. For Sally and little James' sake, I had to accept what happened and find a way out of this mess.

I asked my Marine Recon Officer career advisor at the Pentagon for help, especially the need for continuing medical care for my wife. He suggested I ask to extend my term of service, to sort things out and take advantage of the free medical benefits.

I agreed.

The Pentagon let me stay on at Camp Lejeune, granting an extended "compassionate leave" until Sally could be discharged from the hospital and go home to the care of her parents. I knew the Johansson farm was the only place for my wife and son. But, quid pro quo, to get the time I needed to get her well enough to move there, and to keep our benefits, I had to agree to an additional four years of active duty with Force Recon.

What was certain: Sally needed help. James needed a mother. And I loved them both.

I also knew that I needed to be somewhere else, not in the middle of her healing process. I stayed in the Marines so my family could have a chance, for I knew on my own I did not have the tools needed for either Sally's recovery or James' formative years. But someone else did: Abigail Johansson took her daughter in, and in time, brought her back to life. Sally's father, James Johansson, who even with age had platinum blonde hair and bright blue eyes, was six foot five and three hundred pounds of muscle. He was known as "Big Swede" to his friends. Grandpa Johansson took little James under his wing. I had to smile as I watched them together. James was the spitting image of his grandfather.

I assured Sally that I was there for her, that we would get through this together. Slowly but surely, she responded. When I was reassigned and preparing to leave, I felt something growing in me—not free love, but the art of loving freely and without condition. I knew I had to accept our current circumstances and work through them to get us to a better place.

As Sally emerged from the fog of mental illness, the one thing she remembered was that I had stuck with her, that I loved her, and that I did so in the worst of times. Because of that, she stuck by me, too.

~

YEARS LATER, with Sally recovered, we left James with my parents and went to Ireland. I asked her if she was okay meeting "the family," as we had been invited to a birthday celebration for Maureen. It would be my wife's formal introduction to my aunt, my cousin, my sons, and their mother. The FitzGeralds did not know Sally knew our story. Sally and I agreed to keep it that way.

The party was at Kenwood House, in the ballroom. After dinner there was music and dancing, and Gerry cut in to dance with Sally, passing Maureen over to me.

Though I had seen Maureen many times since our weekend in Dublin, it had always been at a safe distance, across a dinner table or riding cross-country. It had been nine years since I last held Maureen in my arms. I tensed, as a crushing confusion washed over me. Touching her again, my heart rate soared. It made my ears ring. My jaw clenched. I was just short of grinding my teeth.

My panic response was a surprise, for I truly considered Maureen a friend. She was as beautiful as ever and looked at me lovingly as she said, "Thank you, Jake," flicking a look toward the children standing with their Grandmother Darragh. "They are wonderful boys."

That was the only time we ever discussed our shared parenting.

In a few minutes, it was over. With a sense of relief, I accepted Sally back into my arms as the band played an acoustic instrumental of Bob Dylan's "Boots of Spanish Leather."

I knew the words and picked up the tune mid-song. I brought my lips close to Sally's ear, inhaling her scent of jasmine and honey, and sang to her—my voice, just above a whisper, a deep, hushed baritone. She sighed with contentment, then I whispered, "Love you, honey."

I stepped back, and in time with the music, raised her hand high and gave her a slow twirl before reeling her back into my arms.

The panic was gone. Everything felt good again.

chapter 12
Tears in the Rain

AFTER LEAVING CAMP LEJEUNE I was reassigned from FORCON—Force Forward Reconnaissance—to SOCOM—Special Operations Command.

Once Sally was released from the hospital and settled into her parents' care at the Johansson farm, I left for two and a half months of highly specialized training at USMC Camp Peary, on the Virginia coast. After a year in Vietnam, losing the baby, and Sally's prolonged illness, part of me was like a wounded animal. That parasite on my psyche I'd vowed to suppress became hair-trigger dangerous.

My Department of Defense Language Aptitude Test—DLAT—score was off the charts, so, based on that and my excellent acquired proficiency in Vietnamese, obtained during my freshman year with Chau Linh and then my first tour of duty in Vietnam, the Corps put me in a month of intensive Vietnamese language and interrogation training at the rural Virginia base. The second month of training at Camp Peary was an extensive on North Vietnamese Army practices and procedures, followed by two weeks of sniper training.

The first month I lived in a sparse room at the BOQ (Bachelor Officer Quarters). Six days a week I was in a classroom, just me and a small cadre of instructors, perfecting my spoken and written Vietnamese. For the second month I was in the field, learning to think like an NVA officer. A former NVA infantry officer who had defected was my instructor. We lived together in a remote cabin, far from any trace of civilization, deep in the woodlands surrounding the base. Together we conducted mock two-man missions, day and night, with little rest. We spoke Vietnamese 24/7. I tried to make friends with my instructor but could not. I asked, in Vietnamese, for his name: *"Tên của bạn là gì?"*

He grunted a firm response: *"Không tên!"* And, just to make his point, grunted again, this time in English, "*NO NAMES!*"

Finally, just as I was beginning to think and dream in Vietnamese, I was extracted from the cabin by helicopter to begin a two-week course, in English with an American instructor, in sniper techniques. I learned the art of getting close without being noticed and the secrets to long-range marksmanship. By the end of my program I could speak fluent Vietnamese, with a Hanoi accent, and shoot a man in the head at five hundred yards, first time, every time.

Training complete, I spent the next year and a half in Vietnam. I was officially classified as a project officer for some obscure training command. The reality: I was assigned to Program Phoenix. I was no longer just a soldier. My new duties involved being an interrogator, an executioner, and an assassin. This was about deliberate dismantling of Viet Cong military and political infrastructure. I was told I'd be "inducing the defection" of high-value Viet Cong targets, but rarely in the Vietnam War did the reality line up with the promise. "Inducing defection" sounds like an act of persuasion, perhaps a bribe, but in reality it was capture, interrogation, and confession—or assassination. This was the dirty part of Program Phoenix—the wet work.

WET, WET, WET!

In my youth, military service had been something I considered honorable and heroic, but that was a childish view crafted more from the flurry of post-World War Two war hero propaganda movies than any well-thought-out version of reality. But even after I had a taste of real war, that reality did not stop me from going forward, for I was drawn to this aspect of my destiny like a moth to a flame.

I have never shared with anyone what I did in Program Phoenix. I even avoided thinking about it, in that way, hiding it from myself. Much of what I did is still DOD classified, but my silence, my avoidance, had nothing to do with *TOP SECRET* and everything to do with shame.

I am ashamed.

AS SOON AS I COMPLETED my stint with Program Phoenix, I was formally assigned to a "shell" Marine Corp Reserve Unit at MacDill Air Base in Tampa, just an hour and thirty from the family farm. I stayed on active duty. My status as a reserve officer was a cover. Except for my father, and Aunt Elizabeth, no one, not even my wife, knew the whole truth. For the balance of my USMC career, I was assigned to SOCOM. I worked a month or two each year in Europe, handing the reins of the business back over to Izzie and my father during Montgomery Racing's slow summer season, but I was at SOCOM's beck and call at all times. SOCOM designed a special operational job just for me, a cushy gig I earned through my Program Phoenix service and my close relationship with FitzGerald Industries.

My service in Program Phoenix confirmed for SOCOM that there was nothing I wouldn't do. Perhaps it was simply in my nature, perhaps it was a reaction to the death of our baby at Camp Lejeune, but on my return to Vietnam, I abandoned myself to ruthlessness. As a reward, I was given a follow-up assignment, one that only I could do. I became a deep-cover extraction specialist for Eastern Europe. "Extraction" was the term for helping defectors cross from East to West. I was on call at short notice should an extraction mission come up in my zone. I received pay, promotions, medical and retirement benefits, all as if I was on full-time active duty. The understanding was that when SOCOM whistled, I'd come running.

Undercover, I was exempt from the traditional Marine buzz-cut hairdo and permitted to sport moderately long hair, consistent with the current style. On those few occasions where I was in the United States and in uniform, all I had to do when a superior officer looked at my non-regulation hair with a questioning stare was to point at my circular red-and-gold SOCOM shoulder patch—the head of a spear. The patch said it all, for SOCOM was outside of the rulebook.

I had a unique skill set: eidetic memory, fluency in foreign languages, mastery of close combat, and the *pièce de résistance*, access to cover as an employee of the Fitzgerald Industries Irish conglomerate. Also, courtesy of a Department of Defense "language lab" in Alexandria, Virginia, I learned to speak flawless Irish Gaelic, with a Shannon accent, and conversational German, Polish, Czech, and Russian with an Irish accent. The training was meticulous. For example, an American speaking German sounds different from an Irishman speaking German. I learned to speak these languages as if I were born and raised in Shannon, Ireland. In the beginning of my transition, I spent two months in my cover personality, living in a house near Shannon and learning not just the local scene but also the schools, churches, parks, and playgrounds I'd have haunted as a boy. To be good under deep cover, you must not only *know* your character but *become* your character.

At SOCOM, deep cover was always a long-term investment. My shadow life was as an Irish businessman buying industrial parts and equipment in the Eastern Bloc for a FitzGerald Industries subsidiary. This permanently separated me from my Marine Corps contemporaries, who ended up on numerous long-term deployments to one hellhole or another. It allowed me to run our racing stable. But perhaps most importantly, I created a structured place for the berserker that now was always bubbling just below the surface. The roles of husband, father, and horse trainer just weren't enough for me—I needed something more, something exciting, something dangerous.

With Lady Elizabeth's cooperation and agreement to secrecy, we created James Gerald Long, a middle-management, middle-aged, Irish Army veteran, and purchasing agent for F&G Tool & Die. I learned to think of myself as Jimmy. "Just call me Jimmy" was one of my opening lines when developing relationships. SOCOM tasked me to go on purchasing visits to factories, always businesses with no military production to avoid heightened scrutiny. I traveled throughout the Eastern Block, and on occasion into Russia. My job was not to cultivate and recruit spies and defectors, but to help high-quality defectors escape the Soviet Bloc. In all the missions I had, I never knew my subject, usually someone with scientific or military expertise, before our initial rendezvous.

My assigned zone was East Germany, Poland, and Czechoslovakia. In that zone, pick-up points were established. They were always away from military- or defense-related industrial areas to avoid heightened security. If I had been nosing around a plant that manufactured depleted uranium artillery shells, the Stasi (secret police) scrutiny would be intense. So instead, I would go to a place as far from such areas as possible to buy industrial rubber hoses or industrial-grade high-pressure connectors—things I could easily buy in England or West Germany, but much cheaper in East Germany...things the secret police couldn't care less about. Once introduced to the sales manager at such a plant, I made follow-up appointments to negotiate and buy whatever they were selling. The visit to the plant was always followed by drinks and dinner. I would build relationships, buy enough goods to become a well-respected customer, and return regularly every summer.

My Irish persona gave me access to industrial enclaves throughout the Communist Bloc in Eastern Europe. It was about going into a place such as East Germany and coming back without the enemy ever knowing an American Marine Corps SOCOM officer had been there. These "business trips" were cover-building exercises. I relished the real mission: saving a life—with a touch of James Bond to boot. Yet, in the years I ended up working the James Gerald Long cover, I was only tasked twice to bring someone out, which I did. Only once was I asked, not ordered, to kill an East German Stasi operative.

I did that too.

My psychological profile for the job was perfect. SOCOM valued that I could do naturally what our marriage counselor, a psychologist Sally and I used from time to time, found so atrocious: disassociate myself from Jake Montgomery. I remember after one session, when, in utter frustration, the therapist looked at Sally and uttered, "I just don't know who he really is."

Sally matched the therapist's frustration with a sarcastic quip: "Join the club, honey. I'm not sure he even knows."

That they said this to my face forced me to acknowledge the issue. I responded with a simple non-incriminating grunt. Rather than lie, I simply avoided sharing with others these secret compartments of my life. I'd become skilled at wearing a "social mask" to hide my autism, and other uncomfortable aspects of myself, from as early as I can remember. So, I was James Gerald Long when I left Ireland on a mission: yes, Jimmy Boy, a single, hard-drinking, Roman Catholic Irishman with an endless repertoire of Irish folktales, homespun wisdom, and the occasional dirty joke.

The Eastern European countries where I worked were mostly Catholic. My dinners with my business hosts typically involved the best local cuisine, an endless supply of vodka or schnapps, and a bevy of flirtatious girls. Eastern European businessmen of that era never brought their wives to such events, and the girls were eager and enthusiastic. I enjoyed myself, but deftly avoided overindulgence, especially drunkenness. With women, I never allowed romantic attachment to enter the picture. Either would have been a slippery slope to breaking my cover.

My character's role was to be fun, interested in doing business, friendly, but also a strict Catholic. I knew from my handlers the local *Polizei* and their national intelligence security service counterparts tracked all business visitors traveling in the Eastern Bloc. I also knew that the women the Stasi served up all reported back to them. So, my alter ego, James Gerald Long, played hard-to-get with the ladies. But in light of some age-old wisdom I had learned years earlier in Ireland—"A hard prick has no conscience"—occasionally, I allowed myself to be had.

When I left these easy-to-have ladies alone in my hotel room, even just for a toilet break, they searched the room. It was a sure-fire test of my cover. Always knowing it was possible, it was one I offered up gladly. As my military handler explained early on, after my second trip to East Germany, "If you keep turning down good-looking girls, the Stasi agents will start sending you boys. If you won't fuck anything, well, that alone makes you suspect and screws up your cover."

But, also in character with my cover, I was always found the day following any acts of drunken debauchery, on my knees in penitential prayer at the local Catholic church.

It was a decade before I saw my two Irish lovers again. I had completed a mission in East Germany around 1978. I had, by then, completely disconnected from those Irish summers, and rarely even thought of them. Then, I received a letter addressed to me at Kenwood House:

> *Jake, I thought I saw you walking near our house in Paris one evening. By the time it registered with me, you were gone. If you are ever in Paris, Colly and I would love to see you. XOXO.*

It was signed with a grandiose looped cursive *M* followed by a phone number.

To survive in the "life role" I'd picked for myself, I'd had to distance myself from Mike and Colleen. You could call it a dishonorable discharge from the sexual revolution. Yet, I regretted having sacrificed the love I felt for them both on the altar of my normalcy.

I discovered that Mike and Colleen had migrated permanently to Paris, leaving Ireland behind. They were founders of *La Commune Anaïs Nin*, or *La Commune* for short. There, a dozen beautiful women and transgender men lived and worked in a palatial nineteenth-century manse a few blocks behind *Hôtel de Crillon*. As a group, *La Commune* led a circle of high-class sex workers in the ultra-luxurious Parisian 16th District. They were getting paid big money for sex parties at the best hotels. It all made for a lifestyle that probably would have made even Anaïs Nin blush.

When I phoned and said I was in Paris, I was promptly invited by Colleen to cocktails at seven.

As soon as I saw them, I was taken aback. I knew then it truly was never going to be the same as before. The person I had known as "Mike" now lived as "Michelle." It was the transformation that shocked me.

Michelle had transitioned to living as a woman—and an extraordinarily beautiful one at that. It was impossible not to love her. It was difficult for me, given our history, not to think of Michelle as a man. "He" was all I'd ever known. Back then, in Ireland, in public, he had appeared masculine, and one detected only a hint of a gay man, an effeminate man. In private, one on one, he was what might be termed "feminine" with me, not in appearance but in nature. The confusion of memories and experiences overwhelmed me. Then, and even now as I look back, I had to remember to say "her" instead of "him." I had to coach myself to respect her choice.

I wish I could explain the feelings I had that day, seeing Michelle. I wish I could justify them, but I can't. To me, at first, it felt like the person I loved was gone. Cosmetic and reconstructive surgery had transformed Michelle into a svelte beauty whose face was still the spitting image of Elizabeth Taylor. Michelle was as magnificent a courtesan as ever graced the grand hotels of Paris, but she was not the same person I had fallen in love with all those years before. At the time, I felt guilty, fearing my feelings were because of her transition. But now I see that *none* of us were the same people we had been when we first fell in love.

Married, father, soldier—battle-scarred killer—yes, *none* of us were the same.

During our summers in Ireland, I had eventually become not just Michelle's lover but a true friend. We had filled emotional spaces in one another, like yin and yang puzzle pieces. As much as I tended toward fierce, she tended toward gentle. As much as I was wild and untamed, she was calm and erudite. We connected intellectually. She was a superb storyteller, and it was only natural, given her background in English literature, that she turned me on to the great writers of our times, often giving me from memory ad-libbed recaps of book after book, quoting memorable passages verbatim. I am certain my love for her was wrapped up in adulation of her worldview, supported by books I would never have read had I simply lived my life as a back-country horse trainer reading James Bond paperbacks.

Over the years, I'd kept an image of Michelle, the person I loved, clear in my mind. All that time, I'd thought Michelle was the only man I'd ever love. Because our love was so evolved, so spiritual, for me it transcended issues of anatomy. Now, seeing the beautiful woman before me, I was left wondering if I had ever loved a man in the first place.

At the end of the evening, we had an exceptionally fine French whisky: Michel Couvreur, Rouge Spécial. It glowed golden red in the crystal decanter. The drawing room at *La Commune* was grandiose, with a framed portrait of Anaïs Nin painted by Michelle hanging in a lighted cove on the back wall. As you entered, it was the centerpiece. Anaïs had the look of a gorgeous 1920s flapper, the kind of girl who partied until the break of dawn. Michelle explained that her books and diaries made her both famous and wealthy in the post-WWII world, and that *The Diary of Anaïs Nin* and her infamous lifestyle were the inspiration for the commune. Nin had died in 1976 after a long, rich life. The backstory, truth or fable, was that Colleen claimed Anaïs had been her lover.

Beneath the portrait was an Anais quote, in French, deeply etched into a bronze plaque: *"We do not see things as they are, we see them as we are."*

That caught my attention, especially given the circumstances of the evening. And while Nin was an unknown to me then, within a year I'd read everything she'd ever written.

ONE OF OUR LAST MEETINGS in Paris followed a difficult and dangerous mission in East Germany. The assignment had been perilous, and up to the last minute, the outcome had been uncertain. I had been thinking of Michelle...thinking I wanted her. I just couldn't bring myself to say so, even to myself. I was in a tense mood, wanting to see her but not knowing what to do.

We visited for a brief thirty minutes at La Commune, and then Colleen and Michelle excused themselves for an important "business meeting." If ever a man had no right to judge anyone, it was me, yet my cynicism had kicked in. I said to myself, *Just another paid-for fuck.*

"Paid-for fuck"—I know now what my fears were then. It was not jealousy that caused my anger. It was not some misplaced moral outrage. It was *the price*, the emotional price I'd have to pay for a renewed relationship with Michelle. It stopped me, and what I thought were my desires, in my tracks. Why? Because, I just didn't think I could pay the price.

As we all stood to leave, Colleen stepped close and stroked my face. Her touch was gentle. She whispered, "Love, you look so tense."

Then, she excused herself and went into her nearby office, and after several minutes with her secretary, she emerged with a dark-blue Ralph Lauren raincoat in hand. Michelle, Colleen, and I left the building and walked together for a few blocks along *Boulevard de la Madeleine*. It was empty. No people. No cars. It seemed as if we were the only people in Paris, braving the cold misty drizzle on this gray night. Then we reached a crossroads: they were going left to a taxi stand and then on to *Hôtel Georges Cinq*, I was turning right toward my hotel. Even in the wet, there would be no taxi for me—I wanted to walk. On a street corner of the

Madeleine, we said goodbye, and something about the moment told me it was for the last time. I remember tasting lovelorn regret as I kissed Michelle on the lips. Then, Colleen turned to me for a kiss of her own. She held the back of my neck so I couldn't pull away, and ever so daintily bit me on the lower lip.

The drizzle turned to rain. I pulled my cap forward to protect my face. Thinking only of them, I walked through the dark and dismal night, embraced by memories and regrets, working through my feelings. I allowed myself to admit that I still cared for them, and because I did, I felt a profound emptiness. It reduced me to tears. I rubbed my eyes to wipe them away, though in the rain it really didn't matter. Wiping away tears in the rain—that summed up my situation nicely.

The never-ending twilight matched my emotional state. I didn't blame my lost lovers. It was me, all me. My heartache flowed from a dark place deep inside of me. Because I did not know what to do, I did nothing.

Anaïs Nin perhaps said it best: "Love never dies a natural death. It dies because we don't know how to replenish its source."

Chilled to the bone from the rain, I turned up the heat in my hotel room, then showered and changed, putting on a well-worn T-shirt from a Shannon pub and a pair of Irish Army exercise pants. Nothing in my Irish-businessman's suitcase even hinted at my American roots. I turned on the TV to an American movie channel and poured myself a large whiskey, straight up, from a pint bottle of Johnny Walker Black I found in the minibar. As I wallowed in this cocktail of regret and self-pity, someone knocked on the door. I opened it to find Aimée, Colleen's administrative assistant, her "Girl Friday." She was a young, short, pert, and pleasantly plump half-Moroccan and French Parisian with cinnamon skin and an ebony pageboy haircut. Her big oval eyes were beautiful, shaped like a fresh-caught sole, with irises dark as night.

"*Bonsoir, mon amour,*" she said with a sly grin. "*Madame* Colleen asked me to come by and keep you company."

"No, Aimée," I replied, wagging my finger.

A widening of her eyes and a hand gesture asked *Why?* without ever uttering a word.

"I'm m-m-married," I stammered.

She laughed. "Almost all *La Commune's* clients are m-m-married. But do not be afraid, I am just a secretary." She began to push her way in. "I won't bite."

I blocked her and she put her hand on my chest, feigning helplessness. "Please, Jake, don't make me go back now. It is horrible out there, cold and wet. Colleen said you were sad and depressed. They had to go to work, a party for some rich Saudis at the *Georges Cinq*. She did not want you to be alone. I promised her I would put a smile on your face."

She pushed again, and this time I didn't resist. Instead, I thought of Colleen and how she'd nipped my lip in our parting kiss. It now made me smile.

"I *am* smiling," I said as I let her in, "but I am not…"

With that, she put her index finger in her mouth, like a popsicle, then, pulling out with a "pop," touched my lips with the tip of her slick finger. She giggled and, with a wicked tone to her voice, said, "Oh, don't worry, *Madame* Colleen has told me all about you. I know you are married. I know you are depressed. Not a week goes by without Colleen or Michelle sharing a story about you when you were a young man. Yes, I know everything, so I will have to try very, very hard to be a good girl."

She took off her coat and tossed it on a nearby armchair. "But I must tell you, I find it cute the way you keep saying, '*Non, non*, I am married,' but then I see you look at Michelle. Haha, why are you really in Paris, eh?" She turned to the TV as she removed her shoes, then sat on my bed, propped up a few pillows, and lay back. "*Bon*, my married friend, let's watch some TV. *Merde alors*, look! It is Steves McQueens."

I was standing at the foot of the bed, watching her, not Steve McQueen. She made herself comfortable, wiggled her perfectly manicured toes, her nails a shiny dark-rose color, then raised her right knee. Her bent leg formed the two upper sides of an equilateral triangle, with the mattress below as its base. I began stimming on the shape—its perfection. Then, gravity caused her dress to settle to her waist, the silken folds slipping down, as if in slow motion. She wore no underwear, and spread her left leg several inches, revealing herself—a second triangle, this one of hair, black and wild, shimmering at her core, signaling she was wet with excitement. I took a deep breath to calm myself, to try and disconnect from the tide of passion rising within me, but I was trapped in a loop. Her spread legs, her sexiness, captivated me. Then, epiphany: this was it, this feeling, the "Delta of Venus" of Anaïs Nin. Aimée looked up at me and our eyes met.

We both knew what would happen next, so I just blurted it out, "*Veux-tu faire l'amour avec moi?*"

"*Oui*," she responded, her voice now an impassioned purr.

Without another word from her, I walked to the TV and turned it off. Keeping my gaze on her, I eased off my T-shirt. She seemed mesmerized by my battle-scarred chest. I tugged at the drawstring and allowed my jogging pants to fall to the floor.

"*Ohhh*," was all she said as I stepped out of the joggers and came to her on the bed, singing *a cappella*, my voice now low and soft. With a flourish of my arm and sway of my hips, I invited her to join me in a dance.

"Ah, ha!" she exclaimed as I pulled her into my embrace. "Now I see you." She laughed, soft and melodic, like a wind chime in a gentle breeze. "I see you now. I see the boy from all the stories they told me."

I held her in my arms, and we danced a dance as old as time.

THREE YEARS HAD PASSED since my last visit. Aimée called from Paris, sobbing as she told me the news, "They have very little time. They are dying." Michelle and Colleen were dying of AIDS—*le SIDA*, as it was called in France. It was the beginning of the epidemic, and death came quickly to the infected.

A profound silence hung on the line as I processed her words; then, when I spoke, my voice was a rasp of emotion. "Where are they? *À l'hôpital*?"

"*Non*, they want to die in bed at *La Commune*."

"Ask if I can come. I want to be there," I said urgently.

"Jake, they want to see you. It was Colleen who asked me to call."

"I'm on my way."

"You may not know it, but you have always been a very important part of their life. They always talk about their time with you. You are a 'little brother,' a third musketeer."

I struggled for self-control. "I will be there in two days." My voice cracked. "I will fly out tomorrow night."

"We have an extra room at *La Commune*. Stay here."

"I will. Thanks. Aimée."

"*Mais oui*. No problem."

I lied, telling Sally it was business, then I packed and caught the next flight, nonstop Orlando to Paris. Thank God for Disney World—the new Orlando International Airport was now a major hub for all the big carriers, domestic and international.

When I arrived at *La Commune*, I was ushered to the large

bedroom they shared. I tried not to show it, but their appearance startled me. AIDS, untreated and in its late stage, was brutal. The disease seemed to suck the life force from a body, leaving behind an emaciated, battered, and wasted shell. They had removed their king-size bed from the room and were now in separate hospital beds. Both had numerous tubes for oxygen and feeding attached.

"*Bonjour, Michelle, Bonjour, Colleen!*" I said, as brightly as possible as I entered their boudoir.

Their smiles were faint. I went first to Michelle, who was upright, her hospital bed adjusted to a sitting position. As I held her in my arms, I couldn't believe how light she felt, like a feather. She had tubes in her nose and throat. Tears brimming, I kissed her forehead. At that time, no one knew how AIDS spread, so there was an underlying fear related to any contact with the infected. I felt it but dismissed it. The disease had ravaged her at every level. What hair remained was wispy gray and closely cropped. In her gaunt beauty, I saw her, to the soul.

"I am here, my love," I whispered to her.

"*Mo fear álain*," she said in a tremulous voice. That was Mike's pet name for me years before; it meant "my beautiful man" in Irish Gaelic.

Then I went to Colleen. Not a word was spoken until I kissed her forehead.

"Thank you for coming, love," she said. "It means so much to us."

"I'm sorry, Colleen," I whispered, almost losing my words. "We missed so much. We missed so much life together."

She managed a smile. "Well, thank God you missed this, Jake, for I cannot express the horror of this disease."

"You are so beautiful, both of you," I said quietly, as I moved an overstuffed armchair into the space between their beds. I had asked Aimée to find me an acoustic guitar, knowing it was likely one of the

La Commune residents would have one. She entered the bedroom and handed me a Yamaha, then brought Colleen's bed into a sitting position.

"I have come to stay for a while," I went on, as I tuned the guitar. "For as long as you'll have me. First, I want to play one of our favorite songs."

I continued tuning the guitar. The high E string was stubbornly attracted to an out-of-tune D sharp. Then, once it was close enough, I began to strum a slow, steady rendition of the Beatles hit "Michelle." Michelle clapped, and I winked at her. "This is for you, my darlings," I said, and began to sing, the words to the song's simple melody transported us back decades to our summer of love.

The next day, I spent every waking hour with them. They were near the end. As word spread, the room filled with a procession of friends, lovers, and clients. All came to say goodbye. As the Parisian twilight settled, in dappled tones of gray and blue, Aimée and I were left alone to watch over them. Michelle died first, quietly. She was breathing, but so weakly it was imperceptible. I noticed her death first because of a feeling in the room. It was as if the evening light filtering through the big window had changed. I turned and looked at her, her complexion now like alabaster. Colleen cried out when Aimée told her. I went over and took Colleen's hand in mine. Just a few hours later, Colleen passed with a deep rattling groan.

The world lost something special when Michelle and Colleen died. Back at the beginning of our relationship, we had talked about "free love" as part of our life philosophy. It was a mixed bag: a social experiment, a religion, and often just a game. But never, never ever, did we contemplate *Le SIDA*—AIDS. The AIDS pandemic, fueled by governmental indifference to what many characterized as a gay affliction, mushroomed out of control. It caught the world of "free love" by surprise.

The virus did not discriminate either. Homosexual, heterosexual, bisexual, or pansexual; black, white, Arab, or Asian—the virus loved us all equally. I knew that could have been me in that hospital bed, had I not taken a different path.

With the deaths of my old friends, I felt a deep and disabling sadness twisting and tearing at the cords of my soul. I was grateful, though, for in the end we three were together. We were able to share and celebrate our love one last time.

Aimée pleaded, "Jake, please stay with me. I cannot be alone right now."

She cried herself to sleep with me cuddling her in an innocent childlike embrace, me on my back and Aimée's head nestled near my heart, my chest wet with her tears. Love and compassion were the only balm for our pain.

I lay there, envisioning that first weekend Mike, Colleen, and I spent together on the beach at Kilkee. They were so beautiful. I remembered their art, their magnificent paintings. I remembered the literature. In my mind's eye, I could clearly see Mike, quoting James Joyce as we all lay on the sandy beach in the shadow of the Cliffs of Kilkee. I could see him lying there, first looking out to sea, then back at me and Colleen, his thick, black hair in tangled plaits, awash in saltwater and sand. I could feel Colleen cuddled against me. Mike had been reading to us from Joyce's book of short stories, *The Dubliners.* A story called "The Dead": *The moments of our secret life together burst like stars upon my memory.*

Burst like stars upon my memory. Beautiful people, beautiful times, beautiful memories. *Stars upon my memory.*

The room silent as a tomb, I fell asleep.

AS I NOW THINK of that moment on that long-ago beach, a certain wisdom comes to me as I write this WET journal. We can live life as if it is a story, written with a finger in the sand on a beach at low tide. We can live as if what we do and who we are make no difference, because the high tide, in due course, simply washes it all away. Gone forever. But I refuse to accept that Michelle and Colleen's lives have been washed away like sand before the surf. My love for them still lives on. It lives within me to this very day.

chapter 13
Crom Abú

HOW I KEPT THINGS TOGETHER over those years, I'll never know. With my assignment to SOCOM and some freedom to spend extended time "at home," Sally and I vowed to chart out a "normal" life for our family, including having more children. We moved in with my parents on the farm in Ocala, expanding the existing house to accommodate all of us. Following a four-year hiatus after our baby's death, we had two daughters just a year apart—Katie and then Cassandra. Pa called them our "Irish twins," a somewhat disparaging reference to siblings born within the same year.

Playing parent and running the farm was like a new identity for me, a new role to play. We had a solid family life, like a *Better Homes and Gardens* magazine cover with parents, three smiling kids, and two dogs. Church, PTA, Little League baseball, we did it all—the whole shebang. James evolved into a tow-headed, extra-large athletic force of nature. By the time he was eight, one could not look at the boy without reflecting on his striking resemblance to Sally's father, Big Swede. The girls did have the look of twins and of Ireland, with dark auburn hair, milky-white complexions, and hazel eyes. But the resemblance to each other ended there. Katie was quiet and serious. In time she became a champion gymnast and a winner in eventing competitions on horseback, declaring at an early age her intention to be a soldier. Cassandra was her polar opposite. A bubbly vivacious socialite who ruled the soccer pitch, she was our family party girl. Also an accomplished rider, she loved barrel racing and rodeos.

When the FitzGerald clan arrived at our farm to visit for the first time, Jake and Sally Montgomery—and the family we created—were pillars of the Ocala community. I enjoyed the simplicity of it. Of all the roles I played, of all the masks I wore, this was the one that came naturally. This was what I had given up Michelle and Colleen for.

The Florida visit was Sally's idea, flowing from an ever-building relationship between her and Elizabeth. I considered the implications. They were two of the smartest women I had the pleasure to know—certified geniuses. And both had tremendous organizational and political skills. They were leaders of their families, albeit in different ways, due to circumstances.

Every culture has tendencies toward matriarchy or patriarchy. Broadly, I have concluded that British and Irish cultures tend toward matriarchy, with family matters often the domain of the alpha females. Often, all this is done with the males under the false impression that they are in charge.

My great-grandmother, Mary Inez Mortimer, is an excellent example. She lived until I was eleven and I remember her well. We visited her once a year, staying in her farm's guesthouse. The cottage was perched on a high point jutting out into the Allegheny River. On the opposite bank were the cliffs, with a park that had a scenic overlook. It was called Brady's Bend, named after an early settler and hero of the French and Indian War, Colonel Matthew Brady. Here the river rushed down from the mountains, slowed, then flowed south to its terminus in the Ohio River.

My great-grandmother grew up in that valley, born on the same farm her family, the Randolphs, settled in the late 1700s. She married Daniel Mortimer, her neighbor who lived a couple miles down-river. His family had settled there in 1754 when it was a true wilderness at the edge of the European frontier in North America.

She was six feet tall and had fourteen children, twelve of whom survived to adulthood. The pioneering clans—Randolph, Mortimer, Armstrong, Brady, Sinclair, and Montgomery—were all interrelated, primarily due to the romantic constraints imposed in the eighteenth and nineteenth centuries by the travel restrictions of Western Pennsylvania's harsh mountain geography in the days before the Pennsylvania Turnpike and the automobile. Well into her nineties, there was no doubt in anyone's mind about who the matriarch was in the valley at Brady's Bend, Pennsylvania. All paid my great-grandmother homage, and it wasn't respect due to obligation but earned through decades of leadership and wisdom.

Outwardly, to our Ocala social and business communities, anyone would tell you *I* was the head of the Montgomery household and "wore the pants in the family." Sally cultivated that impression but, truth be told, just like with Great-Grandma Mortimer, almost every major decision in our family was shaped by her. I rarely did not seek her viewpoint, and vice versa. Accordingly, we rarely fought, unlike some couples we knew, perhaps because by working things out together we had the ability to figure out what was right for our family, and right or wrong, we were comfortable that, as a couple, we did our best.

Lady Elizabeth traveled a far different road as matriarch. She was, in the minds of many—I had heard it voiced more than once by male detractors—an autocratic bitch. There was some literal foundation for that personification, for no alpha female wolf could be more ferocious than Elizabeth when it came to protecting her family and her business interests. If need be, she would rip an enemy's throat out. As her nephew, I was fortunate because she treated me as one of her own. So many avenues were opened to me by her, and I knew she had my back, no matter what.

In Ocala, while Sally created the façade of me being in charge for my benefit, I knew that Elizabeth never had that option. One had to think: what was it like being a widow, with a baby and a great fortune, in post-WWII Ireland and England? I always admired the fact that she believed in herself enough to not settle with finding another man to run her life. She refused to comply with what was expected in the 1940s, snubbing even the most illustrious suitors. Her path to her destiny and that of her son was something she and her late husband Fitz had agreed to. They were a team, and Fitz dying changed nothing about the plan.

It was winter in Florida, postcard perfect, with blue skies and pleasantly cool temperatures, and this FitzGerald and Montgomery family reunion made all the sense in the world. However, I was stressed. Maureen's boys barely knew who I was, and of course the fact I was their father was to remain secret. The idea of getting to know them, and vice versa, had me on edge. During my semi-annual business trips to Ireland, I would sometimes see one or both of them—it was usually just a handshake and off they went. More often than not, they were away at boarding school.

However, when Lady Elizabeth arrived in a rented minivan with her two grandsons, it broke the ice. All I felt was happy. Gerald, the older of the twins by four minutes, had taken on the nickname "Fitz," like his Grandfather "Fitz" FitzGerald. Montgomery Randolph, the second born, was known to all as Monty.

Monty vaguely resembled my father, only smaller and darker. Any similarity to me was washed out by the huge difference in size. In color, we were different too. My hair was brown, with a rusty auburn topcoat. His hair was jet black. I was white, with a ruddy glow, whereas his skin tone was a light golden brown, even after a winter session at Eton where there was rarely any sun. He didn't take long to turn nut-brown in the Florida sun. And my eyes were hazel, while his were a startling cornflower blue.

Young Fitz was another story. He had my size—perhaps one day he'd be even bigger—but the resemblance ended there. The boy also didn't look at all like his brother; he was blond and blue-eyed. That they were twins was almost unbelievable when one looked at them side by side.

One day after Monty and I finished off some friends in a tennis doubles' match, my father, who had been watching and smoking one of his hand-rolled cigarettes, took a draw, exhaled a few well-formed smoke rings, and pointed to Monty. "That boy is what people call 'Black Irish.'"

"Isn't that Irish with gypsy or Spanish blood?" I asked.

"Oh, hell, no," he replied. "That's just people being ignorant. The original people in the islands of Britain and Ireland weren't 'white' at all. They were brown-skinned, with dark hair and blue eyes."

"Oh, Pa, come on now," I said with disbelief. "Where do you get this stuff?"

"Yes, boy, it's true. Read the old tales; the first people of those islands were just like Monty—maybe even a few shades darker. You can bet more than one father went out hunting for a gypsy to blame when one of those babies popped out, but the 'black' in Irish will never go away. In Wales, they relish it as part of being Welsh, but not the Irish. Ha, they all want their children to look like Vikings." He chuckled. "But trust me, every family has one of those dark ones sooner or later."

Pa rarely talked by then, mostly keeping to himself and walking along the paths of the farm, but when it came to family or English history, sometimes you couldn't shut him up.

"Son, you need to understand these things. It's a part of your heritage. I mean, look,"—he pointed at Monty—"you can see it right there! The boy looks just like me, he even rides a horse like me, but he's got the skin tone of a friggin' Turk."

It was the only time Pa ever even hinted at the boys' paternity. It was something we had never discussed.

"How can that be?" I asked.

"Do you remember when I took you to Mortimer's castle? Ludlow?"

"Sure, Pa."

"Do you remember I showed you Roger Mortimer's grave? We also saw the tomb of his father Ralph and his mother, Princess Gwladus Ddu."

"I remember."

He was on a roll. "Now pay attention, son. *Ddu* means 'black' in Welsh. You remember me telling you about the Black Prince, the eldest son of King Edward III? Same thing—dark complexion cropping out. Not a black heart, like many say; the man was perhaps the noblest creature ever birthed in England. He was just dark—*Ddu*."

I stopped to think about it a moment. "Sure, Pa, but what's the point?"

"The point, boy, is that Gwladus Ddu was dark-skinned. Ralph married Gwladus the Black. The Black was the daughter of the King of Wales, Llywelyn the Great, and his queen, Joan Plantagenet, daughter of England's King John. Gwladus was walnut-brown, for Christ's sake. That is what the original people looked like three thousand years ago. They were brown-skinned. Same thing with the Black Prince. It just pops out now and then. Monty has that look."

I changed the subject.

"It is hard to imagine twins looking so different."

WE HAD A COVERED LANAI next to the pool, with a fire pit close by. At night we stoked a bonfire as the kids goofed around in the water. Lady Elizabeth and Pa each told their own tales of our ancestors, going back a thousand years. Fact from fiction, who knew? What counted was we all were enthralled.

Elizabeth was quite the storyteller, and she wove a lyrical tale of the FitzGerald Clan, a Norman band, and how they first settled on the River Maigue in North County Cork nearly a thousand years ago. She described the tribal battle, and how the FitzGeralds conquered the O'Donovans and took their rich riverfront lands at the point of the bend, called "The Crom"—the ancient word for such a bend. It made me think of my great-grandmother and the Randolph family farm at Brady's Bend in Pennsylvania.

Over time, *Crom* came to stand for something more, a concept of home and family—a clan—the FitzGerald Clan. *Abú* meant "forever," thus, said Lady Elizabeth, the FitzGerald motto—like the Montgomery motto I'd learned from Pa—became *Crom Abú*..."Family Forever."

Elizabeth looked at each one of us, young and old faces bright from the light of the bonfire.

"Friends may come and go," she said, "but we are all right now looking at family. I want you all to be there for each other, always. *Always* remember this moment. Family Forever! *Crom Abú*!"

"*Crom Abú*," the twins dutifully repeated, much the same way I had once repeated, *Garde Bien*.

"I can't hear you," she roared. "*Crom Abú*!"

We all joined in, shouting, "*Crom Abú*!"

chapter 17

The Black Stallions

FITZ, WITH HIS LOOK OF AN ELEGANT English aristocrat, wanted to follow in his grandmother's footsteps and run FitzGerald Industries. Monty was different; he was a horseman, through and through. It was his passion and his art. With his slight build, he became a champion over jumps by the age of sixteen.

In the mid-eighties, I sent my prize mare, a daughter of the great Secretariat, to Ireland. My plan? Breed her to Old Pete. A mare's gestational period is eleven months. When the foal was two, Lady Elizabeth and Monty came to Florida to see Old Pete's coal-black colt

Using the FitzGerald visit as an opportunity to see Monty in action, I took the colt for a practice run at the Ocala Breeders Sales track, using three of my successful racehorses as "company"—the race term for the competition. Monty was riding my colt for the first time. He looked calm and relaxed, just like his mount. Sitting astride my big black-and-white pony horse, Shiloh, I think I was the only one at the track racked by nervous excitement.

Monty and the colt smoked the field of four at a mile and established an embarrassing lead at a mile and a half. The black colt was a natural born long-distance racehorse. Monty was enamored, unadulterated exhilaration written across his face. A rumor started...by me, I confess...that I was offering the young black stallion for sale, pre-auction, at seven hundred and fifty thousand dollars. This was before Elizabeth raised the issue of buying him. I know that seems like a lot of money, but when the official time for the colt's third breeze at a half-mile in 44.2 seconds was published in the OBS "official works," the news spread like wildfire. Elizabeth said he was the horse she wanted. She offered eight hundred thousand dollars.

Up until that moment, we had all been acting as if it was just business. I took her aside and said, "I can't do this. Not like this."

"What do you mean, Jake?"

"You want the horse for Monty, right?"

"Yes."

"Look, regardless of this alternate reality we have created, Monty is still my son. I cannot sell you a horse, meant for my son, for eight hundred grand."

"Jake, it has to be that way."

"Sorry, but I don't feel good about it."

She flicked a look to the side to ensure we were alone. "How could you explain, publicly, why you are giving away what is probably a million-dollar horse?"

"Elizabeth, I know what you're saying, but sometimes it isn't about money. I don't need the money. I can keep the horse and Monty can ride him."

"I want that horse, not just for Monty, but for me too. Just like Pete made Gerry a champion, I want the same for Monty." She paused, allowing it to sink in, then gave me a look worthy of a Svengali. "Jake, you know what he will do with him. Your mare put amazing speed on top of Old Pete."

"I know, and Pete was the fastest horse I've ever ridden. That's why I sent her over for breeding."

"Well," she exclaimed, "that freakish speed will have every stable in England, including the queen's, bowing to us. Monty will be a world-renowned grand champion."

"Old Son could do it," I concurred, then added, "The stable staff call the colt 'Old Son,' I guess because I told them about his sire, Old Pete, and how the 'son of Old Pete' had the same calm demeanor. Somehow, 'son of Old Pete' evolved into 'Old Son.'"

"Jake, forgive me, but this is an Irish issue, too. In honor of my husband, may he rest in peace."

At that, I looked at her and saw her features had hardened; I knew from watching her over the years that it was her "tell" when she prepared to close a deal by force of will.

"I want an Irish name for the horse. When Monty wins on Sean Mac..."

Good grief, I thought. *She has already named him.*

"...my Fitz will be smiling from above. You know, for me this is not just about the two-million-dollar Grand National purse. England's best will have just been beaten by an Irishman on an Irish-bred horse. That Irishman will be Monty, your son, my grandson. Now does *that* work for you?"

She was talking, but I had drifted, stimming on the name when she dropped it. I liked "Sean Mac" and silently chanted it with an image of the black colt in mind as she talked. *Sean Mac,* in the dialect of the south of Ireland, means "Old Son." This was how Elizabeth negotiated. Since she couldn't set the hook with money, she was calling down Irish pride and family honor. Ironically, Lady Elizabeth was probably more English than Queen Elizabeth herself. I knew if I agreed to the name Sean Mac, then all that was left to discuss was the amount. Perhaps

Gerry had been right with his advice to me so many years ago on how to deal with his mother: *Just go along*.

An idea arose. "Look, Elizabeth, the horse is going to the auction at OBS in a month, so I can't stop you from buying him."

This laid down the fact that there would be no pre-auction sale to her or anybody else.

"I'm sorry to hear that, Jake. You know what this means to me."

"I do, and Aunt Elizabeth, I know I owe you at least that, and much more." I took a deep breath and offered an alternative way forward. "I want to propose something that might give everyone what they want. You and I own the horse in a partnership. I ship him to you in a year. We don't race him here as a two-year-old but let him mature. Send Monty here as often as possible this coming year, so he and the horse can connect. Then, we ship Sean Mac to Golden Miller Stables, and you take on all responsibility for training and racing for the next four years, more if he's up to it. We split the net winnings, seventy-five to me, twenty-five to you. When he retires from racing, if he's successful, we syndicate him and put him out to stud, which you will broker, conditioned on him standing stud at Golden Miller. We split the proceeds of the syndicate fifty-fifty."

She looked at me for a long moment, her features finally softening. "Jake, you've become not only a fine man but quite the businessman."

"I learned from the master. I was paying attention, not just carrying your briefcase, on all those business trips we made when I was a teenager."

"This is why I am so glad you are a part of our family, and I know it's not always easy under these circumstances. Your gesture means a lot to me, but it is also an incredibly smart move. I have no doubt, if the colt stays healthy, four years from now you will have two million or more out of the deal, and you deserve every penny. Your share of the syndicate will bring at least another two million to you. And I insist on giving a quarter-million up-front payment, so the deal is fair all the way around, since you are taking on the huge risk of injury or illness before he peaks, versus cash-in-hand."

"Okay," I responded, taking no time to consider it. "I appreciate the money up front, because there is always a big risk. But in that same spirit of family fairness, we'll split the purses fifty-fifty instead of seventy-five-twenty-five. Agreed?"

She smiled. "What can I say? Thank you for that. Done!"

"Done!" And like my father, and generations of horsemen before me, I spit on my right palm—Elizabeth doing the same with hers—and we shook hands. It was all the contract we would ever need.

When the down payment for Sean Mac arrived by wire to refresh my farm operating account, there was another surprise. I thought we were talking dollars when we made the deal, but she wired British pounds, slightly over half a million dollars at the exchange rate of the day. I called her up and said, "Elizabeth, thank you, but you sent me pounds instead of dollars. I think there may have been a mistake."

"No mistake, dear boy. I want a generous transaction, and I cannot be taking advantage of my favorite nephew."

I laughed at that and pointed out, "M'lady, I am your *only* nephew."

"All the better!"

WITH A FATHER'S EYE and a father's pride, I watched Monty develop. No one ever admits it, but every father has that "apple of my eye," and Monty was my favorite. Again, in both his look and demeanor, he reminded me of my father. He attended Eton College in England. "College" in England had a different meaning than in the United States.

It was a rough equivalent to a private high school for students over the age of sixteen to prepare for admission to a university. Monty graduated from Eton with distinction. As a fencing champion, he led the Eton team to capture the All-England Hampton Trophy, and as an individual, he won England's Junior Saber Championship.

Consistent with our plan to bring him on slowly, Sean Mac started racing as a four-year-old. In America, the top racehorses started as two-year-olds, but for jumping and distance, waiting until three was far better for the horse. With Monty up, four-year-old Sean Mac won a couple of starter-level stakes races in Ireland. Then, as a five-year-old, he won both the Irish and French Nationals. In the English Grand National that year, Monty and his black stallion were sorely and deliberately fouled by two English competitors who were clearly working in concert. Even though it was deliberate, there was rarely any meaningful recourse in the steeplechase for a protest. It was a forty-horse free-for-all—rules be damned. Still, Sean Mac surprised us all in what turned out to be the equine version of a vicious rugby maul.

It was racing drama at its best. Sean Mac was blocked, with a slowing horse on each side, their riders raining blows with their leather bats. Monty's public-school fencing skills saved the day, deflecting blow after blow with his own racing bat. Still, he saw no clear way out, trapped in an ever-pressing equine vise.

Then, Sean Mac lunged to the right and bit off the blocking gray gelding's left ear, leaving the injured horse screaming and spraying blood. Monty, in an equally possessed moment, instantly took advantage of his adversary's shock, slashing his racing bat across the face of the gray horse's jockey. It broke the man's nose and sliced open his cheek. The wounded gelding reared up and threw his equally injured rider to the ground. Sean Mac then sprinted through the chaos-driven gap and sought to take the lead, but he couldn't make up the lost time. He came in third by eight lengths.

At the time, Andy Warhol's famous expression came to my mind: "In the future, everyone will be famous for fifteen minutes." This Grand National melee looked like Monty and Sean Mac's fifteen minutes of fame. Actually, "infamy" is the proper word. All of England's prominent but notoriously muckraking newspapers smeared big front-page photos of the critical moment of Sean Mac biting and Monty slashing. Rider and horse were quickly branded by the English press as "The Savages" in sports page headline after headline.

In an act of bald-faced temerity, the two English riders who incited the melee filed a protest, seeking to ban Monty and Sean Mac from future competition in England. By the grace of God, an up-and-coming English filmmaker had videoed the whole incident, start to finish, for a documentary he was doing. He sent copies of the tape to both the track stewards and the BBC. The stewards, who were "the law" on the racetrack and unwilling to bend to chauvinistic pressure, exonerated Monty and Sean Mac, and in a rare act censured and fined—*sua sponte*—both English jockeys. The BBC backed the stewards by repeatedly broadcasting the video, including a follow-on stamp of royal approval with a video clip of the Prince of Wales, stating: "In England, we believe in fair play and good form."

It seemed there was justice for an Irishman, and an Irish horse, in England after all.

As a six-year-old, winning every race he entered, Sean Mac was invincible. Sally, Katie, and I traveled to England for the following year's Grand National and were seated in Viscountess Spennithorne's box, near the royals. It was a family affair, with Lady Elizabeth, Eamon Cavanaugh, Rory and his wife Glenda, Gerry and Maureen, and Fitz with his date and future wife, Lady Margaret. A royal cousin, Maggie was craquant, smart, and funny, and beloved by her grand-aunt, the queen.

With Sean Mac's fame, for the first time "Jake Montgomery" stood publicly as a player on a European stage. Even though I avoided public attention, interviews and the like, my increasing public profile was a problem with my undercover career. I was co-owner, trainer, and breeder of Sean Mac, rapidly emerging as the most famous horse in Europe. SOCOM, without even consulting with me, took me off field duty. When I voiced a half-hearted complaint to my handler, a thirty-something civilian who was probably an NSA or CIA bureaucrat, insult was added to injury with, "You are past twenty years of service and getting too old to do the job anyway."

With that, the Marine Corps promptly promoted me from Lieutenant Colonel to Colonel, setting the stage for my imminent retirement. James Gerald Long was retired too, with a fake death certificate (heart attack) and a marked grave at Shannon's Lemenagh Cemetery. These were his only rewards for years of service. In a goofily macabre hat-tip to my Irish alter ego (may he rest in peace), I visit him every now and then to lay flowers on his grave.

AS A PART OF MY MAKEOVER, my public coming out, when I arrived in London for the English Grand National, I sported a new look. First, in an offering to the retirement gods, I put on an extra fifteen pounds. That was all it took to soften the lean-and-mean look. I draped the new me in a neat close-trimmed full beard, a tailored gray Canali day suit, a matching suede flat cap, and Ray-Ban Aviator sunglasses. Not a trace of my secret alter ego could be seen. The aging movie star look was my newly crafted public persona, my new mask. I liked the look! Been that way, with an ever-growing touch of gray, ever since.

The Grand National was a true extravaganza. We didn't have anything like it in America—a free-flowing festival, with more than half a million people converging on Aintree Racecourse, near Liverpool. In the Grand National race, there was no starting gate, and the field of competitors was always enormous. Sean Mac was the favorite among the mob of thirty-six entered horses. The race had two false starts before getting the runners away clean.

Monty, not wanting a repeat of what happened the previous year, quickly took the lead, showing tremendous early speed for a race of more than four miles with thirty jumps. The field then broke into a six-horse pack and thinned out from there. A hush overtook the crowd, with murmurs that the fast pace couldn't be maintained for the distance. Then Monty and Sean Mac put down more early speed, leaving the pack behind. It reminded me of the greatest race I'd ever seen, when Sean Mac's grandsire, Secretariat, won the Belmont by almost a furlong in world-record time.

Monty struck for home, leaving the number-two horse, Escalon, a furlong behind with only half a mile left to run. Wire to wire, I thought it a bold move and I knew it was a complete departure from the pre-race plan laid out by Rory. As they neared the finish, Monty tried to slow Sean Mac to preserve the horse. The win was secure, but the stallion was not slowing down. Yes, this was Old Pete's son for sure, running the race *his* way. Sean Mac increased the pace for the finish, finding a reservoir of blinding speed. Monty did the only thing possible: enjoy the ride. Gerry and I looked at each other, beaming with pride in our son and our horse as they blazed across the finish line. Like two teenagers, we shared a high five.

That race was the pinnacle of my professional life as a horse breeder and trainer. I came up with the idea for his breeding. I helped birth him. Within minutes of birth, the long-legged mousey-blue colt was up and prancing in the foaling stall. I knew then he would be exceptional. I knew then that he would be raven black, as all truly black horses are born with a distinct bluish coloring. The colt had an aura of speed that I saw from the start.

I was a horseman, and Sean Mac was my masterpiece.

I screamed so loud at the finish that my voice was gone for hours. I smiled so much that my jaw ached for days. Monty and Sean Mac broke the record books, perhaps for all time.

In the winner's enclosure—"winner's circle" to us Yanks—Monty, still atop Sean Mac, held the horsehead-shaped trophy high and told the press, "I want to thank this great horse. He is the world's best! I want to thank my family, my grandfather and trainer, Colonel Rory Darragh, my parents, Gerry and Maureen Fitzgerald, Lord and Lady Montgomery... and a special thanks to my grandmother, Viscountess Spennithorne, Lady Elizabeth FitzGerald, and my cousin, Mister Jake Montgomery, the breeders and owners of Sean Mac. THANK YOU!"

RECOUNTING THIS VICTORY is accompanied by a bittersweet memory, for it was my last time with Gerry and Maureen. Several months later they died at a FitzGerald chateau in the Swiss Alps. It was thought to be an accident. Gerry came home late and, according to the toxicology report, he was dangerously high on a perfect storm of whiskey, cocaine, and Seconal. They had separate bedrooms. Maureen was sound asleep. The coroner's report concluded that Gerry stumbled to his bed and passed out. In his drunken stupor, he forgot to turn off the Land Rover parked in the garage. Carbon monoxide filled the house. They never woke up.

Only with their passing did I fully appreciate how much I cared for them.

Katie and Cassie went to the funeral in Ireland with me. James remained behind to run our farm while Sally went to South Carolina to be with her mother, who had fractured her hip in a fall and was recovering from surgery. I only stayed in Ireland for a day after the funeral to pay my respects, needing to return on a direct flight from Shannon to Newark. A horse I trained was racing in a big-money Grade I stakes race at Saratoga. To be honest, I was grateful for the excuse to leave. The urge to console my boys as their father, not a cousin, was overwhelming.

My daughters stayed behind in Tara for several weeks after the funeral. Then, they returned with Monty to Ocala's Jim Taylor Field, what is now called Ocala International Airport, in the big FitzGerald Industries private jet. At first I thought the use of the jet was ostentatious, but quickly dismissed it with, *If you've got it, why not?* However, in a follow-up act that reeked of impulsiveness, Monty bought a two-and-a-half-million-dollar racing farm in Ocala, just a few miles from us.

Elizabeth called me, concerned about Monty's move to Ocala. She told me she had cautioned Monty years earlier about flirting with Katie, during one of her high school summer vacation visits to Kenwood, saying she was off limits because she was his cousin.

I shrugged the whole thing off, saying, "No worries, they're just best friends." I reassured myself with my observations that over the past twenty years, Katie had never seemed to have *any* romantic relationships, male or female.

"Too friendly, if you ask me!" Elizabeth retorted.

"What do you mean?"

"Monty was cavalier with me—'No worries, Mhaimeo,' he said to me, 'we are all kissing cousins in this family, and I do like her very much.' I did not know what to say to him, so...so I said nothing."

"They seem to just be friends," I said, cautiously now. "I mean, and please, this is just between us, but Katie doesn't seem interested in men."

My assessment of Katie's sexuality was not shared by Aunt Elizabeth. She replied, her tone conveying clear doubt in my judgment, "Let's hope so."

Once settled into his Ocala farm—Monty followed the seasons. He summered in England and Ireland, along with a circuit of jump races in the northern United States. Winters were spent in Florida. His farm trained steeplechase horses for the American jump race circuit, and as a sideline, he conducted clinics for difficult horses at the nearby Florida Horse Park arena in the winter. I'd been to several of his seminars, which were like a magic show for horse aficionados. People would bring their wild or maladjusted horses to the clinic, and Monty played the role of a faith healer. Without rehearsal or other prearrangements so common to the fake faith healers at a camp revival, he asked for only the worst problem horses to come forward as subjects. "The badder the better" was his slogan.

First, the owner of the problem horse would get his animal from a nearby holding stall, lead him up to the microphone, and tell his tale of woe. Then, keeping the horse and sending the owner back to the audience, within half an hour...sometime in just minutes, Monty would be riding with the animal calm and well-behaved under saddle.

As "Uncle Jake," Monty and I became close. In fact, because as horsemen we shared the same profession, I spent more time then with

Monty and Katie than any of my other children. She was running both our farm and Monty's farm, called Tara, when he was away on the road teaching and racing. Katie lived in a guesthouse near the front gate of the luxurious Tara estate. It felt like Monty made an extra effort to be with me too. A frequent guest at family dinners and a regular at our home racetrack, Monty soon became that which was his secret birthright—a part of my family. It meant the world to me.

AFTER MY RETIREMENT, an adrenal substitute for my SOCOM service came fast in the form of a stallion we called "The Black." I won't mince words—this black stallion was the meanest and most dangerous horse I have ever encountered. Cunning, with a mind like a predator, he was a throwback to atavistic qualities rarely seen in the modern horse.

The Black was a refugee from Hurricane Andrew, a Category 5 storm with one-hundred-and-seventy-five-miles-per-hour sustained winds and bands of embedded tornados. It devastated Miami in August 1992, killing sixty-three people and more than a thousand horses as it cut across South Florida, leaving in its wake a twenty-mile-wide swath of destruction. The predominately agricultural southern area of Miami-Dade County had no power for more than a month because the electrical grid had been obliterated. Telephone lines were down, with entire neighborhoods flattened and flooded.

Stabled horses died in barns destroyed by the hurricane. Horses turned out in fields panicked and ran through storm-damaged fences into flooded streets and fields, often drowning in the swollen canals that crisscrossed the region. Countless others died of trauma from flying debris. It was like a nightmare straight from hell.

Our farm in Ocala, almost four hundred miles north of Miami, was unaffected by the storm. With evangelic zeal, Sally organized local racehorse farms in a volunteer strategy to rescue Miami horses in need of shelter. She ran the money end of our farm, from basic bookkeeping to managing our investments. There were many years when her profits from real estate and stock market investments exceeded what we made on equine operations. But I was especially impressed by her volunteer initiative, seeing a need and almost overnight creating something from nothing. She convinced Ocala's big racing farms to commit to an act of charity, one Ocala horse farms were in a position to provide. (The organization Sally founded that year lives on, evolving into an equine rescue that rehabilitates for adoption almost a hundred abandoned and abused horses every year.)

Montgomery Racing Stables agreed to take in six horses, the capacity of our biggest horse trailer. Back then, a horse cost, all averaged out, three hundred dollars a month to keep. I did the math—six times three hundred—it was almost half my monthly Marine Corp retirement pay. When I pointed that out to Sally, indicating my reason for saying we could not take in six, all I got in return was silence and a sour look. Much of our marital communication by this time was nonverbal. We both used words wisely. This suited my neural profile, and this particular look was well deserved at the time. She knew that Montgomery Racing's net income was always well into the seven figures.

We were going to the farmlands just south of Miami's urban center. It was the area hardest hit by the storm. Most of the horses affected by Hurricane Andrew weren't racehorses. They were pleasure horses, pets and companions, whose owners had family ranches. Some were from small equestrian training centers and boarding barns. Before the storm, this beautiful suburban, agricultural enclave was a hodgepodge of horse farms, vegetable farms, ornamental plant nurseries, and fruit groves. After Hurricane Andrew, it looked as if it had been run through a blender. The closer we got to the center of the storm track, the worse the damage. Where houses once stood now lay fields of rubble. Some home sites were reduced to a scraped concrete foundation. Trees were stripped, not just of leaves and branches, but even their bark, all peeled off by the ferocity of the wind.

The statistics were shocking. Before the storm, there had been around five thousand horses in Miami-Dade County. In a pre-storm exodus, owners moved fifteen hundred out of the area. Many went to Ocala, which was a natural haven. It was far from the storm's projected path and with all the amenities of the "horse capital" of Florida. Of the remaining horses, more than one thousand were killed in the raging tempest. Another two hundred and fifty were injured so severely they had to be euthanized by volunteer veterinarians and animal control officers. Many more were never found. Some were drowned and swept out to sea. Others were stolen. Just as the storm brought out the best in people, with tens of thousands volunteering to help, it also brought out the worst. Roving bands of thugs caught loose horses and cattle and shipped them out of state to meat-processing plants.

All the horses we rescued were Paso Finos—the same kind of horses Izzie had ridden for rich owners back in the El Yunque. Paso Finos are a popular breed with the large Caribbean and South American ethnic communities of Miami. Imported from Spain with the conquistadors, they were descended from a colonial horse bred over centuries for use as a light working mount on the plantations of the Spanish-American colonies.

The Paso Fino was a smaller breed of horse, typically standing fourteen to fifteen hands tall at the withers. They were sturdy and sure-footed, their equine ancestral roots from Spain a blend of Arabian, North-African Barb, the gaited Spanish Jennet, and Andalusian. The breed was preserved by aficionados, primarily in Puerto Rico, the Dominican Republic, and Colombia. It was thought by many that Pasos had the smoothest and most refined four-beat lateral gait of any of the "gaited" horses in the world.

Four of the horses on our rescue list were owned by the González family, who we met at a temporary holding facility in their area. I labeled the horses, with good cause, the "House Pets." Mr. and Mrs. Gonzalez had only moderate roof damage to their well-built concrete-block home, but their wooden barn had been destroyed. Mrs. Gonzalez, to her credit, had insisted—over some protest from her husband—that the horses weather the storm inside their house. When it was over, the entire Gonzalez family, horses included, were safe. But the property had no electricity or running water. Their fences had been knocked down and the barn had simply disappeared. So, amidst tearful goodbyes, they helped Sally and me load their horses onto our trailer. The Gonzalez family had a look on their faces that reminded me of soldiers in Vietnam: shell-shocked and traumatized. But they thanked us profusely. I knew then we were doing the right thing. I also knew that, as soon as possible, this family would be on its way to Ocala for their Pasos. Just the thought of their four horses camping out in their living room made me smile.

Before he left, Mr. Gonzalez took me aside, pointing to a nearby Animal Control horse trailer, where two officers waited to speak with me.

"Mister Montgomery, I know of this black horse in their trailer. He is very bad. Dangerous. Be careful."

I was taken aback by the ominous warning.

When the Gonzalez family departed, the two officers from Animal

Control, middle-aged men in khaki uniforms with badges and side-arms, approached us. They both had a military bearing.

"Mr. and Mrs. Montgomery, I'm Officer Reggie Forman and this is Officer Manny Cejas."

We exchanged greetings.

"We only have one horse for you to transport. The other one died."

"Sorry to hear that," I said. "I've only ever seen damage like this in the war."

"'Nam?" Officer Cejas asked.

"Yep." I sensed he was a veteran, so went on. "Marine Recon. Khe Sahn and Dong Ha. Colonel, just retired."

He snapped me a quick salute, smiled and thumped his chest "Third Division too. *Semper Fi,* Colonel."

By reflex, I saluted and completed the ritual greeting with a guttural, "*Semper Fi!*"

Officer Foreman half-heartedly raised his hand and offered an almost apologetic, "Army," then began what I could tell was a speech he'd rehearsed. "Sir, ma'am, we must put you on clear notice about this horse." He motioned toward the Animal Control trailer. "He was running loose and was extremely aggressive to anyone who approached. We finally had to bring him down with a tranquilizer dart."

"Actually, it took two," Cejas added. "He's very strong."

"Look, he's drugged now, but as soon as he comes out from the tranq, he'll go crazy." Foreman paused. "Because he was abandoned, he's yours to keep. Here is the paperwork." He shook a few pages in his right hand. "He was never reported missing, so we don't think anyone is coming for him. If you agree to take him, we have four syringes of an Alpha-two sedative prepared for his transport. We just injected him. Don't go more than three hours without hitting him up; otherwise, he is dangerous.

When you get home, I advise putting him in a pasture by himself. He goes completely crazy in a stall." Foreman met my eyes. "Now, if you *don't* want to take him, we'll understand. We are prepared to euthanize him, if need be, since we have no facilities for this kind of stallion. If you take him but later you decide to put him down, you will have our full understanding. So, like I said, sign here and he is your horse."

The words, "You keep him," were on the tip of my tongue. Sally knew that. After so many years together, she was able to read my mind, and she knew I'd inherited a practical business sense from my father. This was not smart business. But before I could utter the words, Sally grabbed the sleeve of my shirt and tugged me aside.

"Jake, I created this project. All the big farms are in. My reputation is on the line. I am not going to have one of my first rescues put down."

"Honey, this is crazy. You heard the man, didn't you?"

"Listen, Big Boy." She tapped me on the chest with her index finger. "I know you, and I know you can do it. Do it for *me*."

Truth be told, I would do almost anything for her.

My father never had a horse on the farm that didn't have a meaningful business function. Every individual animal was part of some plan. The plans didn't always work but each horse had one.

"Pa is going to shit himself when he finds out," I said to her. That was my way of agreeing.

Animal Control led the drugged horse out of the trailer. He was jet black, except for a white "8" on his left shoulder. The mark had been made when the horse was just a few months old by shaving the hair in that spot, then using a copper branding iron dipped in liquid nitrogen to freeze-burn the skin. When it healed, the hair grew back white.

SOCOM, out of our Tampa base, deployed resources in Colombia, so I knew the "8" stood for the horse's breeder, Fabio Ochoa, founder of the infamous Medellin drug cartel. It was the symbol for all horses born at the Ochoa farm in Medellin, Colombia. I also knew that drug dealers in Miami coveted an Ochoa horse the same way they sported solid gold Rolex watches and Lamborghinis. So we were probably rescuing a horse that at one time belonged to a dangerous criminal.

The black stallion's head hung low, and his legs were wobbly, all signs he was well sedated. I'd helped veterinarians castrate young horses using a similar drug cocktail. The process was called "standing castration." With sedation and local anesthetics, a vet could surgically remove a stallion's testicles as the horse stood, calmly, without even a flinch or groan in the process. This type of procedure was far safer than using general anesthesia and the post-surgical recovery was swift, with the horse capable of light workouts in just a few days.

The stallion was a dynamic black, like a slice of midnight in the bright afternoon sun, a chiseled block of glistening ebony. He had perfect conformation, complemented by one thousand pounds of rippling muscle and only minor cuts and scrapes. I could see in him a flashy equine elegance that was rare. The horse had to have been expensive. He made the González family's Paso Finos look inferior, like Chevys compared to a Ferrari.

"Officer Foreman," I said, gesturing with my thumb at the stallion, "this clearly is a very valuable animal. Are you saying no one has reported him missing?"

He flicked the papers once more. "It's been more than a week since the storm, and nothing."

That was all I needed to know. The horse loaded onto the trailer without an issue, and we headed home. Sally looked at the papers as I drove, which left the horse unnamed, with just "black stallion" scrawled on the form that had been signed by me and Officer Cejas. As children,

Sally and I had both been big fans of Walter Farley's novel *The Black Stallion*. With a clear sense of relief on leaving the disaster area behind, we got to making comparisons between Farley's stallion character and the drugged horse in our trailer. From the first, we called the unnamed miscreant "The Black," just like in Farley's book.

I called the farm from a payphone at the Turnpike's Palm Beach Service Plaza and had one of the grooms track down Izzie.

"What's up, Jake?" he asked.

"Hey, Izz. As planned, I'm bringing up four horses for that big pasture over by your house, all from the same home, all Paso Finos."

"Got it. I'll have everything ready. What was it like down there?"

"It's bad, really bad."

"I started out on Pasos. You remember?"

"I know, and I'm going to need your help. I have one more. A stallion. A completely loco Paso stallion."

"What?"

"I'll explain later. I have him drugged. We need to put him in that big foaling stall in the west-gate barn. We'll figure out what comes next once he comes to. Please have Lloyd get things ready for us."

I decided to ignore Foreman's advice to put the stallion in a pasture because I refused to have to shoot a horse with a dart gun to catch him. The west-gate barn was at the far northwest corner of the farm. It was remote and rarely used, except when we were in overflow mode. The extra-large foaling stall would suit the plan I was hatching to work with The Black.

"Trying to hide him from the old man?" Izzie asked with a chuckle.

"Caught me."

"Won't work."

Sally injected the stallion one more time at the Okahumpka

Service Plaza, and forty-five minutes later we unloaded him at the west end of the farm. He came out like a lamb. The González "House Pets" were released without incident into the big pasture nearby. They seemed content as long as they were together. After a few minutes, the horses were playfully dodging and leaping in a vast field of bright green grass, celebrating as if Hurricane Andrew never happened.

"When can I ride him?" Sally asked after inspecting The Black.

I responded with a nervous laugh.

Izzie intervened, "Give him a few months, *Patrona*."

With a flick of her head, she tossed back her long strawberry-blonde locks. It was one of her signature moves. She gave me a seductive look. Then, holding up the truck keys with a jingling shake, Sally said, "I'm going to see the kids. Don't be gone long, Big Boy!"

She gunned the truck and left in a cloud of dust. Izzie started laughing and in a mocking falsetto said, "*Oye*, don't be gone long, Beega Boy." He chuckled at his own joke, then, in perfect English, said, "I think Sally has plans for you tonight, Jake."

"Let's hope so. It's been a long hard day," I replied with a laugh.

However, it was the horse, not sex, on my mind. His new stall was the size of two big stalls—a space normally used for birthing. A thick layer of specially ground fresh wood shavings covered the clay surface, and thick rubber floor mats had been attached to the walls to protect foals from injury. It was the perfect place for a potentially crazed horse—his own rubber room, big enough for the two of us but small enough to catch him, by force or tranquilizer, if necessary.

Lloyd, one of our grooms, joined us. I put him to work. "Lloyd, run over to the shop and grab some gate chain and a padlock."

Izzie gave The Black a final injection for the evening as I filled a water bucket and laid down a couple of sheaves of coastal hay. After enduring the storm, being shipped from Miami, and injected with so much drugs, high-quality feed or hay could induce colic (a bad stomach ache) or even a bout of laminitis, which would damage the horse's feet. Both issues could be fatal. Coastal was a cheap, low-protein hay, and the perfect feed after a stressful event.

Lloyd returned with the padlock and a curious audience—two of our Mexican exercise riders. To looks of disbelief, I proceeded to chain and lock the stall entrance.

"This stays locked until tomorrow," I announced. "I don't care what happens, and nobody goes in but me. *Lo entiendes?*" I slipped the key into the right front pocket of my jeans.

"Your poppa is not going to like that lock on the stall," Izzie said.

"If he has a problem, have him see me."

All the men nodded their agreement.

chapter 15
Garde Bien

WITH THE BLACK, I had to learn new skills. It was daunting, as it'd been a minute since I'd had to learn anything new when it came to handling horses. I needed Monty's advice, but he and Katie were in England for the summer horse sales. It was "hunt season." Through Monty's enduring fame as a now two-time Grand National champion, he'd become a sought-after celebrity fixture in England during the summer hunt season. Katie could ride the hunt almost as well as Monty and was a welcome guest. And while there, she could do business. Like my father and me before her, she sold our farm's racehorses and Monty's jump race babies to England's elite.

Without Monty's "horse whisperer" expertise to turn to, Izzie and I decided to start from scratch. The stallion was aggressive in his stall, not just hard to handle. He charged at anyone who dared enter, teeth bared. Before we could get to the round pen—a safe and secure training space—we had to be able to lead him. So the first sessions were all conducted in the big foaling stall. Our first problem? How to safely get into the stall. Izzie knocked the head off an old polo mallet, securely duct-taped a streamer made of strands of fluorescent orange marking ribbon to the end of the stick, and handed it to me.

I looked at him, puzzled. "Why are you giving this to me? To hit him?"

"God, no, don't hit him. He will kick your ass in that stall."

"Come on, Izzie, you are the Paso expert. Maybe you should do it, eh?"

"No fuckin' way," he stated in perfect English with a North Florida drawl. "If you think I am going in there with that crazy stallion, you are crazier than he is. You brought him here. You need to do it."

"Do what, then?"

"Jake, that fucker is crazy. He needs to be respectful, so you go in big and be twice as crazy. Move to make a space as you enter. Go for it. Hit those buckets. Hit the wall. Yell. Make him respect your space. But stay away from him. Respect his space. For now, you stay out of his space, and please, do not hit him! He will not walk into your space if you are carving it out in the air with the stick. All we need to do now is teach him to respect your space."

I looked at the streamers on the end of the stick, shaking them like a pom pom for effect, then said to Izzie. "You're joking?"

"No, you need the horse to be thinking, 'Who is this lunatic?' Otherwise, he will try to stomp you to death."

"Stomp me to death?" I repeated. I glanced over to the shed row wall at the shotgun we kept for the occasional snake or coyote. "Okay." I pointed at the gun. "But please shoot him before that happens."

I wasn't joking and Izzie knew it.

At first, the horse and I were in a stalemate. I could occupy half the stall space, but only because of my fearsome display. On the third day, we caught each other's gaze, and just for a moment, I sensed a seething malice. It was both hypnotic and suffocating. The Black stared at me, pawing the floor in a cloud of rising sawdust. Real or imagined, the smell of ammonia was almost overwhelming. I struggled to breathe; my throat constricted like in the first stages of an asthma attack. I was spacing out, but it was no place for an autistic freeze. I knew I had to do something, fast.

Izzie's advice came to mind. I broke the spell by smacking the feed buckets repeatedly with the polo stick, stimming on the arc of light created by the orange florescent tape and the rapid back-and-forth motion of the polo mallet, forming a firey figure eight like a forcefield between us. Then, the horse and I connected. He knew: *Come inside and we fight.* Had I let my guard down, I'm sure I'd have been at his mercy.

As soon as I could track Monty down, I asked him the best way to handle The Black. His simple suggestion was to get the horse into the round pen, turn sideways and wait, for as long as it took. Once the stallion made clear eye contact, I was to reciprocate for just a moment, but no staring, and then wait for him to relax before moving slowly, no strong pressure, "like a dance, Uncle Jake," he said. "Think like a slow dance where you connect with a woman, not just physically but emotionally. Both of you as one, like two lovers. Just whisper to yourself and to the horse, 'both as one,' over and over."

To me, his instructions sounded like hocus pocus, and I said so.

I heard Monty chuckle over the phone as he responded, "Trust me. It works—and even better on the ladies. And, Uncle Jake, whispering 'both as one' is for *you*, to get *you* in the right place, not the horse."

I trusted Monty, so the next morning I began the exercise in patience that was catching The Black and somehow leading him to the farm's round pen, a fenced circle with a sixty-foot diameter. Once there, I was aided by the fact that a round pen seemed to be a familiar space to him from prior training—that and the fact he probably looked forward to moving outside the confines of a stall. Nevertheless, it was not without incident. As I unclipped the lead rope from his halter, he reached out, teeth bared, and bit down on the bill of my red ball cap. It was so fast it startled me. The feisty stallion then pranced in a circle along the pen's wall, his nostrils flaring, his tail up in a flag of excitement as he proudly carried this bright red trophy in his maw for all to see.

Keeping my expression neutral, I stood in the middle of the pen, calm, waiting for The Black to stop and connect with me. Whispering to myself, *Both as one,* was challenging, as *Drop the fucking hat* was at the forefront of my mind. Thankfully, after just a few minutes, he stopped, dropped the hat, and looked me over. I turned sideways, took a deep relaxing breath and whispered, "Both as one," aloud and in earnest. His head dropped an inch or two as he relaxed. Still sideways, I moved back a little. As I moved back, he moved forward, toward me. I stopped. He came to me, and I eased my hand to his neck and scratched him—my touch gentle, all the while whispering, "Both as one." Then I reconnected the lead rope, ending the lesson on a high point, and took him back to his stall. Remarkably, The Black acted like a well-trained horse on the way to the barn, telling me then that his dangerous behaviors were not uncontrolled but deliberate.

I still preferred untrained wildness to deliberate maliciousness.

Nevertheless, things got better day by day. In a week, The Black seemed not just to recognize me but to accept me. He allowed me, but only me, to clean his stall, bring in food and water, lead him to the round pen, and move him through his gaits using body language. But even though we made steady progress, there were still problems. I was bit, stepped on, and shoved into a wall. Not all at once and nothing serious, and I escaped with just scrapes and bruises. It was even good for a little marital humor—once, The Black reached out and nipped me just above my left nipple, clamping down on my chest for a moment. It didn't break the skin, so I paid it no mind. However, later, when showering after the day's work, Sally saw the bruise. She had been sitting on the marble edge of our Jacuzzi tub, talking and watching me shower. She came over, reached in, and pointed at the perfect purple dental imprint on my left pec. "New girlfriend?"

I laughed. "No. The Black."

She smiled and responded with a velvety growl, "In that case, let me kiss it and make it better."

We never made it into the bedroom. Even though she was fully clothed, I pulled Sally into the steam filled shower. Slowly, gently, while standing behind her and whispering to myself, "Both as one," I kissed her neck and massaged her lower abdomen. Taking my time, I rubbed, twisted, and worked my way up the front of her wet blouse as one after another, buttons popped open. Her blouse slipped off, and then she took charge, removed her bra and panties, and turned to face me. I remember her kiss, it was sweet, tasting of strawberry jam.

IZZIE AND I WORKED TOGETHER, trying to fix The Black. Izzie's attitude made the job easier, for he was still one of the most happy-go-lucky men I'd ever met, always with a smile on his face and a song in his heart. At first the horse was calmed only by injectable sedatives or Izzie singing an old Spanish song called "*Doce Cascabeles*," meaning "twelve bells." Izzie would often sit on the front-porch deck of his double-wide trailer, play the guitar, and sing the same song to his rotating harem of lady friends.

The Black, and Monty, taught me techniques in the round pen that have served me well ever since. The key was that I learned to move the horse without ever touching him. The old-fashioned style of "breaking" a horse with ropes and whips, brute force, and rodeo-like first rides was, to me, ignorant and cruel, and unnecessarily dangerous for both horse and rider. I had long employed a light-intensity, round-pen-based, ground-training technique, using long lines. But Monty's no-touch technique, abandoning ropes and lines altogether, and eliminating any direct pressure—no touching, pulling, or pushing—created a positive environment where man and horse could act in harmony. It also created a setting where trust could grow. Enough trust to connect.

Even though my focus was on creating a bond with The Black, our lessons together were forcing me to grow too. I was training with the round pen and body language, but also with love—love for a horse that was hard to love.

The Black was smart, and with a few subtle cues, he learned in the round pen to follow orders for gallop, *corto, largo*, and walk—the four gaits of a Paso Fino. These gaits were on tap with simple and subtle body language commands. It might have appeared to others to be telepathy, but really his reactions were based on shifts of my body position and energy. I was pleased, even proud, of our progress. He would come to me on a verbal command when I said, "*Ven!*" which meant "come" in Spanish. But it was really my body position and energy that cued him: when I turned sideways, hands down, and took a half-step back, he would walk to me. But if I raised an extended hand, or took a step toward him, he would stop, and once stopped, if I took another step forward, he would move out again along the wall.

Staying within my circle, if I moved to get in front of him with my body and gently waved the lead rope I carried, he would stop, then turn and move in the other direction. Getting him to move, turn, and move again, then getting him to stop on cue, all without ever touching him, was the method. However, I was not trying to tire him out, a form of punishment, but using negative reinforcement—which sounds bad because of the word "negative," but actually just means I was training him through the application and then removal of subtle pressure. Postive reinforcement then came in the form of praise. I was always watching the horse for the telltale signs that he got the message and heaped praise on The Black for even small steps forward. With him, I learned to read horses more carefully, to watch every small cue, from an eye movement to a flip of the tail. I learned to be always alert—*Garde Bien*—and to use that information to direct my horse.

Garde Bien—"pay attention"—became a daily mantra as I went from basic round pen work to putting a saddle on The Black. Once I made the transition from the ground to riding—with a few tips from Izzie on Paso Fino equitation, such as using my legs and reins to engage the horse's hindquarters, thereby creating a proper headset and an optimal ambling lightness in the front—I experienced something I never expected: The Black surprised the hell out of me. He was *magnificent*—fully trained, and at what seemed to me to be a world-class level. Not once did he misbehave when I was riding him. All our problems were on the ground.

The Black's fast gait, called a *largo*, was smooth as silk and at a speed of close to fifteen miles per hour. We cruised through the Ocala forest for hours, just for fun. Fun for both of us. *Both as one.*

Gait is what made Pasos special. Like Montgomery Racing's Spotted Saddle Horses, The Black didn't have a "typical" horse trot. That two-beat motion, the hooves and the earth like a muffled bass drum, beating out *clip clop, clip clop*, always has two diagonally placed feet in the air. A rough trot could shake every inch of a rider, until the rider learned how to post and move in sync with the bounce of the horse. In the Paso, instead of a rough two-beat diagonal trot, the intermediate gait had a smooth four-beat lateral movement. You could be moving fast and drink from a glass without spilling a drop.

Gaited horses, like our Spotted Saddle Horses and the Pasos, were smoother to ride than Thoroughbreds, for example, because, while all four feet moved rapidly, only one foot was clearly off the ground at a time. I had learned growing up on Geronimo to just feel for the right rhythm, and Izzie taught me how, with light-handed adjustments to headset, to find the perfect four-beat motion. He told me to repeat, *Paco Perry, Paco Perry, Paco Perry, Paco Perry,* or as an alternative, *tik-a-tik-a-tik-a-tik-a* in my head as an aid to help me feel each of the four hoof beats.

Once I felt The Black was ready, Izzie and I put Sally up, as she had asked. She was an accomplished equestrian, so I wasn't worried. She took the stallion around the farm. He was perfect. Upon return, she dismounted and said, "Thank you, Jake. Thank you, Izzie. This means a lot to me. He's like a different horse."

But then, several days later, as I walked the stallion out of the wash-rack cross-ties after a long trail ride in the forest, I made a mistake. I dropped my guard. I trusted him too much. Without warning, the horse rose on two legs, aiming to strike at my head with his forelegs. I was looking the other way, but I felt him rise in the tug of the lead rope. In an instant, both of us had departed the plane of reason and operated on pure instinct. I turned to meet him, dropping the rope. The Black stood eight feet tall, and we looked into each other's eyes. His eyes were like dark diamonds, black and brilliant.

People accept that animals succumb to primal forces but rest comfortably in the delusion that humans are above all that. Not me. I knew that I shared with The Black an atavistic demon within. There was a raw, raging force that would always be a part of me and a part of him. In an instant, we slipped back to a place and time when horses and men were both wild and savage. *Both as one.* The flash of silver from his shod hoof as it targeted my face—a kill shot—was met with a right-handed rising block I'd learned in the special forces, called *jodan uke* in karate.

I was wearing a pair of sunglasses that day. The Black's strike was aimed to hit me square in the face, but my block partly deflected it. He sideswiped my head, breaking off the right arm of the sunglasses. The glancing blow cut my upper right ear, slicing it. By instinct, my block was followed by a strike of my own. While he was still on two legs, I hit him with a hard left to his nose that staggered him. Knocked off balance, he teetered, so I rammed him with a shoulder block to his exposed chest, taking him to the ground. As he fell, I dropped to my knees on his neck. I knew I couldn't let him get up. If he were back on his feet, he might kill me. So, I put every possible ounce of my two hundred forty-five pounds on his neck, gathered the lead rope, and waited, not sure what would come next.

From start to finish our fight lasted, at most, twenty seconds. Izzie was schooling a young Thoroughbred nearby, and they were both frozen in shock at the sight. An older woman, one of Izzie's best friends—a sleepover buddy—sat nearby in a lawn chair watching her Adonis. She screamed at the scene, jerking back to the point the chair tipped over. From my holding position on the stallion's neck, I blinked several times to regain focus. All I could see were the woman's legs twitching above the toppled lawn chair as she cried out for help. I didn't know whether to laugh or collapse with emotional exhaustion.

The stallion struggled to get up, but with me on his neck, all he could do was flail his legs and grunt. My weight prevented him from gaining traction. Then, after a minute, he gave up. As the struggle subsided, I whispered in his ear, in my best Spanish, to be calm—"*Cálmate, Papá, cálmate*"—and then started humming the tune to "Twelve Bells." I could hear his heart rapidly thumping, then slowing. We stayed that way for what seemed an eternity. I closed my eyes and slipped into a daze as the beat of his huge heart reverberated within me. *Calm, calm...* I was stimming on the beating of his heart.

Izzie tied his horse to a fence post, and after helping his girlfriend to her feet, came to me.

"Jake... Jake... Time to let him up, Jake. Jake?"

I opened my eyes to see his extended hand. It took effort to regain clarity and stand. When I helped the horse to his feet, with a gentle tug on the lead rope, there was no more fight left in him. I was drained too.

Izzie took the lead rope from my hand as I struggled to regain my composure. All he said was, "Jesus, Jake," turning his palms up in a non-verbal question mark. "Look at your ear. What happened?"

"I'm getting too old for this shit," was all I could say as I brushed the dirt from my knees.

"No joke," Izzie exclaimed.

I stripped off my shirt and undershirt, folded the undershirt into a compress, and held it to my ear to stop the bleeding. "I think I'm going to need stiches. Is the vet on the farm?"

Izzie's girlfriend exclaimed, "You've got to go to the emergency room!"

I ignored her.

"He's over at Barn Three. I'll get him," Izzie said.

"No, I'll go," I said, taking the lead rope and control of the stallion. I put The Black in his stall and gave him some Bute, an oral paste painkiller. "I'll send the vet to check on him," I told Izzie, who nodded from where he stood at the stall door.

I DID TWO THINGS IMMEDIATELY after the fight: I removed The Black's metal shoes and castrated him.

Gelding him was the proper thing to do; the removal of his testicles wasn't vindictive, but rather responsible. I was done playing the stallion-domination game. It was simply too dangerous. If he could do what he had done to me, he could kill somebody else.

After the castration procedure, the vet said that the stallion had the biggest testicles he'd ever seen on a horse. His comment jogged a memory of what the Greek horseman Xenophon had written in *The Art of Horsemanship* three thousand years before: *Never buy a horse with overly large testicles, but if you do, remove them.*

Ancient wisdom.

The removal of the shoes, I confess, was solely for my peace of mind; I would never forget that horseshoe coming at my face.

I took care to assure The Black's courage and spirit were not broken. I treated him thereafter with the utmost respect. After our one-round title bout, he and I never fought again.

A month later, the González family were ready to get their horses. They had been checking in on the House Pets by phone every week, and though we never requested it, every month a check for a thousand dollars to cover feed and expenses arrived in the farm's mailbox with *Thank you* written on a note that accompanied it.

Mr. González arrived right on schedule, but with two trucks, and two big horse trailers, instead of one. I approached to greet him, curious about the trailering arrangements. Mr. González introduced me to a man who stepped down from the passenger side of the bigger rig. "Don" Miguel Pérez was a Miami businessman, Mr. González said, who was also well known for riding and breeding the *crème de la crème* of Paso Finos in Florida.

He was The Black's owner.

Don Miguel had a couple of grooms with him, and the truck's driver, and they looked more like Mafioso bodyguards than horse attendants. The hairs went up on the back of my neck for a moment. However, Miguel was affable, even charming. He showed me the registration papers.

"Pirata del Ocho is his name," he said in reference to The Black. "He comes from Colombia, the farm of Fabio Ochoa, the greatest Paso

Fino breeder ever. Did you see he has a white '8' freeze-branded on his left shoulder?" I nodded, and he smiled, saying, "The Ochoa brand."

I had known when I first saw the "8" that the horse had probably come from the Ochoa farm. A flicker of worry went through me, given the likelihood of this businessman's business practices. But he made me feel at ease, complimenting me on my achievement in returning Pirata "to honorable service."

Miguel recounted how Pirata's first three years were spent with a big-time Colombian drug dealer in Miami. Such men took pride in their fine Paso Finos, but few were true horsemen. They were Miami's "cocaine cowboys," and the Paso Fino was their signature horse.

Pirata had been purchased in Medellín as a weanling for a quarter million, Miguel said, and imported as a yearling to the United States. As a two-year-old, the horse had broken the leg of his trainer, Bebe Ticaroua, and to add insult to injury, also bit the man several times. *Harsh training techniques sometimes have consequences,* I thought. I felt no pity for the man, for he was probably the reason Pirata had learned to fight to survive.

Miguel had acquired Pirata shortly afterward, having taken the horse to cover "fifty thousand dollars' worth of debt" after the stallion's drug dealer owner had been found dead, floating in a canal, with three shots to the head.

Miguel confessed the horse was so malicious that he had thought about putting him down, but couldn't, "because the stallion was so beautiful, *porque era tan bello*."

"You're here with a horse trailer," I said, deciding to be direct. "I assume you want him back, right?"

"Legally, he is yours, Mister Montgomery. But I would like him back, if you agree."

"Please, call me Jake."

"Of course," he said, then, pointing to himself, "Miguel."

"Miguel, can you tell me why you never reported the horse missing?"

"I have never been one to go to the authorities," Miguel stated, looking me right in the eye. "I used my resources to find him, and after hearing of the amazing progress you were making with the horse, something I simply could not achieve, I decided to wait."

"I gelded him. It was necessary."

He nodded his understanding. "Probably long overdue."

I took a slow, deep breath, pondering how he could have known I was "making progress" with the horse. As I exhaled, I said, "I am inclined to return him to you, but I have to check with my wife. Taking Pirata in was her idea. If she agrees, I have one condition."

"If it is money, of course, no problem."

"No, no money." I held my finger up, and at that he smiled. "I would like you to stay here for a week or two and learn how to handle this horse. He is still very complex. I've put too much into him to see him go backward again. Plus,"—I gestured to my recovering ear—"he can be very dangerous. I don't want you getting hurt."

"Agreed, Jake," he responded without a beat. "And I assure you, I am a very good rider."

"I can tell," I replied.

"I confess," Miguel said, "I acquired Pirata out of what was misplaced ego. He was infamous in my circle of friends as being beautiful, magnificently gaited, but dangerous. Being able to master him makes a big statement. *Muy macho*. I underestimated how tough, intelligent, and vicious he was. *Muy malo* meets *muy macho* is a bad scene."

WITHOUT A SECOND THOUGHT, Sally agreed to Pirata leaving. After our near-death melee, the horse had gained a new status with her. Anything that tried to kill me got on a special "Be gone as quickly as possible" list, and my crusty scab of a right ear was still a reminder of the incident.

Don Miguel and his ever-growing entourage took over an entire floor at the Ocala Hilton, and I spent the week getting Miguel and his crew accustomed to Pirata. Miguel was, as he had said, a masterful rider. With him in the saddle, Pirata seemed more relaxed than ever. They were composed and refined, pure elegance in motion. Under his light and well-trained hand, Pirata's energy was now focused.

I told Miguel about "Twelve Bells," indicating it could soothe the black horse.

"I know that one!" Miguel responded with enthusiasm, and he began to sing it with perfect pitch and tempo, like a Pavarotti. Pirata nickered his approval.

I felt comfortable with Pirata going home with Miguel. I could sense it would be okay between them.

"Jake, he is a different horse," Miguel said. "Thank you."

"Miguel, be alert with him," I replied. "Always."

"*¡Siempre alerta!*" he said. "Always alert! You know, my friend, that is my business motto."

I said, "Safe travels."

A MONTH LATER, TWO MEN arrived in a Lamborghini LM002, a five-hundred horsepower, custom-made Italian SUV. It was towing a bumper-pull Avanti, a gleaming aluminum two-horse trailer with an angular aerodynamic fuselage, also from Italy. A man had phoned Sally a few days earlier and arranged for the visit, announcing he was Don Miguel's personal assistant.

The two men exited the Lambo, the driver leaning casually against the door as the other approached me and Sally where we waited outside the barn closest to our house.

"I am Luis, and I come on behalf of Don Miguel," the man said. He was just over five feet tall, but I could see his muscular build beneath the custom suit. A gold cross glinted against his chest where his white shirt was open at the collar.

He said nothing more as he handed a letter to Sally, waiting as she opened it. I read it over her shoulder: what I presumed was Miguel's handwriting, thanking her for her good work in setting up the horse-rescue program. Luis then presented a black S.T. Dupont leather briefcase, turning it on its side and cracking it open in front of us. It was full of hundred-dollar bills, fresh from the bank, in wrappers denoting two-thousand-dollar increments. When I began to protest, Luis shook his head, and handed me a photo of Miguel riding Pirata at his Miami hacienda with "Thank you, Jake!" written across it. Along with the photo were the signed registration papers for a Paso Fino yearling colt—I had to assume it was the one pawing restlessly in the trailer.

Luis and his driver unloaded the yearling as Sally and I watched in stunned silence. He stood in the sunlight, a glistening equine beauty. Then, Luis said, "Mister Montgomery, this is for you. His name is Resortissimo, a son of Resorte Cuatro."

The big sable bay colt was simply magnificent. I gaped at his perfect conformation and walked forward, proclaiming my surprise at the incredibly generous gift. Luis gave me a half-smile.

"Don Miguel repays his debts," he said. He gave a little nod of farewell and climbed with his nameless driver back into the Lambo. As they pulled away, Sally turned toward the house, briefcase in hand, and I walked the colt to a stall in the barn, taking a few minutes to settle him in. I threw a few sheaves of coastal hay in the corner and brushed his gleaming coat, thinking, *Both as one*.

I RETURNED FROM THE BARN to join Sally in the house and talk through the unbelievable events of the morning. However, as I approached, I became aware of an escalating debate in the corner of the family room. Undetected, I backed up a step to watch as Pa pointed at the briefcase with the cash.

"Sally, you know, don't you, that is probably drug money?"

"Don't think so," she replied.

Pa jabbed his forefinger at the case. "That's dirty money."

"First of all, Mister Montgomery..."

Her tone was clearly contentious, and she paused mid-sentence for emphasis. Standing in the background, my jaw dropped. She hadn't called Pa "Mister Montgomery" since she was twenty years old, when I'd brought her home the first time to meet my parents. On the few occasions she called *me* "Mister Montgomery," I had to endure a maelstrom of fierce logic, with each and every fallacious opinion I held shattered on the hard edge of her intellect. One of the things that kept me with Sally, once the overwhelming infatuation subsided, was her brilliance. While we never discussed it, I accepted early on that she was "the smarter one." I learned to use that to make better decisions. We would hash through ideas, exploring options and alternatives, some of which I never would have considered on my own.

Pa could only stand and look surprised at her tone. He was rarely challenged, and never ever, to my knowledge, on his own farm.

"Mister Pérez—"

"Don't you mean *Don* Miguel?" my old man said, his response followed by a derisory snort.

"Mister Pérez owns a chain of drugstores, numerous supermarkets, and a dozen tire stores. This money from him will make a big difference for horses that have been mistreated or abandoned."

"I still think his money is dirty. It is from drugs, and you know it."

"And I think you're being hypocritical."

"*What*?" His face went beet red.

"Let's just go over the facts. You're giving me a hard time because you think some of this money might come from people who have fallen into a vice. Drug use, right?"

I cringed once she started asking him to agree to facts, knowing from personal experience that this was the beginning of the end of the argument. Since they hadn't noticed me, I backed up a few feet, deciding to slip out and spend a little more time with my new colt, instead of entering the fray.

As I snuck out the door, I heard her bring the hammer down. "Gambling is a vice. Look around you! All this is built on *gambling*—that's what horse racing is, *gambling*. Who are we to judge?"

An hour later, when the old ship's bell mounted on the back patio rang out, I returned, happy to see our normal family dinner routine. All was well; the skirmish seemed to be diffused, though only time would tell. I smiled as I entered the kitchen, and Ma and Sally, the two favorite women of my life, smiled back. Feeling the rare contentment of being at complete peace with the world, I gave Sally an intimate sidelong glance, then focused on my mother and asked, "How can I help, Ma?"

MIGUEL AND I BECAME FAST FRIENDS. Over the next two years, we spent more and more time together. I was in Miami frequently, racing at two of South Florida's racetracks: Gulfstream and Calder. It all started with me visiting Pirata to check on his progress. From there, our friendship evolved to a point where I became his houseguest when in Miami. Yes, my father was one hundred ten percent correct—Miguel was no normal businessman. He headed an empire of both legal and illegal activities, the laundering of cartel money from cocaine sales being at the top of his list. But even when I understood that fact as truth and not simply suspicion, I neither judged him nor shied away from spending time together.

From our first meeting, we had both sensed a compelling affinity. We built our friendship on that feeling. Miguel's life was much more complex than mine had become. He juggled the demands of a criminal empire while maintaining a façade of respectability and philanthropy. I knew from experience that kind of ruse was no small feat.

We were close, and in a way I know many may never understand, I loved Miguel. I loved him like I loved Izzie. It was never sexual. Though neither of us ever expressed it, I am certain he loved me too. There was never a quid pro quo in our relationship other than good company, civility, and humor. Neither of us expected more.

When I explained to Sally that I wanted to be with him, to spend more time with him, she challenged me, asking if he was my lover. I said no, but knowing my past, I think she was dubious.

I also think she knew she had no choice.

chapter 18

The Art of Horsemanship

SHILOH WAS ONE OF THE GREATEST loves in my life. He was born on my forty-sixth birthday. As farm manager, I was only called to the foaling barn when there was a serious problem, and Shiloh's birth was problematic. I stayed all night with the mare until we got the job done. The delivery was difficult, principally due to his size. He was enormous, a throwback to his ancestor Ajax. If it hadn't been for our foaling team helping him safely work his way down the birth canal, both mare and foal would have died from the tearing and consequent hemorrhaging in an unassisted birth.

It was well worth the work. The colt was a drop-dead gorgeous black-and-white Spotted Saddle Horse. He had a black face, with a white patch on the tip of his nose in the shape of an arrowhead. Within moments he was on his feet at his mother's side, sucking at her teats.

Shiloh was my favorite from that day on—it just took me a while to admit it. By that point, my parents had handed the entire business over to us. Running a business, I had to separate myself emotionally as a buffer from the hard realities of the racing game. Horses were bred and trained to race or be sold. Racing was a deadly sport, equally dangerous for horse and rider. Horses sometimes got injured, and on rare occasions, needed to be put down. It was now fully my burden, the dirty part of the business.

When Shiloh was five months old, we began in the round pen with his first training lesson. The big colt stood his ground as I approached him, halter in one hand, lead rope in the other. This youngster had a striking presence. Most colts at that age were, for want of a better word, "skinny." Shiloh's dose of Percheron blood gave him girth and musculature, even at an early age. That he had inherited traits from his draft horse ancestor was also evidenced by his fledgling feathered fetlocks, the beginning of a plume of white hair sprouting just above his hooves.

Xenophon wrote about use of the round pen in *The Art of Horsemanship.* Horse training started with moving the young horse in circles. These were the sacred circles that first connected man and horse, the circles that had connected me with Pirata. Now, with Shiloh, it was our turn.

Most of the weanlings on the farm had been imprinted and halter-broke in the day-to-day interaction of bringing the broodmares and babies in from the fields at night. The routine was the perfect time to slip a halter and lead line on the foal and begin leading him alongside his mother. This colt, however, followed his mother blindly and would not allow the stablehands to touch him. It was only the rare case—the "tough nut" of a horse—that ended up in the round pen without this most basic part of training already confirmed. But we couldn't wean him until we could halter and lead him.

I approached Shiloh. Many young horses initially move away as you move toward them, with an instinctive respect for space, but not this one. He evaluated me—assessed me—coolly. We were eye to eye, me and this eight-hundred-pound tough guy. At five months, he was almost as big as a mature Paso Fino. I released a low chuckle, barely audible.

One thing was for sure, I admired the colt's bravery—his defiance. It was clear that he would fight me if I pushed too hard. There would be no running away.

Shiloh was tense, his muscles corded and nostrils flared, as he snorted *STAY AWAY* trumpet-like warnings. Though the colt was a fighter, he was not mean-spirited like Pirata. He was just alone and afraid, he wanted his mother, and his nature prevented him from giving in to a threat. How I handled him now might make the difference between a great horse and one that was totally unmanageable. Pirata had probably had a similar inflection point in his early training, where he learned to fear and fight instead of love and trust. The way Shiloh was wired, he simply *could not* back down. We'd used his mother as the lead horse to bring him into the round pen, and as all foals do, he followed her without issue. However, it is a gross understatement to say he was unhappy as his mother was removed from the round pen. He became enraged at her removal.

I sensed his strong fear as well as his desire to break out and find "Mom," so I calmed myself with slow, deep breathing. To me, the signs were clear as he began to relax: the twitch of an ear, a slight lowering of his head as his neck softened, and a slowing of his breathing pattern to match mine. Good progress.

In my mind, I always tried to picture what I wanted from a horse. It is believed by many that horses, as well as many Autistic people, think nonverbally, in images. It's true, that old saying, "A picture is worth a thousand words." Because I used mental visual imagery just to manage day-to-day life, I was perhaps more empathetic toward and telepathic with horses than most people. As a horseman, I learned, more and more over time, to control my feelings and picture what I wanted from the horse.

The mental image I crafted for Shiloh in that first round-pen session was of a horse, head lowered, viewed from the side. To the inexperienced, this image would mean nothing; however, it was classic horse body language. It was what a horse does when meeting another for the first time in a field—he signals, "I am no threat," by turning sideways. Sideways, all the horse's offensive weapons, teeth and hooves, are directed away. It was an image that meant, if you made it a declarative sentence, "You be nice, and I will be nice."

With this picture in mind, I turned sideways. I looked at the colt, making eye contact over my shoulder, mimicking the body language of two male horses meeting for the first time in a pasture, trying to be friendly, to say with my body, "I am no threat."

With my posture, mental image, and my calm and happy demeanor all broadcasting my good intentions, I approached the colt, maintaining the sideways posture. I closed the gap with a final few shuffling side steps, saying his name, my tone soft, breaking it down phonetically: "shy" then "low," whispering again and again, "Shi-loh." He relaxed some more and dropped his head several inches. Then I slipped the oiled leather halter on without incident.

Shiloh made direct eye contact and held it—a rare thing for a horse. And, at that very moment, I felt something, something deeper than just a sense of favoritism or the affection I'd immediately felt for him when he was born. It was something deeper than I'd ever felt with another horse. From that first sense of connection, I knew he was *my* horse, not just an agricultural product. Just as he was mine, I, too, was his. But this wasn't simple possession in the way of man, like the title to a car. I knew in that moment Shiloh would never be sold or discarded. Divorce or separation would never come between us. We were forever bound together in a way known to so few in the thousands of years of relations between man and horse.

Shiloh was a part of me.

Izzie watched from the elevated viewing platform on the south side of the round pen. "That went smooth," he said in the low soft tone of one who makes a living by not spooking horses. "Thought he was going to charge you."

I chuckled. "Pretty sure it crossed his mind, Izz."

Shiloh turned and looked at Izzie as I slid the blue nylon lead line from over my shoulders, and slowly and cautiously hooked it to his halter.

"Come on in," I said. "Let's see if we can get him to walk."

Lead-rope training, getting the horse "halter broke," started with getting the young horse to accept the halter. Step two was to get him to walk with you on a lead rope, at your right side, the horse's head beside you. Easily said, but a typical, full-grown horse can weigh anywhere from a thousand to almost two thousand pounds and can pull a Cadillac with ease. By anyone's standards, I was a big and strong man, yet despite my strength and size, I'd had a two-year-old Thoroughbred rear up and lift me right off the ground when I wouldn't let go of the lead rope.

Izzie, even after retirement from racing, was still a remarkable athlete. All wiry muscle, still with the balance of a cat, the horses loved him. Rather than go around, through the gate and into the pen, he hopped over the top rail from the viewing stand and dropped to the soft dirt inside the pen.

"Careful, Jake, he could still blow up."

"Will do," I said, standing at the colt's left side. Horses were customarily trained so almost all ground interaction came from the left.

As Izzie and I had done with dozens of young horses before, he approached Shiloh from the rear, off his left flank. He made a loud clicking sound, the onomatopoeia *ta ta coo coo* resounding from the roof of his mouth like a knock on a door. Most horses would move out when he made that sound. By nature, they run when threatened. However, Shiloh wasn't moving. As Izzie got closer, the horse tensed, his neck muscles tightening as he realized I had him by the head with the lead line and that Izzie was coming from behind. His ears went back, and his haunch muscles twitched, a sure sign a kick from the rear was imminent. I held out my right hand, signaling Izzie to stop.

"Gonna blow up, you watch 'eem," Izzie whispered as he stopped dead in his tracks about five yards behind the colt.

I took a deep breath. My father had taught me that, with a horse, when it seemed like things were going wrong, no matter how bad, to take a deep breath, be calm, and smile. The horse could feel what I felt, and my fear would become fear for the horse. But it worked the other way, too—my own calm could serve to calm a scared horse. The deep breaths had worked with Shiloh already, as I had first put the halter on him, so now I once again calmed myself by slowing my breathing. As I did, Shiloh relaxed. I realized he had trusted me just a few minutes ago, so now it was my turn to trust him.

I turned my back to him.

"Careful, Jake. Be careful," Izzie advised.

Once more it felt like it was just me and Shiloh. Horses, unlike most people, lived in the moment, and in that moment, the only thing in our world was each other. Nothing else seemed to register. *Both as one.* I visualized us walking to the wall of the round pen. Just as I visualized it, we did it. Mission accomplished, I looked at Shiloh over my shoulder and smiled, showing no teeth. I swear the horse smiled back.

By the age of three, Shiloh was huge and doing well under saddle, so he became my trail-riding replacement for Pirata. And like Pirata, Shiloh had a comfortable four-beat gait, but without the explosive attitude. Shiloh and I loved to go on Saturday rides deep into the state forest north of our farm. Despite his large size, or perhaps because of it, Shiloh was athletic, able to jump obstacles with ease. He seemed to sense what I wanted and just do it.

Just for fun, we rode all over the Cross-Florida Greenway, the state forest system that abuts my farm's north boundary. As a biosystem, it is the most diverse in Florida. Its landscape varies from rolling hills, thick with stands of oak and pine, to verdant lakes, huge sand dunes, and deep impenetrable swamps, along with steep walled rock mining ravines and crystal-clear springs. The thousands upon thousands of acres are an explosion of pristine flora and abundant fauna. From a recreational horseman's perspective, the Greenway Trails are Florida at its best.

If a horse and a man could exist as soulmates, with Shiloh, this was our time. We rode as one, in body and spirit. We traversed the forest, galloping for miles, jumping fallen trees, fording streams, climbing oak-canopied hill trails, and sliding down sand dunes. Riding for the joy of riding. We, and I mean *we*, always felt the better for it.

YEARS LATER, RACING a promising two-year-old colt at the Gulfstream Park Racetrack near Miami, we lost big, by twenty lengths. My colt was injured coming out of the starting gate. The horse to his left cut right and smashed into him, almost knocking him down. The young colt stumbled, but to his credit, he raced his heart out to the finish line. However, that only exacerbated a deep cut on his shoulder. He crossed the line bleeding, and it took fifty-five stiches for the vet to close the wound. Depending on how he healed, his racing career could be over before it started.

After the horse was stitched up, I loaded him in the trailer and dropped him off at the track vet's hospital, just west of Fort Lauderdale, then headed for Miguel's hacienda thirty minutes south, in Miami. I almost called to cancel my visit. I felt off; a sense of foreboding twisted my gut. I dismissed it as a reaction to seeing my horse get hurt.

The entrance to the estate, named *Finca Soroa*, was a broad drive with a guardhouse in an exterior island in front of an ornate double gate. I was a known visitor, and greeted warmly by Gustavo, the gate guard. Nevertheless, he and an associate did a quick search of my truck and trailer. The big three-level Cuban colonial style house, half a mile down the drive, shimmered in the afternoon sun, framed artfully in a lush array of palms and other tropical trees.

Miguel and staff stood waiting as I parked. A valet carrying my bag to my room and a groom took charge of my truck and trailer. I was never sure where the truck went but after every one of my prior visits, it was returned to the front drive with both truck and trailer gleaming with a fresh and thorough wax job. This ritual was the same every time, and was so gracious and hospitable that I looked forward to it. I was treated like a king—that summed it up.

Miguel and I walked through the atrium and down the broad hall that traversed the manse, leading to a veranda and outdoor bar. Miguel offered and I readily accepted a glass of Glenlivet 15, French Oak Reserve. I was on my second glass of scotch—self-medication for my track disappointment—when I received the call.

Sally was sobbing, slurring her words.

"Jake, I'm so sorry. Ma and Pa are dead."

"What?" My chest tightened.

"A car accident," she choked out. "Horrible. At the intersection of 475 and 32nd Street."

My parents were dead.

My parents had been killed on a sunny afternoon at an intersection not far from home.

"Jake...it was a drunk driver. He ran a red light."

The glass fell from my hand as I heard her words. All I said was "I'm coming home now." Then, I dropped my cell phone to the floor. It landed in the pool of scotch whiskey and broken glass with a hollow thud. I looked to the ceiling, like a wolf howling at the moon, and from deep inside came an explosive primal spectrum-driven scream.

Miguel immediately offered to drive me home. He picked up my phone, wiping the face with a towel from the bar, handed it to me, then led me to his big Mercedes sedan. His security team followed, two gunmen in a chase car, with a ranch hand bringing up the rear of the convoy in my truck, towing the empty horse trailer. We barely spoke during the five-hour trip, yet, in that way, he was more supportive than imaginable. "I am here for you," infused the silence.

As he drove, I drifted off, half asleep, thinking of my father. I knew he'd loved me deeply, but he was a hard man. I thought about the days after my humiliating seventh grade beat-down, when Pa had begun his campaign to make a "man" of me. His one-on-one Army Ranger martial arts training had been combined with consistent and ruthless psychological conditioning to suppress any emotional response. Crying had not been an option. It had worked. Even when my infant son died, I never shed a tear. When Michelle and Colleen died, nothing.

I occupied this semi-dream-state until we arrived in Ocala. When we got to my farm, two marked police cars—a sedan and an SUV—were in the big circular drive in front of the house, along with several cars of family and friends.

Miguel didn't get out, but as I exited the sedan, he said, "Jake, my condolences, brother, I go back now. I am going to make an offering for your parents in Miami."

With that, he and his entourage left.

I walked in the door. Sally and the kids were red-eyed from crying. I fell to my knees and laid my head in Sally's lap.

~

MA'S NEPHEW, JIMMY PETTIGREW, had been fifteen years with the Marion County Sheriff's Department, rising from a patrol deputy to detective to Chief of Emergency Operations. The next day, Jimmy drove me to the morgue. He had already identified my parents, but the coroner insisted on the next of kin. This was a vehicular double homicide and Jimmy, while kin, had an arguable legal conflict because he was also law enforcement.

Even today, journaling this memory after all these years, I hesitate to recall the sight of my parents' bodies. It was a horror my mind rejects. My parents were mutilated. My father was almost unrecognizable. My mother...I got weak at the knees when I saw her. Jimmy could tell. He took me by the arm. I was broken.

We left the morgue in silence, the cold gray windowless fluorescence of the morgue replaced by the sizzling hot Ocala afternoon sun. I shielded my eyes and turned to my cousin, with only one question.

"Who did this?"

"We have him in custody, Jake. His name is Ray Marty."

"I know the guy. A half-assed shit-talking groom at Bright Oaks."

Jimmy, talking to me now as my cousin, not a cop, explained, "He's a drunk and drug addict, with a string of DUIs as long as my arm. He hit and killed a kid on a bicycle ten years ago, served three years at a prison farm near Raiford. Drugs, too—horse tranquilizers, crack. You're right, he was working at Bright Oak Farm but got fired just a few days before the accident for stealing horse tranquilizers. He had half a bottle of vodka and a recently used crack pipe in his car." Jimmy then pinched the bridge of his nose and grimaced; it was painful for him to say. "His pants were around his knees. The accident reconstruction guy says he was masturbating when he ran the red light. The fucking asshole wasn't even hurt. He was trying to escape, but was too fucking drunk to leave the scene, so fucking drunk he kept tripping on the pants around his ankles."

Hearing the facts drove me over the edge…infuriated me beyond comprehension. Jimmy, a natural-born cop, knew what I was thinking.

"Don't even think about it, Jake. Let the law take care of it." He wagged his finger at me.

My response wasn't subtle. "Don't wag your fucking finger at me, Jimmy. I want this motherfucker dead. Dead! You hear me?"

"No, Jake! For the record, I didn't hear you say that. Now, come back home with me. Your family needs you."

IT WAS A MONTH LATER that Jimmy came back to the farm. I was at our practice track, watching a client horse we were prepping for a race run a fast breeze. Racing folk live by a known schedule, and this was the time for New York racing. We were getting ready to go to Saratoga.

When I saw him approaching, I could tell from the look on Jimmy's face he had bad news.

"Ray Marty is out on bail. The judge reduced it, and his lawyer bailed him out." He shook his head, and I knew worse was coming. "Looks like he might get off. His lawyer found some potential legal loophole with the blood test they took and used that argument to lower the bail pending an evidentiary hearing."

"You telling me that motherfucker is loose?" I snapped.

"Jake, please listen."

"I'm done listening! You saw what he did. That was your aunt and uncle, Jimmy. You fucking saw!"

"Jake, I know. I know."

"I want him dead!"

"Everyone in Ocala knows that, too, Jake. Stay away. Let me handle it. One way or another, I'll make sure justice gets done here. I promise you, cousin."

I'd been pushed to my limits. It was as if I was a tree and my roots had been cut out from under me. I couldn't rationalize or forgive.

I was in Saratoga, the most beautiful racing venue in the country, celebrating two wins that day, when Jimmy called to say that Ray Marty had disappeared. His rental car had been found with light blood splatter on the steering wheel, windshield, and dashboard.

My jaw muscles strained. I ground my back teeth and held the cell phone in a death grip. "What do you want from me, Jimmy?"

"Well, first thing, cousin, I wanted to make sure you were in fact in New York at the time of his disappearance. I suspect foul play but am going to treat him as a bail jumper. Marty's lawyer, Coolridge Cassidy, may not buy that, though."

"Where does a piece of shit like that get a high-priced defense lawyer like Coolridge?" I asked. "Where does he get seventy thousand in bail money? This is bullshit, fucking bullshit. That lawyer and I played tennis at the Country Club of Ocala. He used to brag about not taking a case unless he was paid fifty grand up front."

"Beats me, but I know crime scenes, and trust me, a lawyer isn't going to help Ray Marty now. I will pull down the race replays showing you in the winner's circle and check your cellphone records for location and activity. That gets you out of the lineup as a suspect. I'm trying to track down the family of the kid he killed but everyone from that case left town long ago. The parents divorced a year after the accident. In the meantime, please don't do or say anything stupid."

I did not respond to his advice but answered his implied question. "Watch the race video replays. You'll see me standing in the winner's circle at Saratoga—twice! So I don't know anything about it. But if you don't find him, rest assured, I *will* track his ass down."

After winning a purse in a stakes race at Calder Racecourse two weeks later, I planned to return to Ocala right after the race rather than visit Miguel, but he said he needed to see me, that he needed my advice, that it was important. So I called Sally and told her I was staying over. I could tell she was displeased, for her response was a barely verbal, "*Hmmpf.*"

Dinner finished, Miguel and I sat on the veranda, sipping cognac, cigars in hand. As we smoked, I asked, "So what can I help with?"

He said, "I told Jaime to get the horses ready. Let's go do a little riding."

As we walked into his massive covered arena, Miguel's voice dropped to a conspiratorial whisper. "Jake, I hope you will understand what I have done. It cannot be undone."

Pirata and a large bay stallion were there, saddled, at the ready, with grooms by their sides. Pirata looked me in the eyes. He knew me. Both horses were fired up. Pirata's coat glistened black, wet with nervous sweat. It took a moment for me to accommodate the full scene. A big dark-blue tarp, a fifteen-foot by fifteen-foot sheet of thick canvas, took up the center of the covered arena. A naked man was staked out on his back in the middle. I couldn't see who, but my intuition told me. I was drawn forward, compelled to walk closer, to look him in the eyes.

A dozen bruises testified to a prior beating. He had a rubber ball gag in his mouth. Each limb was secured by a rubberized cuff, and he'd been tied flat like a gelatinous white "X" on the dark tarp. In an epiphany, I understood exactly what had happened. Miguel had hired the attorney Coolridge through some front, bailed out Ray Marty, then kidnapped him.

When Marty saw me, our eyes met. The terror in his eyes was unmistakable. My eyes, I'm sure, were hard and cold—a killer's eyes. Over and over, he cried out a gag-garbled, "Please, please, please…" but, from my grim visage alone, he knew there would be no reprieve.

"Thank you, Miguel," I said. "I couldn't have done this myself. Everyone was watching me."

"Jake, you are a brother to me. I could not allow him to get away with some slap on the hand and a few years in prison. Your parents deserved more. They deserve justice."

I didn't need convincing. There was a two-tone white-and-red Chevy pickup in the arena, and it had a shovel leaning against it. I walked over and grabbed it, a weapon so familiar to me, prepared to beat the loser to death, saying, "Let's get this over with."

"Wait, Jake!" Miguel exclaimed.

Ray Marty's eyes were wide, then shuttered tight at the spectacle of his impending death as I raised the spade to strike him dead.

"No, Jake," Miguel shouted. His strident tone stopped me. I turned to him.

"Jake, we are horsemen. You know my passion—I study cultures surrounding horsemen. Perhaps the greatest… the Mongols…do you know how they dealt with a criminal like this?"

"No," I said, my biceps twitching in explosive anticipation triggered by the heft of the shovel.

"It was a ceremony. The Mongols rolled him in a carpet, tied it tight around with rope, and then the warriors of the injured family trotted their horses over him, breaking every bone, but taking hours to do it. Eventually, the offender would drown in his own blood. And justice was done."

I met Miguel's intense gaze, then followed his hand as he pointed at Pirata and the bay stallion.

"These two horses have a *fino* gait of more than one hundred ten beats per minute and a four- to six-inch extension," he said pointedly. "They are shod, steel shoes, so the impact is tremendous. You know what it sounds like when we ride across a sounding board in competition? Like rolling thunder." He paused, then said, "Well, in dealing with the occasional associate who has betrayed me, I have modified the Mongols' technique. No carpet. Just stretched out on the canvas. That way I can see the terror, feel the pain. As it should be." Now one corner of his mouth lifted in a slanted sadistic grin. "The Paso Fino was born for this. If you will allow me to do this with you, we will ride together as brothers and each hoof beat will bring justice. When done, we will never speak of it again. Agreed?"

I drew in a deep breath. The berserker made his choice.

"Agreed."

I remembered for a second the battered face of my mother on a metal gurney at the county coroner's office.

"And thank you, thank you, my brother," I said.

"Jake, take your time. Break this pathetic excuse for a man slowly. Do not step on his head or his heart. Let him suffer as he so richly deserves."

Ray Marty, hearing our discussion of his fate, moaned pitifully through the gag.

I walked to Pirata. The insides of his nostrils were red and flared. His blood was up. I sensed he knew what was coming. Perhaps he had done it before.

In a moment, I was in the saddle, riding a tight *fino* gait straight for the prostrated man. I would have killed him with my bare hands, torn his throat open with my teeth, if I had to.

Miguel rode alongside as we made pass after pass over Ray Marty. Bones snapped. The horses' hooves were covered in blood, its spray rising like a crimson mist below me, along with the screams, muffled by the gag. Ray Marty's face was twisted in pain and terror, his agony so intense the energy was palpable. The hoof beats sounded like tribal drums. I was locked in a vicious, blood-drenched freeze loop. I couldn't stop.

We rode back and forth over him for fifteen minutes. Then Ray Marty died. Miguel moved off to the side and dismounted. I didn't. Stopping for me was not tied to Ray Marty's death. I had been steeping in a hate-fueled rage for weeks and couldn't stop riding until that rage was washed away. It took another ten minutes before I was spent. Pirata and I left Ray Marty's body pulverized beyond recognition.

Miguel's grooms took the horses away. His security staff took off the dead man's head, hands, and feet with large chopping machetes. Then they dismembered his limbs, wrapped the bloody heap in the canvas tarp, and loaded it in the back of a pickup truck. I looked from the bundle to Miguel, then back again.

"For the big incinerator," he explained. "We burn him and then grind the ashes, teeth, and bones."

We walked back to his veranda for another cognac.

Once again ensconced in post-colonial splendor, "To justice," Miguel said, raising his drink. The crystal glasses rang clear, like a chime.

"Thank you, my friend. I couldn't live without doing this for my parents. I know sooner or later I would have killed him, consequences be damned."

Miguel nodded, swirling his drink in his glass. "A man cannot live with honor unless he does justice for his family." Then Miguel, having a well-developed sense of criminal evidence, said, "Jake, go now to your room and change. Wash yourself. Clean carefully. Leave your bloody clothes, boots, everything, in the shower. I will have them placed in the incinerator. Dress for dinner, and tomorrow morning, when you leave for home, it will be as if it never happened. *¿Entiendes?*"

"*Sí, hermano. Sí, yo entiendo.*"

During the winter racing season, I had my own room at Miguel's place and kept a few changes of clothes. I stood fully dressed in the shower and stripped, littering the shower floor with my blood-stained apparel. Despite my satisfaction with the night's events, I scrubbed and scrubbed...feeling unclean long after the sweat and blood had flowed down the drain. *WET.*

ONE DAY, MIGUEL CAME TO ME to buy a horse. We walked together trackside. He told me Miami was in an ever-escalating drug war amidst the worst government crackdown ever. While he had started out as a smuggler of marijuana, he had long ago left the direct-distribution drug trade. For him, there was no more smuggling or dealing—only processing the cash from the business for its Colombian and Mexican overlords. Because the drug wars in Miami stepped up federal pressure, bribes were no longer safe harbors.

Miguel had decided to retire from a business with a notoriously poor retirement history. He used old age, poor health, and early-stage Alzheimer's as his excuse. It was a clever ploy, as no one wanted a money launderer who might forget where he put the money. Miguel performed an audit. His customers were satisfied.

His explanation of his future plans to me to me complete, he then asked, "What is the most you ever sold a racehorse for?"

"Two and a half million," I replied.

"Do you have a horse worth that?"

"Not now. Those are few and far between."

"Close?"

"I guess so, if we had a runaway auction. Sometimes these *nouveau riche* hedge-fund guys go crazy. It's not a horse I could sell you at that kind of price."

"Look, Jake, I am going to disappear. I have liquidated everything possible, and now I want to buy a yearling horse from you for two million. You pick the horse, but make it your very best. We will have a written contract for the sale, lump sum upfront, and a separate contract for the training. When I go, I will simply disappear. After a few months of nonpayment on the training contract, I want you to sue me. Then, take the horse back—a lien action—and sell him again to someone else."

"But why, Miguel?"

"I may need the money later. Take the after-tax amount you net on the deal, and put it safely away. I will contact you."

"Is that legal?"

"Of course not," he replied. "You will probably at some point be visited by the DEA or the FBI. Do not worry. Meet with them. Cooperate. Show them the written deal on the horse, show them the lien lawsuit, even send them to your lawyer. But do not tell them anything."

I tried to take a minute to digest his plan, but he continued without a pause.

"If someone calls saying they are me, or calls for me, it is bogus.

Do not even respond. If the FBI, DEA, CIA, or even your old SOCOM people—whatever, whoever—says I said something, that is a lie. The only way I will ever contact you is if you get a call from Claude Girardeau, from Rouen, France. That will be me. If you hear that name and recognize my voice, it is me. If I want my money back, I will tell you of a horse I have for sale. If I want something else, I will ask to see you. Someplace safe. Understand?"

"Yes...okay."

"Repeat the name, Claude Girardeau."

"I got it, Miguel."

"Listen, this may not work. I have enemies. I may not make it back, between old age or, well, you know the risks. If everything goes right, I may not even need the money. So, if you do not hear from me in five years, you put the money to good use. Five years. If you and your family want it, use it. If not, find a good charity."

"Don't go, Miguel. You can stay with us."

He looked at me with an expression of sadness and grief. Funeral eyes welled up with tears that could never flow. "No, Jake. It must be this way, or it never ends."

I thought about the situation. Miguel was sixty, and I wasn't far behind. He would soon leave everything behind to start a new life, never to return. How does one do that? I found it difficult to get my head around it.

"So, this is goodbye?" I asked.

"Will you help me with this?"

"Of course, Miguel."

"Then this is goodbye, Jake."

"What about Pirata?"

"Do you want him?"

"Who else could care for him?" The answer to my question was self-evident and Miguel simply nodded his assent.

Before he got in his car to leave, we embraced. I loved him. His departure broke my heart.

I never saw Miguel again. Pirata arrived a week later and began the life of a retired gelding. With age and retirement, he became calmer and for the first time in his life... fatter. From time to time, with Sally on Resortissimo at our side, we would ride together through the forest.

As Miguel predicted, the FBI came to me a year later. I showed them the legal documents, the contract, the lawsuit, and even made copies for them. As planned, I said, "I'm not much on legalities, but as you can see, I had a lawyer for this deal and the lawsuit. His name is Zachary Zoberman in Orlando. I will tell him he's authorized to talk freely to you."

They visited ZZ and collected copies of the litigation documents. I never heard from the feds again.

Five years later, I put Miguel's money where I thought it might do some real good. I built a Catholic mission church, with a community hall for a food bank, immigration clinic, and medical clinic. The structure was a new home for an existing program being run by a priest from Guatemala and a group of Nicaraguan nuns out of a huge dilapidated abandoned barn for farm equipment. They served Central American migrant farm workers growing vegetables on the muck farms near Lake Apopka. The Catholic Charities director was effusive at the multi-million-dollar gift. He asked if I had a name in mind for the mission, maybe a favorite saint. A lyric from the Rolling Stones song "Sympathy for the Devil" and its poetic juxtaposition of sinners and saints came to mind.

"Please call it The Mission of San Miguel," I replied.

chapter 17
The Light

FOR WELL OVER TWENTY YEARS, Shiloh had been my equine partner. Not just working on our training track, but as a real part of my life. The love we shared was healing, particularly after my parents died. But for Shiloh, my rage may have never subsided. My PTSD therapy sessions at the VA only scratched the surface, directing my attention to and awareness of what they described as C-PTSD or Explosive Anger Disorder. Just acknowledging my explosive anger as an issue primed the therapeutic pump, but I think having Shiloh and his unconditional love was the key.

After my parents died, I fell back to where I was right after 'Nam, and I was perhaps even worse. My progress toward psychological well-being had been dislodged in the severe trauma of seeing them slain and by my vengeful and sadistic killing of Ray Marty.

I think back on that night, the night I killed Ray Marty. My monster had come completely out of the closet. My anger was spent, but the fact of it, my loss of control, the brutality of it, left me cold and distant. I turned more and more farm responsibilities over to Katie and spent more and more time as a caregiver for Sally and on trail rides with Shiloh. Riding Shiloh gave me a sense of peace that I found nowhere else.

Once, long ago, one of my business friends, a Japanese racehorse broker named Toyo "Yoshi" Hideyoshi, took me on a trail ride from his horse farm near Mount Fuji. Yoshi and I rode through the foothills of the mountain into a magnificent virgin forest. Mount Fuji, rising high above the forest in snow-capped splendor, was one of the most wondrous sights I had ever seen. Yoshi told me that the Japanese had a word for the special feeling that comes from riding through the forest: *shinrin'yoku.* It means "forest bathing." One uses the energy of the deep forest to cleanse one's aura.

"Little is better for the soul," Yoshi said.

In exactly that way, Shiloh was good for me. That was his gift, a gift he shared not just with me but with anyone in need. He was always content to let a child ride him. He was a paragon of gentleness with young kids and a perfect gentleman with children in a therapeutic riding program I offered from the farm. These were kids who were all too often underestimated and deprived of opportunities, the ones who dreamed of seeing the world from horseback.

Because of my own autism, I always made a point to reach out to help Autistic children in our community. I knew that many of them were impacted by apraxia, a common neurological comorbidity that disconnected their brains from their bodies. Apraxia made it difficult to speak or even move the way they wanted to, yet these extraordinary children emanated a profound intelligence and inner wisdom without the use of words. I observed in them a reservoir of untapped brilliance, particularly evident in their unique perception of beauty and connection with nature. Together we could be transfixed by the delicate dance of sunlight through the leaves of the oak trees and lose ourselves in the rhythmic cadence of hoof beats.

So it was through Shiloh that I realized how young children, and especially Autistic children, were open to the spirit of the horse. At times, their connection to him seemed miraculous. In the saddle, such children appeared to be transformed, their expressions calming and softening as the tension in their bodies gave way to the fluidity of Shiloh's rhythmic movements. I gave the horse all the credit and rightly so. He grew a fan club. Rarely did a week pass without a visit from some child he had impacted. And he seemed to recognize them all, greeting them with a friendly whinny—and of course they always brought apples or carrots.

But it couldn't last forever.

The big gelding had been fighting a bout colic for days. He was old and I could feel him slipping. We had tried the usual remedies, but they did no good. Our vet said surgery wasn't possible as Shiloh had a month previously suffered an age-related heart attack and now had an untreatable heart rhythm irregularity. That ruled out anything but palliative care. The colic was a consequence of the heart problem, not the cause.

A bitter despair filled me as Shiloh and I walked beneath the ancient oaks in his favorite pasture. Shiloh struggled to breathe but refused to lie down.

I looked about. It was an April morning in Ocala. The pasture grass was high and rich emerald green; shade from the giant oaks dappled the ground. A cool breeze was scented with jasmine and magnolia. Surveying the panorama before me, I took a deep breath of my own. As I soaked in the striking beauty of our surroundings, I rationalized: *If this is his time, there could be no more beautiful day.*

Walking with him, I could not help but reminisce. Some of our trail rides were unforgettable. Once, Shiloh and I took a twenty-mile jaunt to Lake Shangri-La, deep in the Greenway Forest. After a skinny-dip swim in the cool spring-fed lake, we returned home. The sun had begun to set. Ocala sunsets are often a golden extravaganza, painting the dome of the sky in gilded glory. This light changes the forest at dusk. Leaves of green are mystically transformed into shades of burnished gold, copper, and purple, and long shadows crisscross the trails.

Deer, boar, panthers, and bears were at home in this forest. By law, no hunting or motorized vehicles were allowed. Packs of coyotes roamed as well. The typical Florida coyote traveled in family packs, sometimes numbering as many as eight.

Shiloh and I had taken this path home hundreds of times, and I was half asleep in the saddle, my feet out of the stirrups, relaxed and dangling loose at his sides. He knew the way. We were at a leisurely walk, the kind only a big, gaited horse can provide, riding in the cool shade of the dense oak-laden tree line that led back to the north gate of the farm.

Suddenly Shiloh bolted like a racehorse, thundering out of the starting gate. We went from serenity to shit-storm in an instant. I flew off his back. Before I even hit the ground, he was in full stride, heading home. Shiloh had explosive speed. I landed on my backside, shook off the impact, and jumped to my feet.

A pack of coyotes was chasing something through the woods. I never knew what—probably a rabbit. As soon as I saw them, I knew what had happened. They'd burst out of the tree line right behind us, triggering an instinctual response in Shiloh. The scruffy wild canines stood frozen, looking at me, and I think they were as surprised as I was.

Coyotes are intelligent and will only attack easy prey. They stared at me, gauging whether I was a part of their food chain. I knew better than to show fear, so I reached for the scabbard on my belt and slid out the old military KA-BAR fighting knife issued to me by the Marine Corps years earlier. As I touched the knife, I flashed back to the first time my KA-BAR tasted blood in combat. Khe Sanh, in a quick struggle to the death with a North Vietnamese Army sapper. Staring straight at the pack, I whispered our Marine Corps battle cry, "Recon." Then, spreading my arms high and making myself look as big as a raging bear, I transferred all my energy into a loud, snarling, roaring *kiai:* "Recon!"

The coyotes melted back into the woods as fast as they'd emerged.

Nothing damaged except my pride, I jogged back toward the farm. I came over a small knoll and saw Shiloh standing at the gate, waiting to be let in. I whistled. As soon as he heard me, he galloped over and nudged me a few times with his head. I sensed his confusion. He thought he'd saved us from the coyotes by running like the wind and was home before he realized he had dumped me. Head-butting was his way of apologizing. I rubbed his neck, and we touched foreheads.

Reminiscence...I shook it off. The harsh reality left no room for dwelling on the past. As I walked Shiloh in a big circle, he stumbled, bumped into me, and almost knocked me off my feet. Then he collected himself. I could sense his embarrassment. Our barn manager, Big John, stood nearby with the veterinarian.

"John, I'm going to the house to get some beers." The horse had countless bags of fluid intravenously but nothing to drink in a few days. "He must be parched."

"Electrolytes would be better."

"No, John, I think we're going to have a beer."

"Can't hurt, I guess," he replied.

The vet grunted. "That won't be good for him."

"Listen," I said, unable to keep the terseness out of my voice. "You've been nagging me about putting him down since yesterday, and I know he won't be with us much longer, but this old horse loves cold beer, and frankly, all of us could use one."

John chuckled. "You know I don't drink much, but I'll make an exception this time."

The vet suppressed his professional opinion and concurred with a shrug.

Shiloh loved beer. While almost all horses were ridden using a bit—a metal shaft over the tongue connected to reins to control the horse. I never used a bit when riding Shiloh, preferring reins connected to two brass rings on the noseband of a light, close-fitted halter. That way, on the trail, he could drink and browse without the impediment of a steel bar in his mouth. In the heat of the summer, he always looked forward to a cold beer upon our return to the farm. He was a natural comic, gulping it down as I poured it into his mouth. When he'd get excited, he would grab the bottle between his teeth, lift his head high, and chug it in a few seconds. Then, with a quick twist of his head, he'd throw the empty bottle into the grass. Even though I'd seen it a hundred times, it always made me laugh.

His favorite beer, and mine, was Killian's Irish Red. Shiloh was a beer snob. Try to give him a cheap beer and he'd turn his head away in disgust, or worse. In one such expression, he grabbed a bottle of a cheap swill called Old Madison in his teeth and hurled it, with a snap of his head, smashing it in an explosion of glass and froth against the stable wall.

I gave Shiloh's lead line to John and whistled for my dogs, Akeela and Zipper. The two mixed-breed herding dogs had been sitting a respectful distance away, sensing the unfolding tragedy. In a flash, they jumped into the back of my UTV. As I started to pull away, I looked over at my horse. Despite his age and illness, he was still beautiful, his black-and-white coat glistening, his muscles thick and strong. I touched my forehead in a gesture to him, then stopped and got out of the UTV, leaving the motor at a growling idle. The dogs followed at my heel. For what was probably the thousandth time, Shiloh and I bowed to one another and touched foreheads. *Topi*—a symbolic touching of our brows like two old monks in soulful communion at an ancient Himalayan temple—was our way of saying, "I love you." I then returned to the idling UTV and drove away.

When I returned, the vet intercepted me as I approached the paddock with the cold six-pack. He touched my shoulder, a gesture I appreciated. I admired him for his compassion for animals and owners alike.

"Jake, it's time. We need to put him down."

"Please, Doc...you can do it, and I'm sorry I was gruff, but...well, you understand. First...please give us a minute."

He nodded and stepped back. I twisted the top off a cold bottle and tried to get Shiloh to drink. He couldn't.

"John, bring me that feeding syringe, please."

It was a big plastic syringe connected to a tube, not a needle. Together, we injected beer at a slow rate into Shiloh's mouth.

The beer seemed to revitalize him, if only for a moment—a wave of pleasure in a sea of pain. I nodded to the vet, who came and deftly injected his neck.

"Lie down, my brother, lie down," I whispered in his ear.

The big horse dropped to his knees, and I went down with him onto my knees, my arms around his neck. I felt his pain like a shard of glass in my gut. He lay on his side, head in my lap, and I could feel death there, embracing us. As he faded, so did I. The pain was unbearable—a tightness in my chest—so bad, I struggled to breathe. Then it came to me, a vision in my mind, a flowing cinematic montage from Shiloh's perspective: baby horses, Sally, trail rides, the children, grandchildren, carrots, beer, and me. Me! Whether it was Shiloh's projection or my hallucination, I'll never know. As we lay together, my anger disappeared, replaced by an overwhelming sense of peace and love. Shiloh's work was done.

I knelt there with him in the lush-green grass, stroking his neck and mane. A cool spring breeze rustled the leaves in the oaks above.

"Happy trails, Shiloh," I said aloud, my voice cracking. It felt like my heart was being torn from my chest. As he slipped away, I whispered in his ear, "Shiloh, Shiloh... Shiloh."

Then he was gone.

When I think back to the day Shiloh died, I remember the trouble I had standing up. I was on the ground when he passed, but afterward I struggled, unable to stand by myself. Though I was getting on in years, I was still active and athletic. Yet there I was, out of breath, wobbly legs, staggering like a drunk. I drove to the house and Sally met me at the door. I told her Shiloh had passed. Sally's Parkinson's disease was severe by then, so distraction, memory loss, and dementia were a part of our everyday life. Some days were better than others.

"Who is Shiloh?" she asked. Sometimes she did not know who I was.

I felt so alone. I felt helpless.

"Shiloh, our horse, he's dead. Dead!" I barked in a moment of insensitive self-absorbed grief. "Shiloh, the horse."

Sally started crying. My fault. Clearly, my fault. It took me many years to realize that, in such times, there were no words that could help. So, I stood beside her, and without a word, put my arm around her. Then I kissed the tears from her cheek and whispered, "I'm sorry. So sorry." I caressed her hair. "I love you." Sally buried her head in my shoulder, and I embraced her. Soon the sobbing stopped.

That evening at sunset, we buried Shiloh in his favorite pasture. I was surprised by the turnout. My family showed up and most of the farm hands were there. However, around thirty other friends and neighbors came too. There were almost twenty years of children, many now grown, for whom Shiloh was both a therapy horse and beloved friend. Shiloh's unconditional love and acceptance was not forgotten. They all came to say goodbye.

WAR AND OLD AGE are seasons, and I have now seen both.

Shortly after Shiloh's death, Sally was diagnosed with stage 4 liver cancer. My wife had very little time left. The doctor, in private, told me a month, at most, maybe only a week.

When I explained to Sally about the cancer, she clearly understood. I think she knew she was dying. She wanted to go "home," not to our house on the farm, but to her childhood home in South Carolina. She had inherited it, and just a few years before, she had given it to our daughter Cassie, who had lived there since college, cared for her grandparents until they passed, and made it a home with her partner Kristen. We had already been planning a trip to see them because of some good news: both Cassie and Kristen were pregnant.

The Johansson farm was well off the beaten path. It was a nine-hour drive from Ocala. We left at dawn, and by early evening, we reached the rugged upland point near where Georgia, South Carolina, and North Carolina meet. About an hour later, our trip ended just outside of the sleepy hamlet known as Cleveland, South Carolina, population 1,198, just north of the small city of Greenville.

The Johansson place was on an asphalt road that provided access for tourists and state-contract loggers alike—the primary access road to the Mountain Bridge Wilderness Area, a huge state forest on the eastern edge of the Great Smoky Mountains. The preserve consisted of tens of thousands of acres. Both Caesar's Head and Jones Gap State Parks were within the wilderness area boundary.

I had always appreciated the property for its off-the-charts wild beauty. Sally and I were married at an open-air mountain chapel in the nearby, century-old, YMCA Camp, just a few miles from the farm. The locals called it "Pretty Place Chapel," and when we passed by, it was as beautiful as it was when we'd been married there, over four decades before. Before our wedding, when we were in college and visiting the Johanssons, I would jog from Sally's home to the chapel, arriving near sunset. Sally would then meet me there in the car. We'd watch the sun set and ride home.

It was there, during one such sunset, two college students had planned a wedding. There hadn't been another soul for miles. The outdoor altar was on the edge of a vast precipice, with an unobstructed view west across the Great Smoky Mountains. We'd stood there in front of the cross, looking out over the hills. It had been a spectacular evening. We'd kissed, then made love, draped in the golden and purple hues of the setting sun. Sublimely tender and spiritual, it remains the most beautiful experience of my life.

James had been conceived there. It was our little secret—the kind two college kids in love cherish.

A little more than a month later, we got married as planned, standing on that spot. Baby James even cooperated by arriving several weeks late. The only comment on the timing of the pregnancy was from Pa, who had said with a hint of sarcasm, "Didn't waste much time knocking her up, did ya?"

Sally, in a moment of crystal-clear clarity, asked me to stop at Pretty Place first, before going to the farm. Over the decades, Sally and I had aged, changing to the point we were no longer recognizable as that twenty-year-old couple in love. But unlike us, the sunset at Pretty Place was ageless—as rich and vibrant as ever—with pulsating shades of iridescent white, golden yellow, psychedelic blue, and a spectrum of purple, all in a haze of wispy clouds. It overpowered the senses. Magnificent! I helped her from the truck and into her wheelchair. We took a spot, our special spot, overlooking the Great Smoky Mountain range. There was a huge roof-support cross beam near the altar that had the first verse of Psalm 121 engraved on it: *I will lift up mine eyes unto the hills.* I read it aloud to her. Then, searching my memory for the next verse, which was not written above us, I said, "From whence cometh my help? My help cometh from the Lord."

Sally nodded with approval.

I know I've made mistakes, sometimes terrible mistakes. I know I've hurt people. Maybe that is why I'm not one to pray in front of other people. I pray in private. But there, in that moment, I knew words had to be said. Holding Sally's hand, sensing her frailty in its thin translucence, tenderly caressing her palm with my thumb, I prayed aloud, speaking for both of us. I knew we were near the end. We had lived our lives. I asked that, with the time left, God help us to finish properly, and for the sake of our family, show our love for them. I ended with, "Lord, help us, please help us. Amen."

Sally sat transfixed, looking off to the west. I'm not even sure she heard me, but I felt secure that our prayer had made the transition from sublime to divine. The sun was dipping low, and at that moment the purple mountains were decked in high clouds, with rolling layers of fog like a sluggish river of smoke, flowing across the hillsides. The horizon above the mountain ridge, off to the west, glowed in sunset gold and rose-colored highlights. Then, just as the sun sank below our sightline, I saw a sign. To me, some atavistic part of me, it was an affirmation. A brilliant green and gold flash of light just as the sun disappeared. For just a few seconds, it illuminated the western sky.

I blurted, "Thank you, Lord."

Sally added, "Amen," and turned to look at me and asked, "Jake will you please sing me a song, like when we were young?"

"I don't have my guitar, love."

"That's okay. Just sing."

"Sure," I said, "What do you want to hear."

"Lord of the Dance?"

"Sure, I remember it."

She took a moment to look at me, her gaze so intense. "Jake."

"Sally..."

She blinked a couple times as she collected her thoughts. "Please, when I can no longer remember you, when I can no longer remember me, will you try to remember me, the *real* me?" Sally had tears streaming down her face. Soon I did too. We had lived through so much together.

I was crying at last.

We sat, her in the wheelchair and me on the rugged bench, facing the altar. I started singing the old Shaker hymn a capella, holding her hand. She fell asleep, still holding my hand. The cancer had ravaged her to the point where she weighed barely a hundred pounds. Returning to the truck, I lifted her from the wheelchair, cradled her in my arms, and put her in the passenger seat.

It was time for Sally to go home.

That night, I called the children to come to the Johansson homestead. I cut off all the excuses, from business meetings to soccer games, with, "Your mother is dying!" I explained the end was near and that their mother was too weak to return to Florida.

James and his family arrived first, his four boys bursting out of their minivan, rushing me like the defensive line of the Florida Gators. The depressing energy lifted like fog in the morning sun, as with a youthful exuberance they tackled me with hugs in the driveway, yelling, "Grandpa!" then bouncing off to see Grandma.

Shortly thereafter, Katie arrived, escorted by Monty. They were more than just half-siblings, they were best friends, although it remained clear as time passed it was strictly platonic. Katie was by far the toughest of my children. When I saw her, I could see my father. Army strong and Ranger tough. Saying goodbye to her mother, though, it brought her to the verge of a breakdown. I was grateful that Monty had come along to help.

Cassie, a nurse working at Greenville General, and her wife Kristen, also a nurse who owned a hospice service in Greenville, set up a home hospice for their mother. They were her caregivers.

Sally died just two days later. She was surrounded by family in her childhood bedroom. In what was the darkest moment for us, she became the light. She looked at her family surrounding her bed and her last words were, "I love you." Her love for us, and our love for her, infused every moment at the end. She fell asleep with a slight sweet smile on her face. After a few minutes, and it was almost imperceptible, she was gone.

As she wished, and just as we had done for the baby we'd lost so many years before, we spread her ashes to the winds at sunset at Pretty Place Chapel.

I WAS THE LAST OF OUR FAMILY to leave the Carolina mountains—it was two weeks after the funeral that I kissed Cassie and Kristen goodbye. I had always been an overly proud grandpa. When Kristen told me the babies were planned to arrive at the same time, I almost made a quip about "Rainbow Twins," but having gained some wisdom with age, I swallowed the words before they could pass my lips. I didn't want to offend them and, frankly, I had no feel for what might be offensive. What I did say was that I was there for them, one hundred percent. I made sure they knew that if they needed anything, any help whatsoever, all they had to do was call.

I drove south as if in a trance—the kind where you've been on the interstate for hours, but other than knowing you are on I-75 in Georgia, you haven't a clue where exactly you are. I arrived home and it was sunset. It was like the trip had been bookended by sunsets. Evening shadows in shades of purple and gray had settled onto our Italian Cypress-lined driveway as I pulled up to the house. By habit, I honked the truck horn. Katie, with Monty behind, came out to greet me. I wrapped both of them in a big bear hug.

We entered the house, and they gave me a rundown on progress with the horses in training as I dropped my bag by the door and walked across the living room to the bar to pour each of us a whiskey.

"Two fingers neat for me, Daddy," Katie said.

Monty gave an approving nod and signaled a heavier pour for him. We all raised our glasses and, in harmony, toasted, "*Crom Abú*, family forever."

The entire drive south I'd been planning something, something long overdue. I took a melodramatic deep breath and removed the amulet from my neck. The bronze disc was tarnished, almost black, but the Tang horsehead in the center gleamed reddish bronze, probably because I rubbed it with my thumb several times a day, like a nervous habit.

"Katie," I said. "This is for you." I looked at them both, watching my words settle in. "This medallion was given to me by my father, an heirloom passed down generation to generation for a thousand years. Katie, you are both a superlative horsewoman and a warrior, a true warrior. My guess is you will be the first woman in the history of our family to carry this. So, I ask you to wear it with honor, humility, and respect. When the time comes, and you will sense it, pass it on to the next generation, to the one destined to wear it after you."

Monty smiled and said generously, "Excellent choice, Jake." He then raised his glass again. "To the next generation of horsemen."

Then, with hugs and goodbyes, they left.

I settled in for the night. As I lay in bed, sleep wouldn't come. Around one in the morning, I nodded off and dreamed of Shiloh. I was riding him, cantering through a forest glen dappled in the golden hues of sunset. When I woke, or thought I woke, the big house was dark and empty, silent as a tomb. I sensed I was having an out-of-body experience. Dream? Reality? Who knew? For a moment I was afraid, but then I let go. All alone in the darkness, cut loose from my mortal shell, I sensed I was a part of everything that ever existed as I drifted up into a black and infinite void. With my emptiness came a serenity. With it came freedom from fear. I realized that I was no longer afraid of dying. Izzie came to mind. I saw his smile. I smiled.

At last, I was ready.

This light within me carried me up, and I felt I could go forever, adrift in the black void. I recounted all the love in my life, from my parents to Geronimo, from Izzie to Old Pete, from Michelle to Sally, and from my children to Shiloh. The stepping stones of my life. The true markers of my success. Then I stopped thinking, fully surrendering myself to a light that was now the only visible sign of my existence. "The light, the light, the light," I chanted, low and soft, stimming, bathed in its shimmering purity. I had been there before, I felt, and once again, after all these years, I was one with a sacred space. Once again, I was like a child, innocent, free from desire, and in that moment, I knew God was with me and I was with God.

With not so much an act of will but rather an impression of returning, I opened my eyes and lay there in bed, stunned and confused. After a moment, on a silly impulse, I called out, "Alexa!" The blue LED ring at the top of the canister-shaped Echo device sitting on my nightstand lit up the pitch-black bedroom.

I asked, "Where am I?"

My electronic female companion stated, in monotone, "You are eight-point-seven miles south of downtown Ocala."

With that, my spirit settled deep into the comfort of my body. The parable Jesus told in the Book of Matthew, of the farmer who hired workers early in the day, then more workers later in the day, yet paid them all the same, came to mind. I felt I was being called very late in the day, yet by some divine grace, receiving the same blessing.

Though I did not understand it, I appreciated it. I softly muttered, "Thank you, Lord." Then, I assessed my physical state from the prone and cushioned comfort of my bed. With a wiggle of fingers and toes, with the stretching of my legs, and with the flexing of my biceps, I returned to the corporeal world. Not only was everything working but the constant pains that were a part of me being a senior citizen felt like they were gone. It was as if God had hit my "reset" button for a new day.

MY PHONE WAKES ME from a deep sleep, dreaming my horse dream. I'm in my La-Z-Boy, my laptop still open on my legs, an empty glass on the table beside me. The caller ID shows it is Linda, my lead groom and the "midwife" for our foaling barn, but I'm too late to answer. I shake off my groggy haze, realizing it must be important, given the early morning hour. I listen to her voicemail message, which is edged with urgency:

> *Jake, sorry to wake you, but it's an emergency. We need your help with a delivery. That big spotted mare is in bad trouble. The baby is breeched. Henry is here with me, and we've tried and tried, but we just can't fix it.*

As I digest this, my mother's words come to me—the practical, spiritual instruction of a loving mother, and I say aloud, "Receive who you really are. Then, when you receive it, and you will, become that which you received."

As I recite the words, I finally understand a truth so simple it has become lost in the volatility of my life and in the pages of my journal.

I am a horseman—no more, no less.

I call Linda to say I'm on my way. She says to hurry; we are running out of time. As if by instinct, I reach for the talisman around my neck, only to remember that I've given it to Katie. I dress quickly.

Even though it is pitch-black outside, after seventy years, I know the path to the foaling barn by heart. From the house, I traverse in darkness through a thicket of ancient oaks, then turn, and off in the distance the foaling barn glows in a blaze of fluorescent light. As I hurry to the birthing stall, I see tears of frustration in Linda's eyes. Her chocolate skin tone has an ashen pall, and her eyes are bloodshot from exhaustion and crying.

"Let me help," I say as I take over, kneeling behind the mare, inspecting her as she lies stretched out amidst bloody, body-fluid-soiled shavings on the stall floor. Her labored breathing signals *extremis*—she is near the end. Without help, she will die. "Are you sure she's breeched?"

Linda nods. "Yes, and we can't turn the baby."

I know what I have to do. I stand up, ramrod straight, strip off my shirt, then, using the hose outside the stall, I carefully scrub my hands and right arm. Once again, I kneel with the mare. This time I reach up inside her. My long arm and powerful grip allow me, and only me, to save them. When all seems lost and you can do no harm, act decisively. The mare and foal will both die unless I change the equation. So, without doubt or fear, I pull, twist, and jerk until the baby's front feet and head are turned into position. Then, as the pearlescent-white amniotic sac emerges, I uses every ounce of my strength to drag the foal out of his mother and into the light. The sac tears and the foal emerges front feet first from her in a gush.

After I check to ensure the foal is breathing and the mare isn't hemorrhaging, I rise to my knees and pick up the big newborn, his umbilical cord dangling. I embrace him with both arms. As if it is the most natural thing to do, he lays his head on my bare shoulder. Linda, with professional expertise, crushes and breaks loose the umbilical cord and swathes the remnant in gauze dripping of iodine. With that done, I lay him beside his depleted mother. But he is having none of that. The colt jumps to his feet. As if by primordial instinct, the mare overcomes her pain and exhaustion, and with our help, slowly, she rises too. I know now they both will be okay.

The baby is magnificent. His tri-color pinto markings are like a broad-stroke Jackson Pollock painting, with abstract splashes of coppery chestnut, bright white, and blue-gray black, with small coppery "cat-print" spots strewn across the large white diagonal swath that runs symmetrically on both sides from the crest of his neck, across his withers, and down to his belly. Like his uncle, my beloved Shiloh, he is exceptionally big. The aura and energy of the colt also reminds me of Shiloh, and without a second thought, I proclaim, "This will be my new riding horse. Hidalgo is his name. Take good care of him."

The two grooms respond in unison, "Yes, sir," and Linda asks, "What does *Hidalgo* mean?"

"It's Spanish, and it means 'the noble one.'"

I clean my arms and chest off with the hose in the barn's center aisle. Linda and Henry make sure the mother is steady on her feet and the baby is nursing. I look on with satisfaction. Hidalgo senses my gaze, stops nursing, and turns to look at me. An energetic heat surges through me. I *know* that look. I *know* that feeling. We connect. *He is my horse, I am his man,* and I am excited to see our new life together unfold. Something within me is renewed. It is more than just hope for the future, it is a future with *this horse*.

My horse.

I silently stim on his name: *Hidalgo, Hidalgo....*

A piece of me that was missing has been found; for a horseman, without a horse, is just a man.

acknowledgments

THANK YOU to my family, for all they put up with during the creation of the book, especially my constant pleas to, "Please give me an hour...I'm writing," as I woke at five in the morning to get in a page or two before work, and came back to the manuscript again, evening after evening, for almost two years. They were my sounding board.

My deepest appreciation to Martha Cook and Rebecca Didier at Trafalgar Square Books for believing in me and giving me, and Jake, a chance, and a special shout-out to Trafalgar's editor Rebecca for her excellent advice. Thank you to the editors that helped me with this novel (Michael Denneny, Harper Zacharias, and Eamon O'Cleirigh) and my editor/reading group (Hillary Johnson, Ruth Saberton, Ted Carter, Roy Luna, Jud Orrick, Raquel Rodriguez, and Richard Gonzalez) for the many horse stories I wrote over the years that, in many ways, are a foundation for *The Horseman's Tale*. Many thanks to my high school friend Professor J. Budziszewski and his book *What We Can't Not Know: A Guide* for inspiring the moral and ethical battleground that underlies *The Horseman's Tale*. Thank you to my friend of over twenty years and PR specialist Charles Jones for his efforts to share this book and its many messages of acceptance of self and of others with the world.

And finally, but perhaps most importantly, thank you to the many horses I have known and loved over the past seventy years—Thoroughbreds, Spotted Saddle Horses, Paso Finos, and everything in between. My life as a horseman has broadened my life's purpose, made me a better man, and brought me closer to the natural beauty of Ocala, Florida, the home I love. While I've had formal instruction in riding over the years, my true teachers were my horses. Without them, and their love, I would never have learned the way of the horse.

about the author

TOM EQUELS was knighted in the Equestrian Order of Saint Gregory the Great by Pope Benedict in 2012. For decades he has bred and trained winning Thoroughbred racehorses and champion Paso Finos and Spotted Saddle Horses on his farm in Ocala, Florida. He has ridden to numerous championships, including a PFHA International Grand Championship at the prestigious USEF sanctioned Spectrum International. A combat-wounded Vietnam veteran, combat pilot, and instructor pilot, Equels was twice awarded the Distinguished Flying Cross (DFC) for heroism while participating in aerial combat, as well as the Purple Heart. He is a black belt in karate and was named one of the Florida Black Belt Association's 'Four Season Tour' champions, as well as a National Sport Karate Association (NASKA) National Champion. As a lawyer, Equels received numerous federal and state awards for his high-impact pro bono work in civil rights, poverty law, and social justice cases. For over three decades he represented foreign states on an international basis. He also served private companies in the banking, insurance, aviation, pharmaceutical, and construction industries. Since 2016, Equels has served as CEO of AIM ImmunoTech Inc, an immunology research company focused on the development of dsRNA therapeutics to treat cancers, immune disorders, and viral diseases. This is his first book.